FRANCE´   ꓴR

A
CHRISTMAS
CORPSE

ISBN: 1475152973
ISBN-13: 9781475152975

ALSO BY THE AUTHOR

THE PULPIT IS VACANT
DEATH OF A CHAMELEON

ACKNOWLEDGEMENTS

I would like, once again, to thank my proof-readers, Leela, Margo, Jean and Ivor my husband. The latter usually finds mistakes after the book has gone to print but better late than never!

Thanks too to all my friends who purchased my first two books and to those who have even asked to be put on the list for this one.

My friend Marilyn has greatly supported me by buying multiple copies and she doesn't even like fiction!!

My biggest thanks for this book go, however, to my late Mum, Win McGhie, who was famous for her Christmas parties and baffled most of us with her treasure hunts. Mum died in 2004, unfortunately before I had the courage to start writing. She got me started on crime novels at the age of 9 when she gave me Agatha Christie's, "Sparkling Cyanide", to read while I was in bed with measles.

CHAPTER 1

"**I** can't do it. I can't."

"Yes you can, darling. I'll be there to help you and there'll be nobody there who isn't your friend. It's nothing to be scared of."

"But Ralph I haven't had guests since before...."

"...since before your panic attack. I know but this is after it. It's the start of a new life for you. You've been well for ages now."

"This could set me back Ralph. I know it could. I'll get anxious."

"Of course you will. Everyone gets nervous hosting a party but it's natural and I'll be there every step of the way. Come on Sally. Do it for me and for Hazel. You know she would love a party."

Sally Ewing ran nervous fingers through her dark hair. All her life she had been confident and outgoing. She had run the History department at a Glasgow secondary school, Greystone Academy for eight years. She and Ralph had been famous for their parties, especially their Christmas one. They, with their daughter, Hazel, had gone on fabulous holidays and come home full of stories and with ideas for theme parties.

They were in Minorca having a relaxed, luxurious holiday when it happened.

First it was a racing heart, then a terrible sweat. Sally thought she was dying. She had been sitting, wrapped in a fluffy, towelling robe having just had a relaxing bath when it struck.

"A heart attack," she thought immediately. "I'm having a heart attack."

She had jumped to her feet, calling out for Ralph her husband who had come at once from the bathroom.

"What is it darling? You've gone sheet white."

"I …I…think I'm having a heart attack, Ralph."

Ralph had made her sit back down until her colour returned but she was still shaking.

Naturally he had insisted that she see the hotel doctor who had given her the most rigorous examination she had ever had. Far from reassuring her, this had made her if anything more frightened. He had told her that her arm reflexes were too fast and her leg reflexes too slow then given her a letter for her own GP, telling her that he had advised a brain and heart scan once she got home. Meanwhile she was to drink plenty of water as it could have been dehydration which had caused the symptoms. For the rest of the holiday she had had anxiety bursts and even though her doctor had laughed it all off, the damage had been done and she went into a cycle of anxiety followed by depression then more anxiety.

Over the last four years she had been a shadow of her former self and it did not help that everyone said it was not like her to be anything other than fun-loving and confident. At school where she was Principal teacher of history, she remained competent but no one knew of the times spent shaking in the base room, certainly not the pupils who found her, as always, strict but fun.

At home however it was a different story. They had always held parties, she and Ralph, including their daughter Hazel when she was old enough to join them which had been from the age of six. She was a bright, intelligent child and, being an only one, had loved the company of their friends and neighbours.

They had made the excuse of being too busy at work, both of them. Ralph was an accountant and it was true that he often had to bring work home as she did, having work to mark for her classes. Gradually friends had stopped inviting them as Sally was afraid she would spoil the evening and instead of telling the truth, had invented reasons for not going. The only people outwith the family to come into their home now were Hazel's close friend Pippa Davenport who occasionally came for a sleep-over and their neighbours, Sandra and Jim Rogerson.

Sally had eventually been put on medication, valium, which cured her depression after some weeks but did not allay her fears.

She had read once of someone who had blamed her attacks on Pam : Panic Attack Monster and so it was with her. She now lived with three people, Ralph, Hazel and Pam.

After nearly two years of having anxiety attacks she had gone to a doctor while they were on holiday and he had diagnosed her problem and prescribed a drug which after a bad start seemed to have cured her but she did not yet feel ready to return to her old life. Ralph had been very understanding but he wanted a return of their social life. He had suggested that they host a Christmas party in two months' time and she so wanted to do it for him and for Hazel. She had agreed way back in October but now was taking cold feet.

"OK Ralph, if you promise to help me on the night."

Sally smiled and Ralph felt a rush of love for his wife. She had gone through so much. He had too as he tried to understand what had happened to his fun-loving, gregarious wife. All he had been able to do was hold her tight while she shook with fear and could not tell him what she was afraid of.

Invitations were sent out to Ralph's brother Brian, his wife Carol, their twin sons John and Ian who were eighteen and their daughter Diana who was thirteen, to their nearest neighbours, the Rogersons, Jim and Sandra and to Arthur Mackie, a doctor friend. Then Hazel had asked that her best friend Pippa should be invited with her dad.

Sally had laughed, throwing her head back in the way she used to, sending her long hair rippling down her back.

"Why not? Wait though, that makes us thirteen. Can't have that, eh Hazel?"

"Oh no Mum, not thirteen. Maybe Pippa's dad could bring someone. There was a woman at the house once when I slept over. He could bring her maybe."

Sally wrote an invitation to Charles Davenport asking him to bring Pippa and a partner to their Christmas party on 23rd December. Then Ralph asked if he could invite his colleague, Colin and his French fiancée, Aimee. The numbers were finalized as sixteen, Charles Davenport having replied that he would be delighted to come and would bring a workmate called Fiona Macdonald.

The next few weeks were hectic at school. There were prelim exams to plan for in November and to mark in December, school dances to attend and reports to write up. Sally was a one woman department as the school roll was falling. The school had been threatened with closure about eighteen months ago and she has been involved in the "Save Our School" campaign. Having no staff, she had no discipline worries but neither did she have anyone to help her come exam marking time.

Suddenly it was the 20th of December.

Sally felt a small tremor as she started to plan what food she would have for the party but she told herself off as she knew that she could cope with a buffet supper and Ralph would organise the drinks and the games. They had always had games at their Christmas parties and this one was to be no exception. The adults enjoyed these as well as the children.

All that was left was to buy a new outfit. Never fat, she had lost weight over the last few years and had had no need for party clothes. She decided to take Hazel to the shops - never mind the Christmas rush - and buy them both a festive outfit. Hazel was delighted. They went into East Kilbride which was the nearest indoor shopping centre to them in Newlands apart from the Mearns Arcade which did not have the same selection of shops and Silverburn which she had never driven to yet. After touring round Marks and Spencer's and British Home Stores, they found what they both wanted in Debenhams. Sally bought a short black dress which showed off her new slim waist and long legs and Hazel was delighted with her red mini skirt and white top which went well with her glossy black hair. Both also chose new shoes, flat, black patent ones for Hazel and high-heeled black strappy ones for her Mum. They giggled together as they chose new boxer shorts for Ralph, Christmassy ones with Rudolph on them.

"I always got your Dad something when I spent money on clothes. He used to laugh at the pants and socks and said he knew as soon as he saw them that I'd spent a lot on myself."

"What will Dad wear, Mum?"

"He has plenty of smart clothes in his wardrobe, pet. Don't worry about him."

They finished their shopping spree with a cold drink for Hazel, a coffee for Sally and a doughnut each. Hazel looked so happy and Sally determined to make this shopping trip a more regular feature of their life.

Hearing their happy laughter in the hall, Ralph had put up a silent prayer of thanks. This Christmas was going to be their best ever.

Now she was having second thoughts but for Ralph and her daughter she pulled herself together.

"OK. Sorry darling. It'll go fine with your help."

CHAPTER 2

Colin Ferguson had not had much luck with women. Although he had many friends who were girls, he never seemed able to get beyond friendship. Maybe going to an all-boys' school had not helped. His dad was a British consul and had always lived abroad, moving often as his job demanded and his mum had quite naturally wanted to go with him. This meant that from an early age Colin had gone to a boarding school in Scotland. His mum, being Scottish, thought that Scottish education was the best there was. His Dad just agreed as he always did - for peace.

Colin had spent his holidays in various places overseas and had made friends with girls of all countries. He was a stockily - built young man with darkish fair hair and a pleasant manner so his address book was full and his Christmas card list long. He had male friends who had 'little black books' full of names of females but if Colin ever bought a black book he knew it would remain empty.

All this had changed when he went to the Lake District on a walking holiday and bumped into Aimee, literally.

He had been on a narrow path and had been keeping well in to the rock face as the descent on the other side of the path was steep. He had his iPod in his ear and was singing along to one of his favourite tunes when he rounded a sharp part in the rock and came face to face with a girl. Both had been walking quite briskly and could not stop before bumping into each other.

"Owf !" said the girl. Colin had stood on her foot.

"Oh!" said Colin as he realised what he had done. "Oh, I'm so sorry."

He was holding onto her to keep her from wobbling across to the other side of the path.

They stared at each other. Colin thought he had never seen such a pretty girl. Her black hair was fastened back into a shiny ponytail, her cheeks red with the fresh air on the hill. They were about the same height and so close that her face was almost touching his. Without thinking he kissed her on the lips. She smiled.

"I thought that Englishmen were shy," she said.

Colin was so embarrassed that he would have run off had there been anywhere to run to.

"I am so sorry, again," he said almost stammering his apology. "I don't know what came over me. I'm Scottish," he added, blushing again at this complete non sequitur.

Colin's climbing companion Josh had come up behind him.

"What's stopping you Colin?" He could not see the girl hidden by Colin's body.

The girl turned round and spoke in French to someone behind her. From his knowledge of schoolboy French, Colin realised that she was explaining why she had stopped to someone behind her.

"I'll go backwards," he told her and over his shoulder he said to Josh, "Go back a bit Josh. I've bumped into another group coming the opposite way."

Josh complied and Colin stepped carefully backwards until he reached a wider part on the path.

The girl, followed by another girl and a young man, advanced towards them. The young man and girl thanked them then continued on along the wider path. The first girl stopped.

"Josh, go on first," said Colin and Josh went off.

Colin and the girl looked at each other.

"Where are you staying?" she asked him.

He gave her the name of the little guest house and went on to tell her their itinerary.

"We go back to Glasgow on Saturday," he said.

She grinned. "So do we. We leave for Glasgow in a couple of days. I go home to Paris the following Saturday. I am staying with my pen pal's family for a week."

Colin, feeling extremely forward, suggested that they meet in Glasgow as they could not stop and chat here and their companions would be waiting for them.

She agreed and the rest, as they say, was history.

Colin met Aimee in Glasgow. They arranged to meet again, in London, in a month's time. By the time Aimee went home after that month, they were in love and she had promised to marry him. She was across in Scotland again for Christmas, living with Colin at his parents' home and they would make their wedding plans and their decisions about where to live when the festivities were over.

When Colin had broached the subject of a Christmas party at his colleague Ralph's house, he had not been prepared for the delight on Aimee's part.

"Oh Colin !" she exclaimed, her French accent even more pronounced than usual in her excitement. "An English Christmas party! 'Ow exciting!"

Colin corrected her, "A Scottish Christmas party Aimee. Why are you so pleased?"

"I 'ave read about these parties. There will be 'olly and that stuff you kiss under..."

She was dropping her aitches in her delight at the thought of these treats.

"Mistletoe," Colin laughed.

"And we will play silly games and eat turkey and mince pies and Santa Claus will be there."

"Well I doubt that Santa Claus will be there. I think the youngest will be Ralph's daughter and she's ten I think. Too old for believing in Santa."

Aimee had looked disappointed and Colin made up his mind to ask Ralph for plenty of games to compensate for the lack of Santa. Colin still lived at home with his parents in Newton Mearns and Aimee had been staying with him and his family for a week now. They had finalised some of their wedding plans earlier than they had thought. Aimee had wanted to be married in a small country church but when she went to the church which Colin's parents attended in Newton Mearns, she said she would be happy to be married there. They had seen the minister and made a provisional date. Now they needed to find a hotel for the reception but they planned to wait till after Christmas to do this.

Colin could not believe his luck in finding Aimee and having her return his love.

Aimee had not been enjoying her stay in the Lake District, or rather she had not been enjoying the walking part. She loved parties and nights out with friends, not this energetic climbing. As a result she had been walking faster than the others, trying to get the walk over. She had left her pen pal Heather and her brother George some way behind her. She had rounded a corner and bumped into Colin. He was not her usual kind of man - she usually went out with tall, handsome men - but she felt her heart race as she saw the look on his face.

Willingly she agreed to meet him in Glasgow. She had indeed been staying with Heather but in Manchester. As an independent woman who lived on her own in Paris, both her parents being dead, she was used to making decisions and she made this one, to go to Glasgow, on the spur of the moment.

She had enjoyed her time with Colin, basking in that young man's adoration and had been quite content to marry him. As an accountant who had been living at home, he had a healthy bank balance and his job prospects were very good. In her own way, Aimee loved Colin. She went to church, a new venture for her and fell in love with the old building and beautifully kept gardens. Colin was going to take her to various hotels to choose one for the reception. He knew she had no family and he was prepared to pay for the whole wedding.

She really was thrilled to be going to an old-fashioned Christmas party and knew that Colin was pleased at her delight. She knew he loved her accent and if dropping a few aitches made him happy, she would do it on occasion.

She had left her job, in Paris, in a hairdressing salon and would look for a similar job in Glasgow if indeed Colin wanted her to work. So far he had been content for her to do nothing and his Mum had taken her round Glasgow showing her the sights.

She would return to Paris, give up her room in a shared apartment and invite her best friends to the wedding. Life suddenly seemed sweet.

CHAPTER 3

"Four no trump."

Seeing the panic on his partner's face, Arthur Mackie smiled. He had a gentle smile which went well with his white hair and cherubic face. People, when told, found it hard to believe that he was only fifty-five.

"Don't worry, Jean. Remember it's just a game. I won't eat you."

His partner smiled. She was one of his patients, a long standing one who had come to the GP practice where he worked about thirty years previously. He had been just starting then, a raw young GP and she just married and new to the district. She did not know why she still got nervous playing bridge but she did especially when he made an unusual bid as this was.

"Five diamonds," she replied hoping that this was what she should say with one ace in her hand.

"Five no trump."

"Six hearts." Surely this was right for two kings.

"Seven spades."

Arthur enjoyed the hand. It was really simple after he had successfully finessed their partners' only queen.

It was the last hand of the night and as usual he escorted Jean to her car. On impulse he asked her if she was free the following night to come to a Christmas party with him. He knew that it would be OK with Sally and Ralph Ewing as they were always asking him to bring a partner and Sally, before her illness, had always coped with parties and one more guest would not make things any harder for her, if indeed they were hard.

He had treated Sally for her anxiety but not before it had led to depression. He had been amazed at how she had coped with her school career throughout it all and would much rather she had agreed to stay off. However she had managed and now seemed to have recovered though she was still on a mild dose of antidepressants. He had admitted knowing little about anxiety and had been glad when, taking ill on holiday again, she had been treated by a foreign psychiatrist. He had been only too willing to liaise with the doctor.

"Oh Arthur, I'd like that very much. It gets so lonely now with the children grown up and married and Harry gone."

At fifty seven, she was two years older than Arthur and twenty years younger than her husband who had died six months ago.

Arthur made arrangements to pick her up the next evening and went home to ring Sally and Ralph.

As he had suspected, they were only too delighted. The numbers were now seventeen but their parties had usually numbered more than that and Sally reckoned if she could cater for sixteen, then one more would make little difference. Ralph, hearing her on the phone, was thrilled as she confidently told Arthur Mackie to bring the friend.

"Is it anyone we know, Arthur?"

"Yes, Sally. It's Jean Hope, my bridge partner. Remember she lost Harry a few months ago."

Sally could not remember. The name meant nothing to her but she found herself saying that she could as it would make Arthur feel less guilty about foisting another person onto her.

Going into his lounge, Arthur poured himself a whisky and soda. His cat, curled up as usual on his chair, got off with bad grace and took up an offended position in front of the gas fire. He could tell she was offended as she had her back to him and sat very erect as she did when annoyed. Finding the TV remote down the side of his chair, he switched on but finding nothing on any channel to interest him as Newsnight had just finished, he switched it back off. He had decided from day one not to get Sky as it was against his principles to put any money into the pocket of Rupert Murdoch but sometimes he wished he did have the sports' channel. Deciding to treat himself to a rare cigarette, he lit up. He was trying very hard to stop smoking as he felt a hypocrite advising his patients to stop when he still smoked himself but it was hard, especially after a meal. The golf club where they had played bridge was a non- smoking zone of course which made it easier somehow and he always managed not to go outside at the tea break.

Sitting back, relaxed in his chair, he thought of the impulse which had made him ask Jean Hope to the party. He knew that she was lonely. Harry had been unwilling to socialise over the last few years, probably because he had gone a bit deaf and was too proud to get a hearing aid. This had meant that he and Jean had lost touch with some friends.

He did not feel romantically interested in Jean, nor she in him he admitted to himself but surely two middle-aged people could be friends. He had lost his fiancée to cancer many years ago and had never had the desire to get really close to any woman since then.

It was not vanity but he knew that over the years he could have married quite a few women.

He knew without being big-headed that he was a good-looking man, still trim in his fifties and with a good job. He went holidays to exotic places and had had quite a few holiday romances, especially on the cruises.

On reflection, he was glad that he had asked Jean to come with him tomorrow night. He was sure she would not read anything romantic into it.

Sitting in her small sitting room, Jean was hoping the same thing. She was very fond of Arthur Mackie but she was quite content to be on her own. Harry had not been easy to live with over his last few years and she was enjoying the freedom which she had now. He had thought it needless expense for her to have her hair done for example and now she patted her newly blown dry, honey coloured hair and thought how the colour made her look quite a few years younger. She had quite a decent figure she thought - a bit on the plump side maybe for her small height but definitely not fat.

She thought about the next evening and decided that it might be fun. She had heard of Sally and Ralph's Christmas parties and knew that there would be games and good food and plenty to drink, not that she was much of a drinker. She had been brought up in a house where parties meant games and she had always enjoyed them. She did not know Ralph or Sally well, only by sight, but she was going with Arthur and she knew that he would stay by her side during the evening. She had been glad to accept Arthur's invitation and just hoped that he would not think that she found him anything more than just a friend.

They both went to bed, pleasantly anticipating the next evening.

CHAPTER 4

She looked at her bedside clock. Its glowing figures told her that it was past midnight. Did that mean that he was not coming tonight? She snuggled down under her duvet and felt herself relaxing. Maybe he had decided that it was too risky with a house full of people. She had enjoyed her day out, some of it in the fresh air. They had all gone to Rouken Glen. They had a browse round the shop. She had bought a small scented candle and then they had a brisk walk round the pond, looking at the brave ducks who were swimming in what must be nearly freezing water and then they had gone for lunch in the newly modernised cafe. By common consent they all had baked potatoes with various fillings.

On the way home, someone, she forgot who, had suggested that they go up to the Avenue at Newton Mearns as they still had some presents to get, including the one for Sally and Ralph whose party they were going to the following evening.

The Arcade was festive, with fairy lights festooned at the entrances to Marks and Spencer's and Asda. A school choir was singing outside Asda, raising money for a children's charity, she forgot which one now. The kids' faces were happy and they were singing their hearts out.

They had split up. The two of them were sent into M&S with instructions to buy something nice for the party hosts. They chose a beautiful poinsettia and two large boxes of biscuits. Leaving the shop, they met up with the others who had gone to Asda for last minute shopping and were laden with probably unnecessary food. She had noticed in M&S the folk with trolleys piled high and wondered at this almost panic buying. After all, the shops were only closed for two days. Christmas fell on Sunday this year and most of the shops were closed on the Monday as well. She wondered why they called it Boxing Day and asked if anyone could tell her. No one could.

They had struggled out to the car which had been parked in the car park next to M&S and after stowing all the bags and the plant, they decided to treat themselves to an ice cream sundae at the open-plan cafe. It was very busy and they had to stand and wait to get a table. She had thought that she would not be able to get through the enormous concoction of ice cream, meringue, marshmallows, toffee sauce and cream but she thoroughly enjoyed it, even scraping the bottom of the glass.

In the car they all laughed and joked and discussed what they would do that evening. There were numerous suggestions before someone suggested a silly Christmas DVD so that meant going back into Asda to buy one. The two of them were once again chosen to do the selecting and they came back with The Snowman.

The drive home did not take long. There was no chance of anyone wanting dinner, at least not soon, so they settled down to watch TV at around two thirty. It must have been the fresh air which made her fall asleep in her chair and waking about an hour later she discovered that she was not the only one to have done that!

Maybe that doze had rendered her sleepless once in bed or maybe it was the thought that he might come to her in spite of the difficulties posed. She was on the edge of sleep when she heard the creak of a floorboard. She was immediately awake. In the dim light of the room she saw the door handle turn slowly and the door opened letting in more light from the hall window which, uncurtained, let in the bright moonlight. There was a full moon.

"Are you awake, darling?"

"Yes," she answered.

He came in, closing the door gently behind him and moving over to sit on her bed. He lifted her up and kissed her gently.

"We will have to be very quiet my love."

Forgetting that he could not see her in the dark, she nodded.

He lifted her nightdress over her head and said, softly, "I wish I could see your beautiful white breasts."

He climbed in beside her and began to stroke her breasts, moving on down to her thighs to what he called her special place. She stiffened. How on earth was she going to stop calling out?

He entered her. She gasped and he put his hand over her mouth.

As soon as it was over, he slid quietly out of the room and she lay back exhausted.

CHAPTER 5

She was so bored, bored with her job, bored with her life with Jim. Along with boredom she felt guilt at feeling like this. She knew everyone envied her her life with a handsome husband who had a good job, being a consultant gynaecologist at The Southern General Hospital. Jim, with his aquiline nose and almost white fair hair, his slim almost boyish figure, was, she knew, admired by the nurses who also envied her her job which they saw as glamorous. She was a very successful journalist and was always jetting off to what others saw as fabulously exciting places. All she knew was that she spent hours in airport lounges and even more hours on planes. Business class was, for her, nothing special nowadays. That just made the tedium, comfortable tedium. How she envied the mothers and fathers crammed into what her friends called 'cattle class' with their offspring.

She and Jim had never had children. At first they had been too busy getting their careers up and running and then later, in spite of there being nothing wrong with either of them, physically, she had never got pregnant. Now it was almost too late as, at forty-two, her time clock was ticking and ticking loudly. The trouble was that Jim, in spite of declaring that he too wanted children, did not seem to want sex any more. She had given up trying to excite him, thinking it embarrassing for both of them when she failed. She knew she was good to look at, with dark, wavy chestnut coloured hair, a clear skin and a very reasonable figure for her age but that did not seem to make Jim want her, sexually.

Recently she had begun looking at men and wondering what they would be like in bed, wondering if one of them could make her pregnant.

What did life have to offer her right now? It was the Christmas holidays. Jim had suggested that they jet off somewhere glamorous but she did not want another plane journey. She knew that she was being selfish but this time she did not care. Now they had been roped in for one of Sally Ewing's Christmas parties and Jim just loved them, entering into the silly games with the enthusiasm of a child. She would look at the children present and wonder what her own child would have looked like. Would he have been clever like the Ewing twins or would she have been small and plump like Diana Ewing or mischievous and fun-loving like Hazel, Sally's daughter? Could she call off at the last moment? What excuse could she give? If she pled illness, Jim would insist on remaining at home with her and they would then have a monotonous evening in front of the TV with Jim roaring with laughter at some comedian or shouting out answers in a quiz programme.

Yes, Sandra Rogerson was bored.

Jim Rogerson sang as he drove home early from work. He had only four days off work but he did not mind. He loved his job in the hospital and he also was looking forward to the holiday. He would play golf tomorrow with one of his colleagues and tonight there was one of Sally's famous parties to look forward to. He enjoyed the games and had missed all the fun the years that Sally had been ill. He hoped she would play, "The Weakest Link" again. He loved quizzes of any sort and Sally had made a good Ann Robinson at the last party she had hosted. He had done well and been in the final with Carol Ewing. She read a lot, having no job to go to and beat him because he had failed at the entertainment question and sport question in the final. He knew he would have won if he had had her questions. Silly to be so competitive at a party, he knew. He knew that it annoyed his wife, knew too that she was discontented these days. He had become less interested in sex some years ago, ironic in his line of work and knew that Sandra now blamed him for their lack of children. However, he was happy by nature and had persuaded himself that she would settle down when no longer able to conceive.

Jim was content with his life.

"Darling, it's me," he called.

"Silly thing to say," she thought. "Who else would it be? A burglar?"

"I'm in the kitchen," she called back.

He came through to the kitchen where she was preparing the evening meal. She knew exactly how the conversation would go.

"Did you have a good day at work, San?"

"Not particularly. Very boring. Nothing much newsworthy these day."

"Would you like a drink?"

"Yes please."

"Your usual?"

"No, I'd like a pint of arsenic." She wondered what he would say if she said that out loud. Probably would just say, "Right dear" as he was already pouring out her gin and tonic, not waiting for her reply.

His next question would be to do with his mother who was in a nursing home now but would still call every day on some pretext or another. Sure enough:

"Did mother ring?"

"Yes."

"How was she?"

"Fine."

"Will we go and see her today as usual?"

They always visited Jim's mother on Fridays before dinner so this was on Jim's part just another rhetorical question but suddenly something in Sandra snapped and she heard herself saying that she was sorry but a colleague had asked them over for drinks. That was true as Derek, her editor, had asked all the editorial staff to his new flat in the afternoon, knowing that most of their partners would be on holiday by then.

"Oh I couldn't disappoint mother."

"Of course not dear but I would like to go to Derek's for a change so just go on your own."

Jim looked nonplussed. Sandra had never let him visit his mother by himself on a Friday but she was continuing.

"I've bought your mother's present and you can take it with you. I'll no doubt see her on Christmas Day. We'll meet up at the party later."

Sandra was beginning to feel better after her minor rebellion. She had never intended going to Derek's and had a shrewd idea that she might be the only person there, the others being already engaged elsewhere, but why not? Anything would be better than yet another visit to that dreadful nursing home with the stale smell of cooking mixing with the less stale smell of urine and the inane conversation interrupted by the man who was always calling out for Helen. If she could escape for the afternoon, maybe the evening party would be less hard to bear.

Jim realised that his wife was determined and gave in with good grace. He had no idea how bored she had become, neither did either of them realise that Sandra was ripe for something exciting to happen in her life.

CHAPTER 6

The last patient left just after six o'clock and Brian Ewing was on his way home shortly afterwards. Today, December 23rd, was his last day at work for a few days. Being a private dentist, he could take whatever holidays he liked but home was not a happy place to be right now so he had not taken many days off at this time. He knew that come Christmas Day he would probably wish he could have gone to work but who would want to have a dentist appointment then? Christmas followed the same dreary pattern every year. Now that Diana, his youngest, no longer believed in Santa Claus, they opened their presents in the living room after breakfast then they went to church. He was not a Christian but his wife insisted that he go on Christmas day.

After church there was the ritual meal of turkey and all the trimmings. On no other day did they have the dreaded Brussels sprouts! He usually fell asleep after the meal but was always woken up to listen to the Queen's speech. Why, he did not know. None of them were royalists.

Last year Diana had gone off to visit a friend, to exchange presents and compare notes on what they had received. The boys had always left right after dinner for the last four years so he and Carol would sit in front of the TV and watch a repeat of a dreadful film he had never wanted to see once, let alone twice. Later when Diana came home, they would eat again, this time mince pies and Christmas cake.

He turned into Polnoon Street. His house was about half way up the street. He lived in a conservation village and his house still had its original frontage and a gas lamp on the street outside his door. It had electric light but it still looked authentic. Behind the original facade his home was modern and expensively furnished. He turned off the street, thinking for the umpteenth time how lucky he was to have a lane beside his house leading to a garage. Some of his neighbours had to park on the street.

As he stopped, he felt the tension drain out of his shoulders. Perhaps he could have a relaxing time this holiday.

It was not until he was opening his back door that he remembered the party that night. How he hated his brother's parties and how glad he had been when his sister-in-law's mental illness had put paid to the annual event. As if that was not enough, he walked into a row with his wife.

She was in the hall when he came in and he went towards her and attempted to kiss her but she stepped back.

"Don't do that. You're off limits. You've got your floozie for that sort of thing. At least I get peace from your pawing and slobbering."

Brian flushed.

"…and another thing, just tell me why I should go to your brother's stupid Christmas party and pretend that we're a happy family? Tell me. Go on, tell me!"

"Carol. It's not much to ask is it? It's only one night. You won't give me a divorce so at least you can keep up the pretence of us being a happy family," Brian's voice was pleading.

"But these parties are so boring with the silly games. At least when Sally was ill we were spared them."

"I know, I find them boring too - one thing we do agree on - but surely we can pretend for one night!"

Arguments were frequent between Carol and Brian Ewing and had been even before Carol had found out that Brian had been having an affair with his receptionist. He was a dentist in Giffnock and Wendy had been his receptionist for some years, his lover for two of them.

Carol had refused Brian a divorce, claiming that she wanted a united family for her three children though Ian, John and Diana were old enough to understand, he thought, and must surely know that things were not good between their Mum and Dad. The endless rows had been going on for years. Carol did not work but wanted all the luxuries that life could offer for both herself and her children. Diana went to a boarding school in Perthshire, the one which her brothers had attended until recently and they wanted for nothing. Ian and John were members of their father's prestigious golf club although they only played now during the school holidays and Diana had her own horse, stabled near their house in Eaglesham.

"There they are, at it again," said Ian. "Why on earth don't they split up if they hate each other so much?"

"Don't be silly," John said, sarcastically. "Where would mother find someone else silly enough to take on a grasping cow?"

"John!" Diana was horrified. "You can't call Mum names like that."

"Can't I? I just have."

He got up and came over to sit beside his sister on the settee. He put his arm round her.

"Don't worry. I won't let them hear me say it."

"Why are you so hard on Mum? It might be Dad's fault," pointed out Diana.

"Di, what has Dad ever done except provide for all her whims and fancies and ours for that matter? Mum never lifts a finger. She's never worked as far as I know. She has someone in to clean and all she does is go out to lunch and to the hairdresser and the beauty parlour."

"That's all my friends' mothers do." Diana looked puzzled. "What's wrong with that?"

"Other peoples' mothers work and help their husbands. Look at Aunt Sal. I'm sure she's been ill over the last few years but she's never missed her work."

"Maybe they need the money," argued Diana.

"Uncle Ralph's an accountant for goodness sake. He probably earns more than Dad."

"But Hazel goes to the local secondary school and she doesn't have a horse like me."

"And are we any happier with our fancy school and expensive habits?" Ian chipped in, sounding really bitter and John and Diana looked at him in surprise.

"Didn't you enjoy school, Ian?" asked his brother.

"Of course I did and I enjoy university but I don't like it when we come home and no one wants to know us."

Ian got up and slammed out of the room.

Seeing his sister's look of shock at this angry reaction from her usually placid big brother, John explained.

"He asked one of the girls in the village to go out with him and she said no and when he asked why not she said he was a snob. He's fancied her for a while."

"I think I know how he feels," said Diana. "I always feel left out when I meet up with Hazel and her friend Pippa. They talk about things I don't know anything about and they seem so much older than me though I'm a lot older than them. I know I'm fat and small and they're taller than me and thinner. I'm dreading this party, John. Dad's bought me this dreadful dress and I know Hazel will laugh at me. She'll be wearing something modern as usual."

"Dad bought you a dress! Why not Mum?"

"He said Mum didn't have time to go with me so he took me. He was so keen on this dress that I hadn't the heart to tell him I hated it. It makes me look even fatter and it's white and with my fair hair I look like the angel on the top of the tree!"

"Oh. Di. You're too timid. You really must start to stand up for yourself. Never mind, at least Hazel will be on her own at the party."

"No she won't. I rang her yesterday and she said that Pippa and her dad were coming too."

"Don't worry. You can sit with Ian and me."

"I thought you'd told Mum you weren't going?"

"We did but Dad came to me afterwards and asked us to both go for this one last time. He said that Aunt Sal was feeling nervous about having a party again and it would be nice of us to support her. Anyway you need us both now."

Diana gave him a big hug. She and her brothers had always been close. They had protected her until she had found her feet at school and she knew that she had not been bullied as new starts often were because she was the sister of John and Ian Ewing. In their final year they had been figures of hero worship by her classmates and she had basked in their popularity. They were tall and had longish fair hair and were as slim as she was chubby. She knew that they would stay near her at the party and that Hazel who had always adored her two big cousins would not make fun of her when they were present. Pippa was a nice girl and had never been nasty to her. She had seemed sorry for her which in a way had been worse.

"Thanks John. Now you'd better go and see if you can find Ian and calm him down."

CHAPTER 7

True to her word to Jim, Sandra Rogerson had gone to her boss Derek's house at about four o'clock in the afternoon, telling Jim that she would meet him at Ralph and Sally's party that evening. Jim had looked disappointed. He had hoped that she would change her mind and he wondered how he was going to explain her absence to his mother who was in the nursing home because she was frail but was not the least infirm mentally. His mother was a bit of a battle-axe and would probably berate him for allowing his wife to go elsewhere.

However, if he had tried to insist on Sandra coming, she would either have laughed at him and gone her own way or would have given in ungraciously and been moody all evening at the party which she did not enjoy either. Of the two evils he would rather bear the brunt of his mother's displeasure for a few hours rather than his wife's moodiness all evening.

He waved Sandra off. She looked lovely in an emerald green dress, her wavy, chestnut hair setting off the colour of the dress. She had put on her mock fur jacket and a green mohair scarf and had waved happily to him as she got into her car.

He knew her editor from office parties, a divorced man in his early fifties and wondered who else of the staff would attend this soiree.

True to form, his mother criticised him for allowing Sandra to go to a party without him and he spent an uncomfortable time with her as she chose to list what she felt were Sandra's failings as a wife and daughter-in-law. He felt he was letting his wife down by not defending her but he knew from experience that it was better not to argue with his mother. He left the nursing home exhausted.

Luckily there was no one else in attendance to witness the scene in Derek's bedroom that afternoon. He had given Sandra champagne when she arrived and had kept up the pretence of waiting for the other guests until they had both quaffed down two glasses of the expensive bubbly.

"I have a confession to make, Sandra," he had said, coming across the room to sit beside her on the sofa.

"What's that Derek?" She smiled up into his eyes, her green eyes sparkling and he thought for the umpteenth time what a lucky man her husband was.

"There are no other guests coming."

"What! Have they all called off?"

"When you said you would come, I cancelled their invitations. Most had declined having other places to be anyway. I told the others an emergency had come up with one of my children and my wife needed me."

Sandra felt a quiver of excitement. She had felt drawn to this man for some time and had resisted the urge to respond to his obvious liking for her but today she felt no desire to rebuff him, quite the reverse.

Delighted that she had not immediately got up to leave, Derek stroked her neck and, seeing that she accepted that, he trailed his hand down to the V of her dress. Minutes later her dress was off and she was lying on his sofa in her lacy black bra and panties, stockings and suspender belt.

"Did you by any chance dress for me, Sandra?" he asked quietly.

"I did Derek," she said huskily.

At that, he got up and bending over her scooped her up in his arms and carrying her -into his bedroom, laid her on top of the bed. The black lacy bra and panties he quickly removed, leaving her with only the stocking and suspender belt which really turned him on. He got onto the bed beside her and started teasing her with his tongue. Her nipples feeling the soft wetness, hardened and he moved on down. She moaned with pleasure, then sat up and pulled down his boxer shorts.

Soon she was moaning even louder and as she climaxed, she heard herself screaming with pleasure. In minutes he too had reached the peak of his pleasure and they lay, panting side by side.

She must have slept because the sky was darkening when she awoke.

She had expected to feel guilt but surprisingly she felt none. All she wanted now was to know that this would happen again and soon. She said as much to Derek.

"Certainly, my darling. Your every wish is my command. He took her hand and led it to his already burgeoning erection. Is this soon enough?"

The second time was, if anything, even better as she felt less anxious that she would disappoint him. This time he got her to straddle him and they both climaxed together.

"You were hungry for that, Sandra," he said as they lay again side by side.

"Well, it's been a couple of years," she replied, "I've been keen enough but Jim seems to have lost interest."

She felt a small stab of guilt about telling him this but Derek sensing that, told her that he would never tell anyone else or let Jim know that he knew.

Looking at her watch, Sandra realised that she still had another hour before having to leave for the evening's party.

"Do you have to go now?" asked Derek.

"No not right away."

"One more time?"

"Oh yes," she said wondering at how this man in his fifties could be so virile.

He took her into the dining room and bending her over the table took her from behind. She was almost beside herself with pleasure as she climaxed not once but twice. A dining room table would never look the same to her from now on, she thought.

Derek was gentle but masterful at the same time, so different from her husband who had always been almost apologetic in his lovemaking. He led her back into the bedroom and helped her dress, handing her each item tenderly.

Back in the living room, he poured her another glass of champagne and phoned for a taxi telling her that he would drive her car over to Newlands the next day.

Sandra was on cloud nine as she walked up the Ewing's' path. She could have gone home, next door and changed her underwear but she wanted to feel the moistness during this evening of boredom.

"Nice to see you Sandra," Ralph welcomed her. "Jim's already here. Come in."

CHAPTER 8

Charles Davenport had been kept late at work at the large police station called Shawbank where he was DCI in charge of a small department. There had been a spate of small burglaries in Shawlands recently and they had been baffled till, by a quirk of fate, the robber had tried to steal from the top floor flat belonging to DS Fiona Macdonald, his colleague. She had come home tonight to find her door broken and the burglar still inside. He had not been armed and she had found it comparatively easy to apprehend him. She had rung the station on her mobile while standing over the thin, gangly youth and her colleagues PCs Penny Price and Frank Selby had arrived and taken the boy to the station.

Of course, Fiona had had to return to the station to give her account of what had happened and she and her boss had, as a result, been late leaving for the party they had agreed to go to that night.

Charles, tall with thick brown hair and vivid blue eyes, looked smart in his black trousers, blue shirt and black sweater. It was a mild night for December and he had forsaken a jacket. He tooted the car horn at about 7.40 and Fiona had run downstairs and got into the front seat which Pippa Davenport had left for her. Fiona too was dressed for the party, with a white frilly blouse and black velvet skirt. She had lost a bit of weight recently and thought she looked less fat round the middle. Her fair hair had just been highlighted and shone. She was becoming recognised as Charles's partner at their respective golf clubs and at bridge which pleased her, though in spite of going away last August for a week's holiday, there was no relationship as such as both were wary of letting their colleagues at work know of their blossoming friendship.

"Hi, Fiona! We're going to be late," said Pippa, from the back seat.

"It's not Fiona's fault, Pippa."

"No, it's the burglar's fault but let's get there quickly," was her reply.

Charles had driven down from Newton Mearns to collect Fiona in Shawlands and it only took minutes to get to the Ewing's house in Newlands. The driveway already had two cars in it so Charles parked on the street under the light from a street lamp and they got out and hurried up the driveway to the sandstone detached house which had lights on in nearly every room.

As the door was opened by Ralph Ewing, a burst of laughter came towards them.

"Hello, Pippa. Hello Mr Davenport and this must be the Fiona we've heard so much about."

Fiona blushed with pleasure at the thought that Pippa had found her important enough in her young life to talk about her. She held out her hand.

"Pleased to meet you, Mr Ewing. Thanks for inviting me."

"Ralph, please."

"And I'm Charles," said Davenport.

They were escorted upstairs so that Fiona and Pippa could leave their jackets. Charles thought for the umpteenth time how attractive Fiona was with her short fair hair gleaming. He thought she had lost some weight recently and it suited her. Pippa had chosen at the shops last week, a dark blue skirt and a white top which went well with her fair hair tied in a ponytail as usual.

As they descended the stairs, Hazel came to meet them. Fiona wondered if they had collaborated over their outfits as they had similar skirts and tops, though Pippa was in dark blue and white whereas Hazel was in red and white. One fair and one dark, they set each other off beautifully and Fiona felt sorry for the girl who followed behind Hazel. She was a bit older than the other two but was dressed in a young style, overdressed really, in what Fiona would have called years ago a party frock, white with sprigs of flowers over it. Whoever had helped her choose it had little idea of what young girls wore these days. She looked quite timid, the type of girl who would not make a fuss. Pippa said hello to her, introduced her to Charles and Fiona as, "Hazel's cousin, Diana" and the three girls went off together. Sally Ewing, coming up at this point, introduced herself and took Charles and Fiona into the lounge, saying that she would walk them round the room and let them know who everyone was.

"Everyone except our neighbour Arthur Mackie and his partner for the evening, Jean Hope, that is," she laughed. "He's never on time."

When she got to a beautifully coiffured, fair-haired woman in her early forties and introduced her as her sister-in-law, Carol Ewing, Fiona was amazed. She wondered why this woman who was dressed fashionably in this season's long skirt and high boots would dress her daughter in an old-fashioned outfit. Surely she could not be jealous of a very young teenager! The woman extended a perfectly manicured hand then left to go across the room. Sally Ewing gave a small smile as if to apologise for her sister-in-law's rudeness and took Charles and Fiona across to the table where Ralph was dispensing drinks. It had already been agreed that Charles would do the driving home although Fiona had been known to drive his car on occasion, so she asked for a gin and tonic. Charles agreed to have one drink and opted for his usual whisky with lemonade. There were plates with canapés and they helped themselves to these before moving off to chat to the couple who had been introduced as Jim and Sandra Rogerson.

They were in the middle of a conversation about the lead item in that night's Scottish news, the floods which had ruined so many houses in Kilmarnock last week, when the doorbell pealed. Fiona looked round as the last couple to arrive came into the room.

Sandra waved across to them and they joined the group, leaving Sally to hand round the canapés.

"This is Hazel's friend Pippa's father, Charles and his friend Fiona," said Sandra.

They all shook hands, the man introducing himself as Arthur Mackie and his companion as Jean Hope:

"My bridge partner," he added.

"His not very good, bridge partner," laughed Jean and Fiona warmed to this little woman who obviously did not take herself seriously.

Charles realised that he knew this man and asked if he played golf. They discovered that both played at the same golf course though neither had time for the Saturday medals.

"Do you play too, Jean?" asked Fiona.

"Yes that's where I met Arthur socially though he's been my doctor for a long time. I'm as poor a golf player as I am a bridge player and for his sins he got me as his partner some years ago in a fun mixed foursome game.

Fiona and Charles, keen golf players themselves, had started also playing bridge together, so they started talking about the game and Sandra excused herself to go across to the group where Carol Ewing was holding court. Watching her go, Fiona noticed a man pat one of the younger women on the bottom and asked who they were.

"That's Brian Ewing, Ralph's brother. He can't keep his hands off other women. That's Colin's new fiancée, Aimee. Think he'd better leave her alone. Colin's a quiet bloke but these silent types can get heated on occasion," said Arthur, turning back to the group, as did Fiona.

"I wish Sandra would learn golf," Jim was saying. "I used to play a lot at university and would love to take it up again."

"Got the dreaded video camera with you, Jim? If I remember rightly you always took a film of the parties before Sally took ill." Arthur Mackie looked as if he hoped Jim had left the camera at home, thought Fiona.

"Drat! Knew I'd forgotten something," replied Jim.

"Leave it at home."

Sandra had come back to his side and knew what a nuisance her husband could become armed with his favourite 'toy'.

Ralph had taken up position in the middle of the room and an expectant hush fell.

"Right folks, now the serious stuff starts. I've made up one of my famous treasure hunts......."

Groans came from the experienced guests.

"....and I've got names to pin on your backs. You have to try to find your partner without asking what your name is."

More groans.

He went to the door and called, "Hazel, bring your lot through here. Now."

Into the room came Hazel, Pippa and Diana, followed by two tall boys. Jim said under his breath to Fiona and Charles, "Carol and Brian Ewing's trio, Diana and the twins, John and Ian."

Fiona wondered how anyone ever told the two boys apart. They were identical and obviously fond of their sister as one of them had his hand on her arm as they came into the room.

"Treasure hunt time, kiddos," said Ralph and the young ones groaned loudly, except Pippa who loved things like this, Charles knew.

Sally helped her husband pin names onto everyone's back and then he explained that they were not just to wander round the house but had to come to him with a solved clue and have it confirmed before moving into the relevant room. Hoping that he would not be paired off with the cool Carol, Charles smiled at Fiona and she turned Jim round to see the "Jekyll" on his back and ask if she was "Hyde".

The party had started.

CHAPTER 9

Leaving Jim looking for 'Hyde' as he now must have realised what Fiona saw written on the slip of paper on his back, Fiona went round the room looking at what others' names were, then seeing Charles looking a bit lost, she asked to read his name and asked him if she was Laurel. He said that she was not but still seemed at a loss about how to find his partner.

"Charles Davenport! For an intelligent man who solves crimes, you are being very dense. Why did I say after seeing your name, was I Laurel?"

Enlightenment dawned.

"You're the third woman to ask me if she was Laurel and I never realised what that meant," he laughed. "Guess my brain must be in holiday mode."

Birling her round, he asked if he was Jerry although by now he knew he was Hardy. This in turn told her that she was looking for Tom and she was delighted when she discovered that it was Arthur Mackie whom she had liked on meeting him, about ten minutes ago. He in turn, looked pleased and confided that he had been terrified that it would be Carol Ewing.

"She's spoiled rotten and thinks she knows everything. She reads a lot with all the time she has to herself."

"Does she not work?" Fiona enquired.

"Work! Certainly not! She left school as soon as she could with some O grades and set her cap at Brian as soon as she realised that he was going to make money, being a private dentist. I think she may have worked part time for a while but that was all. The children came along and after Diana, she spent all her efforts on getting her figure back. As you can see she succeeded."

"Yes. She has some figure for a woman who's had three kids," Fiona said.

"You must think me a dreadful gossip. Sorry Fiona. I'm just so relieved not to have her as my partner. I hope Jean has someone kindly. I don't think she'll be much good at this treasure hunt. She doesn't do crosswords, so cryptic clues will be a nightmare for her."

He looked round the room and saw Jean chatting to Colin. Fiona saw that it was Charles who had got Carol and she had an inner laugh. Charles hated shallowness in anyone. Besides, being a Guardian crossword solver, he would find this a dawdle and would not let her intimidate him.

Ralph clapped his hands for silence. The various couples and one trio - Jim Rogerson with Diana and Pippa - stopped talking to listen to his instructions.

"The clues are all deductive."

There were some groans from his audience.

"You come to me with your answer and if you're correct I'll tell you where to find the next clue. Understood? No wandering around the house being nosy."

Fiona and Arthur got the first clue right away, it being an anagram which was Fiona's strong point. She did The Herald crossword and had even been known to finish the Wee Stinker on occasion though she had still to win a tee-shirt. She whispered the answer in Ralph's ear and then she and Arthur left the room. As they left, she saw Charles and Carol approach their host. Much to Carol's displeasure, Charles had got the anagram before she had.

Ian Ewing was bright but it was mathematics that was his best subject. He was at Stirling University, in his first year, doing Applied Maths. Aimee had lots of common sense but had never done a crossword in her life and Ian had had to explain what an anagram was while trying to solve it. His brother John, doing an Arts degree at the same university was more au fait with this kind of thing and he had Hazel who knew how her Dad's mind worked and knew the house which helped and they were third to approach Ralph and get his directions to the next clue. Hazel was delighted to be partnered with her favourite cousin. John was an extrovert unlike Ian who was placid and much quieter. Colin, an accountant, grimaced when he saw the clue and it got worse when Jean told him she was hopeless at this sort of thing.

Sandra and Brian came up to Ralph but were sent away to try again. The trio of Diana, Pippa and Jim succeeded next, Pippa being the one to crack the anagram once she knew what was wanted. She was delighted and grabbed Diana's hand as they left the room. Diana was pleased to have been partnered with Pippa whom she liked and the Ewings' neighbour, Jim, who was good fun.

So the treasure hunt wore on, Fiona and Arthur coming in first, just beating Charles and Carol. Carol was not pleased but Charles congratulated the other couple. Last were Colin and Jean who had only solved two clues in the time it took the winners to do six.

The next game was sedentary and Jean won the prize for the general knowledge quiz. She had once been on a pub quiz team when Harry, her husband, was well.

Colin came into his own with Humbug, a game where someone in the team hummed a tune and the rest of his team had to guess the tune. Colin sounded most musical and his team guessed his tunes immediately. Fiona found that she could not hum a tune to save herself and saw Charles turn almost purple with laughter at her attempts.

She got to laugh at him when the game changed to Pictionary as all Charles's animals whether it was a hippo or a cat looked the same, a circle with four legs.

"Right, folks, I think some supper is called for now," said Sally, to a cheer from the guests.

"Oh Aunt Sal, can we have one more game first?" asked John. "Let's have charades!"

Pleased that her nephews, who had not been keen to come, were entering into the party spirit, Sally acquiesced. Jim slipped quietly out of the room accompanied by a frown from his wife who realised that he was off home to get his camera.

By this time, John had nominated his father as the leader of one team and himself as the other. It came as no surprise when he chose his brother first. The teams were, John, Ian, Pippa, Fiona, Arthur, Jean, Sally and Jim versus Brian, Aimee, Hazel, Colin, Ralph, Sandra, Charles and Carol who was decidedly indignant about being chosen last.

John took his team into the dining room, leaving the others in the lounge. There was much discussion in both rooms and much laughter as they practised their little scenes.

"Here we come you lot, with our first word," said John popping his head round the lounge door and the game started.

CHAPTER 10

The boys thought that charades was easy but after the second team had tried their word, Ian said that he thought that they had got the idea wrong so he offered to join them and help out. Fiona was about to call after him to send one of the other team through to even up the teams but he was gone and she did not want to sound officious so she kept quiet and was soon engrossed in her part of the word 'catamaran'. She and Pippa were to act out a scene where she was mother and Pippa was her daughter and Pippa was to call her 'Ma' throughout their scene. 'Cat' had been done already, 'a' would be confusing for the other side as 'a' came into every scene, often and 'ran' would pose few problems for the actors of that scene.

The other team had gone one step further and had raided wardrobes, aided and abetted by Ralph who knew where things were. One of their team was wearing a witch's hat and mask which had been Hazel's for Hallowe'en and another, a white jacket. It was easy to guess that when the third pair mentioned the word 'ring' that their word was 'witchdoctoring'. Fiona wondered why Ian had not explained things better as they were supposed to make it hard to guess the word and they had made it easier by dressing up.

Never mind, it was only a game and when they did their next word, they seemed to have got the hang of things and it was much harder to guess the rest of their words. Ian had obviously explained the game.

Eventually everyone had done four words and they were all back in the lounge.

Sally clapped her hands for silence.

"Right folks! I'm just away in to put the finishing touches to supper. It'll take some time. Have a chat while I..."

The doorbell sounded loud in the silence.

"Who on earth can that be? Our nearest neighbours are here," said Sally, smiling at Sandra and Jim. "Surely we can't have been making so much noise that someone has come to complain."

She looked at Charles as she spoke and Charles, laughing, reassured her that they had not been causing a breach of the peace.

Sally left the room, joined by John. She came back smiling.

"Guess what? Santa has arrived. John is putting him into the study. He's got a big sack of presents for all of us."

She smiled, thinking what a nice surprise Ralph had thought up for them all.

"Right," she said. "Children first. On you go, Pippa. You first."

"Mum, we're too old for Santa Claus," said Hazel embarrassed.

"Hazel, we know that. It's just a joke. On you go, Pippa."

Pippa left and returned with a parcel which she was opening. It was a bright pencil case and she was delighted, loving all stationery things. Hazel came back with an Enid Blyton book and Diana was thrilled with her modern belt.

Colin was first of the adults to go and returned with a pair of Christmas socks, followed shortly by Aimee carrying a teddy bear wearing a red Christmas hat. She sat down and regaled the rest with her meeting with Santa, obviously excited in spite of being an adult. John Ewing was given a festive CD as was his brother Ian. Jim Rogerson went next and returned with a pair of Christmassy socks and his wife Sandra got pretty hankies.

Then it was the turn of Brian Ewing.

While he was away, Ian put on his CD for them to listen to. He left the room to get Santa a mince pie and a drink and his brother came in and switched off his brother's CD and exchanged it for his.

"Ian will probably change it again," he laughed, good-naturedly, running his hand through his fair hair which tended to flop over his face, as did his brother's. Carol made a mental note to ask them to have haircuts before they went back to university. She looked at her watch. Brian was taking an awfully long time with Santa.

Sally left to go to the kitchen, saying as she went:

"I really must see to supper. It should be out on the dining room table soon. Get along there, take a plate and help yourselves to the cold things."

"I'll pop along to Santa's grotto and hurry them up, Sally," said Carol. "There are still half of us to get our presents."

The guests, laughing and talking, left the room and made their way to the dining room. There was some good-natured pushing to get at the sumptuous array of food already on the table. Sally arrived at the door with a tray of sausage rolls which she piled onto an empty plate.

Sandra had a sudden vision of Derek bending her over his dining room table and smothered a giggle.

A horrendous scream startled them all. Sally's empty tray went up in the air coming down on the floor with a clatter. They stood like statues. It was

John Ewing who moved first. He ran out of the room, followed by his brother and collided with Carol.

"It's your Dad. He's dead. In the study. There's blood...."

She collapsed into the arms of John, leaving Ian to run off to the study, followed by Ralph and Charles. The rest stood stunned until Fiona took charge and ushered them all back into the lounge. Sally helped her nephew to half carry Carol along with them.

They were there looking at each other and making inane remarks when Ralph returned, with Ian who was looking white and shaken.

"I'm sorry, Carol, John, Diana, Brian's been murdered. He's been stabbed," said Ralph.

Diana went into the arms of Ian. Carol rallied enough to say shrilly,

"He was just lying there, in the middle of the blood."

"OK Carol, calm down." said Ralph. "Charles is taking charge. For those of you who don't already know it, he's a detective inspector. He's phoning his sergeant to get his team here. Fiona, he wants you to go to him now. He has asked me to keep the rest of you here for the present."

Sally had to stifle a nervous giggle as she thought, "For the present. That's what we all went into the study for, the present."

The door was open and a burning smell came to her nostrils, burning pastry. Her mince pies!

"Can I go to the kitchen Ralph, please? My mince pies are burning."

Suddenly it seemed crucial that she should save the pies. Pippa looked at her. She was not scared; murder was quite a commonplace subject in her house but it seemed silly for Mrs Ewing to be worried about her supper when Diana's father had been killed. She moved across to Hazel who grabbed her hand excitedly.

"It's like a whodunit book," she said.

Hazel nodded, wide-eyed.

"Sorry, Sal. They'll just have to burn. No one is to move," repeated Ralph, moving across to take his wife in his arms.

Sally started to cry. Ralph, thinking that this could set his wife back, put his arms round her.

CHAPTER 11

Charles had locked the study door, after sending Ralph and Ian to the lounge to join the others. He knew that he could rely on Fiona whom he had seen and sent to the lounge, to see that they did not get the chance to prepare alibis. He looked at his watch and was surprised to see that it was only just after 9.30. The games must have taken less time than he thought.

He knelt down by the body, being careful not to kneel in the blood. Brian had been stabbed in the chest. The knife had been removed. Surely, he thought, the murderer must have a lot of blood on his or her clothing. Then his eyes lighted on the sack of presents. Of course, if Santa had committed the murder, then his red gown would have taken all the bloodstains, leaving the clothes underneath clear of blood.

Where had Santa gone? That was his first priority, to find him, if he was still in the house.

He opened the study door, closing and locking it behind him and went to the lounge.

They all looked up at his entrance.

"Carol, I'm sorry to have to ask you a question at a time like this but when you went into the study, was Santa there?"

Carol looked up.

"Santa? What does it matter where Santa was?"

"Carol, Charles is trying to find out who might have stabbed Brian. Give him an answer for goodness sake."

Ralph, visibly shaken at the death of his brother, was curt with his sister-in-law.

"Sorry. Santa? No he wasn't there. There was nobody there."

"Has anyone seen Santa?"

Again Sally had to stifle a fit of the giggles. There had been a murder and the police were hunting for Santa!

Nobody spoke, then John said, "I think I must have been last to see him. I took him a mince pie. Brian went in in front of me and sat down. I left and went into the kitchen to help Mum. I heard Santa saying something like, "Have you been a good boy this year? At least I think that was what he said. That's what he said to me when I went in."

"So nobody else saw Santa?" Charles asked again.

When he got no reply, he continued, "Fiona is my detective sergeant. I want you all to stay here with her until I get back-up from my team. No one is to leave the room for any reason until there is another police person here to escort them."

Saying that, Charles left. He went back to the study and phoned the station, asking the man on duty to contact Sergeant Din and PCs Frank Selby and Penny Price. He gave the Ewing address in Newlands and said he wanted any of them who were reached to come there as soon as they could. He also wanted the Scene of Crime Officers, SOC, here as soon as possible. Next, he phoned Martin Jamieson, the police surgeon, who luckily was at home. He promised that he would get a taxi over to Newlands. He had been drinking and could not drive himself.

Once more locking the study door behind him, Charles went to the front door. It was locked. He opened it and went outside. He looked up and down the street and, seeing an old woman walking her Pekingese dog, he ran over to her and asked if she had seen anyone in the street. She had seen no one. He thanked her and went back inside, walking through the house till he reached the back door. It was unlocked. Outside in the back garden, he noticed that a gate led on to a lane which ran along the back of all the houses in the street, five houses in all he counted from the gate.

There was no one around so he walked back to the house, wishing that there had been snow to show him footprints. The two wheelie bins, brown for garden refuse and grey for rubbish, were sitting quite near the back door. He lifted the lid on the rubbish bin. It was about half full, or half empty he thought, remembering a talk he had once attended where they were told if you thought something was half full you were an optimist and if you thought it was half empty then you were a pessimist.

"I must be an optimist," he thought, then realised that he was mad to be optimistic, thinking he would find the Santa Claus outfit in one of these bins!

Yet, find it he did, underneath some garden refuse in the brown bin. He took it out, holding it gingerly by the neck and trying not to touch the sleeves. He took it into the kitchen and laid it on the floor, noticing that it was covered in drying blood down the front and down both sleeves. Going back out to the bins, he searched thoroughly for a sharp weapon but found nothing. Back in the kitchen, he opened drawers until he found the cutlery drawer but did not remove any of the knives, deciding to leave that to the SOC team when they arrived.

There was a ring at the door. No one came out of the lounge. Fiona was doing a good job. Charles opened it to find Salma Din, his sergeant, on the doorstep. He was surprised to see her trim in her uniform and said so.

"I was still at the station, Sir," she smiled. She was almost as tall as he was. "I had some notes to type up then I got carried away. I typed in the particulars of our burglar on the computer and I didn't realise the time. I went into the canteen to have some late supper and had just left the building when you rang. Phil ran after me and caught me as I was getting into my car."

Charles filled her in with the details so far, and then took her along to the lounge. When he opened the door he saw that the guests had divided themselves into three quite separate groups. The young ones, Pippa, Hazel and Diana were over by the fireplace, sitting on the floor. The women were gathered round Carol, Carol on the settee with Sally beside her, Jean on the other side of her and Aimee and Sandra on the floor at her feet. The men were standing in a huddle near the door, the five of them silent and looking solemn. Fiona was standing in the middle of the room, looking uneasy in her role of watch-dog. He gestured to her to come outside, leaving Salma in the room. Salma took off her hat, revealing her jet black glossy hair coiled neatly at the back of her neck. She smiled round pleasantly and said hello to Pippa whom she knew, as that young lady had been at the station some while back getting information for a solo talk on policing.

In the hallway, Charles was speaking to Fiona.

"Fiona. I want you to go into the dining room."

He opened the lounge door and inquired of Ralph, "Ralph, will I find some notepaper in the study?"

"Yes, in the middle drawer of the desk."

"Thanks."

Charles went back to his DS.

"I'll bring the paper to you, Fiona. Salma will send you everyone here, one at a time. Find out where everyone was just before the murder was discovered. Ask what they thought of Santa, if indeed they saw him. Did they recognise anything about him? It's a pity neither of us went in to see him. When you've finished with each one, send him or her into this room here. He opened the door. It was, as he had thought, the family room and had quite a number of seats in it.

Leaving Fiona to settle herself at the dining room table, he went back to the lounge and told Salma to send the guests into the dining room, youngsters first, starting with Pippa.

As his daughter passed him looking excited, he warned her to tell the truth and not let her imagination carry her away. She looked indignant but said nothing. As she closed the dining room door, he heard Fiona say:

"Hello Pippa, sit down across from me please."

He left to get paper and when he went back into the dining room, Pippa was in full flood, telling Fiona about her time in the study with Santa Claus.

The bell rang again. It was Frank Selby this time, casual in denims and a sweatshirt, looking boyish apart from his receding fair hair. A faint smell of beer and cigarettes came in with him. He had obviously been socialising when he had been contacted.

"Sorry, Selby, to break into your free time but there's been a brutal murder here and I want you to take notes for Fiona in the dining room."

"No problem, Sir. I was at home with some mates. One of them wasn't drinking and drove me over here."

The doorbell rang yet again. This time it was the SOC team arriving at the same time as PC Penny Price, her cheeks red from the cold and her dark curls bouncing. He was just about to close the door when he saw Martin Jamieson hurrying up the path, having paid off his taxi driver. His team was now complete and Charles felt himself relaxing.

"Penny. There's been a murder here. DS Macdonald and I were present at the party. A man has been stabbed. Go into this room. Fiona will be sending you the guests once she's interviewed them. It won't matter if they talk to each other at this point. Just listen in for anything that might be interesting."

He turned to the police surgeon and the two- man SOC team and led them into the study.

Martin knelt down and, putting on his latex gloves, examined the wound carefully. He checked the rest of the body, turning it over to inspect the back, and then he rose to his feet.

"I'll be able to tell you more once I've had time to examine the body in my lab but all I will say now is that he appears to have been stabbed only once. You're looking for a sharp instrument with quite a wide blade."

Charles Davenport felt relieved. The police operation was now in motion. He took Martin into the kitchen where they looked down at the blood-stained Santa Claus outfit.

"Well, I have seen it all now. Santa Claus a murderer!" exclaimed Martin.

"Yes I know it seems farfetched but unless we get evidence to the contrary, it appears that someone dressed as Santa Claus did commit the murder."

"Well, I will get the van round to collect the body, Charles and I will let you have more details tomorrow, if there are any. I have nothing else pressing right now."

Charles thanked his lucky stars for Martin, as he always did. He had known some police surgeons who had taken a delight in making him wait as long as possible for results. He allowed himself a little smile at Martin's very correct speech.

Martin got on his mobile to call for a taxi and Charles asked if he would drop Pippa off at her aunt's house. He would ring his sister to warn her of her unexpected visitor. Pippa would stay the night there and he would collect her in the morning.

He went back to the study. SOC had ringed the body with a chalk mark and fingerprinted the desk, chairs and door handle. Charles made a mental note to ask if anyone had noticed whether or not Santa had worn gloves.

Seeing that they were finished in here, he took them into the kitchen where they bagged the Santa suit, took the cutlery drawer contents, then left, Charles promising that all the guests would be called in for fingerprinting the next day and asking for the fingerprints to be checked against any found in the study and on the suit. Maybe they would be lucky and find out that Santa's prints would be on the suit buttons, if not in the study.

Charles found the silly song, "When Santa Got Stuck up the Chimney" going round in his head. He shook his head to clear it and went into the dining room, just as Hazel was coming out. He went into the family room and told Pippa to get her coat from upstairs and go along with Martin Jamieson.

"He'll take you to Auntie Linda's pet. Ask her for a hot milky drink. I'll collect you from there tomorrow. Will you be OK?"

Pippa, it turned out, was very much OK and was annoyed at being removed from all the excitement. She was however, a sensible child and knew that her dad would be happier with her out of the way, so she followed Martin without complaining.

Charles sighed as he closed the door on them. It was going to be a long night.

CHAPTER 12

In the study, Fiona had asked Hazel if she had noticed anything about Santa.

"Sorry, no," said that young lady looking disappointed.

"What height was he?"

"Well, he was sitting down but he looked quite tall. We were both sitting and his head was above mine."

"What about his voice, Hazel? Was it deep? Did it sound like anyone you know?"

"It was as if he had a sore throat."

Fiona wrote "husky voice" on the pad in front of her.

"What did he actually say to you?"

"He asked me if I'd been good. As if I believed in Santa," she said scornfully.

"I don't think he was being cheeky. He probably said that to the adults as well. It's a Santa thing to say," said Fiona. She thanked Hazel for her help and asked her to go and wait in the family room.

She knew that Penny would entertain her till another person was sent in. As she left the dining room, Frank came in. He told her that he was to take notes for her. He noticed his DS grimace as he was notorious for his badly spelled reports unless Penny had helped him.

"Would you like me to change places with Penny, Ma'am. I saw her go into another room. What is she doing?"

Not liking to go against Charles's wishes, Fiona left the room to ask him what he thought, as these notes could prove important.

She came back and, smiling at Frank, she said that the DCI thanked him for being so thoughtful and yes, he could swap jobs with Penny. He was to entertain the guests who had been interviewed and listen out for anything they might say that would be of importance.

Frank left the dining room and shortly afterwards, Penny came in and sat down at the opposite end of the table to Fiona. Fiona passed down her notebook.

"Evening, Penny."

"Evening, Ma'am."

"Do you know what's happened Penny?"

"One of the guests has been stabbed. You and the DCI were present when it happened." Penny was succinct as usual.

Fiona smiled.

"Well not exactly present or we might have stopped it. We were all in the lounge and Santa Claus was in the study. Some people had been to see him and got presents. Brian Ewing, the brother of the man whose house this is, went along and didn't come back. His wife went into the study and found him dead and Santa gone."

"Whose idea was it to have a Santa Claus Ma'am?"

"I've only interviewed two of the children, Pippa Davenport and her best friend Hazel Ewing, the dead man's niece. When I get to Ralph and Sally Ewing who hosted the party I'll ask them that question. Let's get to work."

Fiona went along to the lounge and asked Diana to come along to the study with her. The girl was subdued and red eyed.

"Sit down Diana. Now all I want is to ask you about Santa. Can you tell me anything about him?"

"He asked me to sit down. His voice was quite quiet, kind of husky. He asked if I'd been good all year. I said I had. I don't believe in Santa of course but I wasn't annoyed like my cousin Hazel. It was just fun. Well it was fun until........"

She stopped.

"Is there anything you could tell me about Santa?"

"He was quite thin, unlike shop Santas when I was wee. I couldn't see his hair or his face because he had a Santa hood and a beard. Wait a minute, he had on black shoes. Is that any help? Santa usually wears boots with fur round them."

Fiona said it was a great help and thanked her, telling her to go along to the study and wait there till all the others had been questioned.

"You'll find Hazel there."

Diana left and Fiona asked Penny to go to the lounge, telling her it was the room to the left of the main door and asking her to bring one of the twin boys along.

"When Penny opened the lounge door, the first thing she noticed was the silence. It was odd to see a roomful of quiet people. She saw two boys, identical as far as she could see, sitting together, one in a chair and the other on the arm and asked one of them to follow her.

"Hello, John, or is it Ian?" said the DS.

"It's John. I'm the good-looking one." He smiled at his own joke. Fiona thought that it probably had not sunk in yet that his father was dead and wondered how his twin was taking it.

"John, sit down please. This is PC Price. She will be taking notes."

John smiled at Penny who smiled back.

"Now, John. Can you tell me anything at all about Santa?"

"Well he dresses in a red outfit, comes in a sleigh pulled by reindeer and brings presents to good children."

"John. This isn't the time for jokes. This man, dressed as Santa Claus, could have killed your father."

Suddenly, John crumpled. His shoulders sagged and his head went down. He mumbled, "Sorry, don't know what came over me."

He pushed a strand of hair back from his forehead and lifted his head.

"What do you want to know about Santa?"

"Did you notice if he was tall, short, thin, fat?"

"A bit taller than me I think. He was looking down at me when we were both sitting. I think he was quite slim as he didn't look plump even in his suit."

"What about his shoes? Did you notice the colour?"

"No, sorry. I didn't."

"Did he speak?"

"Just to say Merry Christmas as he handed me a present. I suppose that was odd. My sister said that he asked if she'd been good but maybe he thought I was too old for that nonsense."

"So is your sister, John."

"Well maybe it was because I was a man."

"Thank you, John. If you remember anything else please let the police know."

John left the room. Penny went with him, telling him to go along to the sitting room. She went on to the lounge and asked the other young man to come to the dining room.

Ian was visibly upset. He sat down, looking at the table.

"Ian, I'm sorry to ask you questions at a time like this but I'd like you to tell me anything you can about Santa, his height, weight, voice, anything at all."

"Well, he was about my height I think. We were both sitting down and his eyes were about level with mine or a wee bit higher. He wasn't fat like Santas were when I was wee."

"Did you see his shoes?"

"His shoes? No I didn't, sorry."

"What about his voice? Did you recognise it?"

"Why would I recognise it? Do you mean that Santa was somebody I knew? I assumed it was someone Uncle Ralph or Aunt Sally had hired to come along and give us presents. Anyway his voice was quiet. I suppose that was unusual too. Santa is usually loud and jovial, isn't he?"

"Who let him in?"

"Mum and John answered the door and John took him to the study. There had been a fire on there earlier and the room was probably the warmest in the house. I imagine that's why Aunt Sal suggested that John take him in there."

"Whose idea was Santa?"

"I'm sorry, I don't know. Must have been either my aunt's or my uncle's, I assume. It was their party and the presents were things most folk wanted. I mean I got a CD of Robbie Williams and he's my favourite and only someone who knew me would know that."

Realising that she would get no more information from the boy, Fiona thanked him and Penny showed him out. She came back in to ask who her boss wanted her to see now. Fiona had been thinking about who else had gone in to see Santa and asked Penny to fetch Aimee followed by her fiancé, Colin, then Jim and Sandra Rogerson. She described them to Penny.

Penny called out Aimee's name and a beautiful young woman rose from the settee. Dark as Penny, she looked excited, rather than upset.

Penny took her to the dining room and asked her to sit down across from the DS.

"Aimee, what an introduction to a Scottish Christmas," said Fiona.

"I know. I 'ave been enjoying every minute of it." said Aimee, then obviously realising that this did not sound right, she hastened to add, "This bit is not exciting, no."

"You went in to see Santa, didn't you?"

"Yes, I did. He gave me a lovely teddy bear in a red hat."

"Can you tell me anything about the man under the red outfit?"

"Well he was wearing black shoes. I thought Santa would wear boots. He was too thin for Santa and his voice was a younger man's voice. I think. Santa, he should be an old man."

"Anything else? Height?"

"He did not get up so I cannot 'elp you with that, I am sorry."

"You've been great help Aimee. You speak English very well. Have you stayed in this country for some time?"

"No but in school we were taught to speak English, not just to write it."

"Thank you. Penny here will show you to the sitting room. Please wait there till we tell you you can go."

Penny showed her out and stood aside to let her DCI enter.

"Fiona, have you finished with all those who saw Santa?"

"Only Colin and the Rogersons left, Sir."

"When you've finished with Colin, we'll let him and his girlfriend go home."

"What about the young girls?"

"It's Hazel's house. I'll tell her she can go to bed though I doubt if she'll want to go till she sees her parents. Diana will have to wait till we've spoken to her mother who found the body. See her after the Rogersons please. We'll leave Ralph and Sally to the last. Pippa's gone to her aunt's with Martin."

"What about us Charles?"

"Quite right. Penny, you've been listening to Fiona's questions. Would you question us after the rest of the guests have been seen? Two more after Carol Ewing: Arthur Mackie the local GP and his friend Jean."

Colin was next. He had little to offer and seemed more concerned about Aimee than about the murder. Asked about the murdered man, he looked mulish.

"I didn't like him much. Too forward with all the ladies. Saw him pat my fiancée's bottom tonight. Was going to speak to him about it. Didn't get the chance."

"Not a man of many words," thought Fiona.

He went to the little family room and collected his fiancée and they left shortly afterwards, promising not to leave the district until told that they could.

It was almost eleven o'clock.

CHAPTER 13

Jim Rogerson looked excited. He reminded Fiona of Hazel and Pippa, almost childlike in his enthusiasm at being part of a murder enquiry. He told them nothing that they didn't already know but was reluctant to leave, adamant about ensuring them that it was the work of an outsider. Asked why he was so sure, he said that no one at the party could have done such an awful thing. Fiona sent him into the sitting room to join the young ones.

Sandra, on the other hand, was quiet and calm. She had noticed Sally smiling when she told them that Santa had arrived. Sally had let him in, so Sandra assumed that having Santa was Sally's idea. That was all she knew. Fiona wondered why Sandra kept looking along the dining room table and smiling to herself. She too was sent to join the others.

Carol, called next, came in looking quite flushed and Fiona suspected that she had been given a stiff drink to calm her down. She asked the woman to sit down across from her and introduced Penny.

"Mrs Ewing, I'm sorry to be asking you questions at a time like this but it really is important that we find out as much as possible as soon as possible so that we can catch the person who killed your husband."

"I understand."

"Tell me what happened when you went into the study, please."

"I was surprised not to see Santa to start with. The room seemed empty. Then I looked down and saw Brian lying on the floor. For a second I thought it was Santa - there was so much red. It was the blood. There was so much...I..."

Into Penny's head popped a quote from Macbeth which she had studied in her last year at school:

"Who would have thought the old man to have so much blood in him?"

Her DS was talking soothingly to Carol Ewing.

"OK Mrs Ewing. Please try not to think about that. All I want to know is, on the way to the study did you see anyone?"

"Only Sally, my sister-in-law. She was going into the dining room with a tray of something for supper. The rest followed me out of the lounge to go for supper. They must have gone to the dining room. Oh, I think all the young ones were at the front of the queue."

"Thank you. Would you mind going into the next room and staying with your daughter and niece. Mr Davenport will let you go home shortly."

As she said these words, Charles came in.

"Carol, take Diana and the boys and get off home. Can you drive or will I get someone to drive you home?"

"Brian was the one who was to drive tonight," said Carol. "I've had a few drinks."

Charles went into the family room where Hazel and her cousins were sitting and asked the boys if either of them could drive. They both could. Ian said he had drunk quite a lot but John had drunk nothing stronger than coca cola so he agreed to take his mother, brother and sister home.

Charles suggested to Hazel that she go upstairs and get ready for bed, telling her that her parents would come up once they had been interviewed. Like her friend Pippa, Hazel seemed disappointed to be leaving the crime scene but Mr Davenport did not look as if he would brook any argument. He was quite different from the jovial man she had met when she had had a sleepover at Pippa's.

He told the Rogersons that they could go home now after getting their address from them, and went into the dining room, asking Frank to come along too after going into the lounge to ask Dr Mackie to come along.

Arthur had not been to see Santa, so was of little help to them, neither was Jean who looked tired and knew nothing of Santa either. Fiona, going into the hall with them, thanked them both for waiting and said that they could now go home.

"Are you the family doctor?" she asked Arthur.

"Only of Ralph, Sally and Hazel Ewing," he said.

"Maybe you should come in to see them tomorrow if possible. There will probably be delayed shock."

Arthur Mackie agreed with her and he and Jean left.

"Who does that leave us with?" Fiona asked Davenport.

"Only Ralph and Sally Ewing."

Davenport went to the lounge and asked Sally Ewing to come to the dining room.

He was shocked when he saw her. She was very pale and shaking quite violently. The sister-in-law was more upset than the wife! He knew that different people reacted in different ways to bereavement and violent death but this woman was distraught. Fiona, seeing her state, was glad that she had asked their doctor to look in the next day.

The door opened. Charles expected it to be Frank but it was Ralph Ewing, followed by Frank who was looking a bit annoyed.

"Mr Ewing, I've told you that only one person is to be seen at one time," Frank was saying. "Please come back to the lounge with me."

"No I won't. My wife is terribly upset and she shouldn't be subjected to any more stress. She's recovering from a mental illness and you can see how this has affected her."

He put his arm round his wife who seemed relieved to see him.

"OK Ralph, but please don't speak while we are interviewing Sally," said Davenport. "DS Macdonald will be as quick as possible and then your wife can go upstairs and stay with Hazel while we talk to you."

Both Ewings sat down. Davenport took Frank outside, not wanting to crowd Fiona and the two being interviewed.

Fiona spoke gently to Sally, "Mrs Ewing, when you went out to get supper ready, did you see anyone in the hallway?"

"I saw John or Ian going back into the lounge. He said he'd been into the study with a mince pie for Santa. He had the empty plate and I took it from him."

"Who was in with Santa at that time?"

"I don't know. Well, it must have still been Brian. I'm sorry, I'm not thinking straight. Of course it was Brian".

Fiona, hearing footsteps in the hall, went out to catch Carol and her family leaving. They had been upstairs to get their coats. Charles and Frank were with them.

"Boys, which one of you gave Santa a mince pie?" Fiona asked.

"I did," said one boy. "Did I not mention that?"

"You told me," said Davenport.

"Which twin are you?" asked Fiona.

"I'm John," said John.

"John. Who was in with Santa?"

"I thought I'd told you. Dad was just going in. Santa spoke to him and then the door shut."

Fiona thanked the boy and went back into the dining room, closing the door.

"OK, Mrs Ewing. You saw John. Nobody else?"

"No."

"Then what happened?"

"I came out of the kitchen with a tray of pies. The next lot got burnt. I wasn't allowed to get them out of the oven."

Ralph took her hand.

"Sal, it doesn't matter about the damn pies."

"Sorry, Ralph. Sorry Fiona...or should I call you DS Macdonald now?"

"Please call me whatever you're most comfortable with," said Fiona.

"Then there was a scream. I dropped the empty tray. Carol came out of the study and said that Brian was dead."

She started to shake. Fiona thanked her and decided to let her stay while she questioned Ralph.

She asked Ralph whose idea Santa had been. Ralph feeling light-headed was tempted to answer flippantly and say, "His mother's," but managed to restrain himself. He needed to keep strong for his wife, not go to pieces himself.

"It was your idea, Sal, wasn't it?"

"No. I thought he was your idea, Ralph," said Sally.

They looked at each other, puzzled.

Fiona thanked them both and let them go, saying that the police would be leaving their home now but that they would be back in the morning. Ralph took his wife's arm and gently led her out of the dining room, making a mental note to call Arthur Mackie in in the morning. Sally was still on antidepressants but she was going to need something extra to get her through this tragedy.

Fiona told the team assembled in the hall that Santa had not been the idea of the host or hostess, unless one or both were lying.

Who had played Santa and whose idea had he been?

CHAPTER 14

It was Saturday 24th December and Davenport's team had assembled in the Incident Room. He had not yet got an enlarged picture of the dead man so the incident board was clear. The phone rang. It was the front desk.

"Sir, there's a call for you from a Mr Rogerson. He says it's important."

"Put me through, Bob."

The others were silent while their boss took the call. He hung up and told them, "That was Jim Rogerson. He's an elder in the local church and someone phoned him this morning to say that they went to get the Santa outfit for the Sunday school party tonight and the outfit had gone."

"So we know where the outfit came from then," said Fiona. "Was there any sign of a break-in?"

"Seemingly not. However, the cupboard wasn't locked so anyone could have taken it, presumably someone who knew where it was kept."

"That only narrows it down to the congregation," said Frank, flippantly, and received a stern look from Davenport.

"The guests who did see Santa got presents that were relevant to them. Well Ian, or was it John, thought that because he got a CD which he liked, a Robbie Williams one."

"But Sir, most young folk would like that CD," said Penny.

"Right enough, young Penny. I remember that Pippa got a pencil case and was delighted but only I and possibly Fiona or her chum Hazel would know that she loved all things stationery so it had to be a coincidence and the others got general Christmassy things."

"So back to the congregation as Frank said," piped in Salma, throwing a smile at Frank and getting a grateful one in return.

"Or to make it worse, anyone who had been told that there was a Santa suit on the church premises. Who would talk about a thing like that?" Davenport looked dejected as he said this.

"Maybe we should get Jim Rogerson in and find out who has been Santa over the last few years," offered Fiona.

"Luckily, I've asked him to come in this morning," said Davenport, brightening up a bit.

It was about eleven when Jim arrived, apologising for taking so long.

"My car wouldn't start and my wife had taken hers out to do some grocery shopping. She got back about half an hour ago and I came straight over."

Asked about who had played Santa over the last few years, Jim looked bemused.

"I did it last year and the year before that it was our session clerk. It's always been a church official recently because of Child Protection. Anyone playing Santa had to have filled in a disclosure form. You must know that Mr Davenport."

"Yes that's true. Anyone else who would know about the outfit being kept at the church?"

"I suppose our families would know."

Thanking him for coming to the station, Davenport said he could go home now.

Fiona had left the room while the DCI had been questioning Jim and she returned to say that there had been a call from Martin Jamieson. The police surgeon had done his work on the body and could now confirm that death had been caused by one stab of a wide bladed knife. The knife had entered the heart and death would have been instantaneous. SOC had tested the blood on the Santa suit and it matched that of the dead man. SOC had also been in touch about the knives they had taken from the Ewing's kitchen drawer. One large knife had been found to have some traces of blood on the blade though it had been washed. The blood also matched that of Brian Ewing.

There were no fingerprints on the handle which in itself was odd as the knife must have been used by the family so the murderer must have wiped the handle. The buttons of the suit had been tested. They too were clean. No need to fingerprint anyone now.

Davenport was grateful for the speedy news. He guessed that things had been quiet for forensics and for Martin Jamieson, though that man always was as speedy as possible. All they knew now was that the murderer had been very efficient.

"Well folks, I'll sum up. The murder was premeditated. Someone went to the bother of stealing the Santa suit and buying presents for the guests. That someone was very organised. The knife and the buttons on the suit were wiped clean."

"So who are we looking for Sir?" asked Penny who could never wait for anyone to finish.

" We are either looking for an outsider who had heard of the party and gate-crashed as Santa Claus to kill Brian Ewing or a guest who took the chance of the party to commit the murder."

"Sir, are we to take charge of this investigation?" asked Salma, "You were, in a way, involved."

"Yes, I contacted the chief constable early this morning and he thinks that it will make things easier that DS Macdonald and I were there."

"Are we working over Christmas, Sir?" asked Salma. "It's OK for me, being a Muslim, but what about Penny and Frank?"

Penny and Frank were quick to say that they were willing to give up their two days' holiday. Charles thanked them both then turned to Fiona.

"You were going to be away this weekend, were you not, Fiona?"

"With my old school chums to Crieff Hydro, yes but I phoned last night and told the one organising it that I'd have to cancel."

Davenport looked round at his team.

"Thank you all. Now let's get started."

CHAPTER 15

They started with Penny doing a brief interview with her two bosses. She asked them to run through the night of the party which they did, outlining the games and the arrival of Santa. Both had noticed Sally smiling and both had assumed that the two Ewings had planned the advent of Mr Claus. With hindsight, they now knew that Sally had smiled thinking it had been her husband's idea. Penny asked what had happened in the run up to Carol's scream and both told her that they had been in the hall, making their way to the dining room.

Asked who they had seen in the hall, Fiona said she had seen Arthur Mackie and Jean and had been talking to them. She thought she had seen both twins as they had pushed in in front of them, eager to get at the food. Charles who had been behind Fiona had seen her talking to the other couple and had been on his own in front of Sandra and Jim Rogerson who had been arguing over a visit to Jim's elderly mother.

Apparently Jim had seen her that afternoon and she had been annoyed that Sandra had not gone with him, as usual. Jim had said that maybe his wife could go the next day by herself and Sandra had snapped back that they were going on Christmas Day and that was enough.

Penny had armed herself with the guest list and asked each one individually if they had seen the three young girls and Colin Ferguson and his fiancée, Aimee.

"Colin was in front of me," said Fiona. "He and Aimee were hugging and kissing. He had taken a piece of mistletoe from the lounge and was holding it over their heads."

"I think the kids were at the very front of the queue," said Davenport "but I can't see any of those young girls stabbing a stocky fellow like Brian Ewing. He wasn't tall but he was very well built. And what motive could they possibly have?"

Penny thanked him and they rejoined the team.

When they were all seated, Davenport asked Penny if anything had come to light from the interviews she had been present at.

"Well Sir, everybody was seen by somebody. The only people you didn't mention were Ralph and Sally Ewing and they......."

"I heard the tray landing on the floor of the dining room," said Davenport, so Sally must have been in there.

"And all the young folk claimed to have seen Ralph in the dining room," finished Penny. "He ran to the study with you, Sir."

"Anything else, Penny, or you, Fiona?"

"Just what you said, Sir, at the end of your interview."

"What was that?"

"You said that the young ones had no motive. I can't see the motive for anyone at all," said Fiona.

"The wife's always the first suspect," chipped in Frank who had been quiet for ages.

"Don't be sexist Frank!" said Penny, knowing her colleague's propensity for being sexist, bigoted and racist though not so much the latter since he had got to know his sergeant, Salma Din.

"No, Penny. He's right. The wife or husband is always the first person we suspect in a murder case and she could have stabbed Brian then screamed." Davenport defended Frank.

"So, Sir, do we get Mrs Ewing, Carol that is, in for questioning today or do we go to her house?" asked Salma.

"I think you and Penny should get along to their house, in Eaglesham it is, and ask her about her relationship with her husband. Not pleasant but it has to be done. She could have got someone to do the killing I suppose. Frank, you go with them and question the kids about their parents' relationship, tactfully please."

"What about me, Sir?" asked Fiona.

"You get the mundane job of typing up all the interviews. Penny's notes are always well-written and easy to read and as you were asking the questions it should be easy for you to fill in the details she might have missed. Penny, leave your notes on our interviews today with DS Macdonald."

Fiona gave a grimace which he noticed. He smiled.

"You and I can go for a bar lunch in Shawlands at midday."

"Good idea Charles."

Frank, heading out of the door behind Salma and Penny, caught this exchange and burst into a bar of, "Speed Bonny Boat." They turned and grinned at him and he hurried after them to tell them what he had heard. Right from the day Charles Davenport had arrived about eighteen months ago, Frank had linked him, Charles, with DS Macdonald, seeing them as Bonnie Prince Charlie and Flora Macdonald. He had found numerous songs which were relevant to this pair and had whistled or sung them so often that he had been chosen, by Davenport, to visit a church locally on their Scottish evening in July, much to Salma's and Penny's delight. Salma had gone with him and they had both been bored stiff but had not dared to tell their boss that Frank did not really like Scottish music.

The three young ones climbed into a squad car. Salma was driving and Frank knew better than to comment on female drivers. Fiona got on with her paperwork and Davenport phoned his sister to tell Pippa that he would pick her up mid-afternoon.

CHAPTER 16

It took the young policeman and women about twenty minutes to get to Eaglesham. It was a lovely, crisp, sunny day, a pleasant change from the wet, windy weather which Glasgow had been having recently. They had been told that Polnoon Street was the first street after The Eglinton Arms Hotel and they found it easily.

The Ewing house was just past a small road called Mid Road and they found a parking space right outside the house.

It was Diana Ewing who answered their ring. She looked hollow-eyed and pale.

"Come in. Mum's expecting you."

She led them through an airy hall to the sitting room. Money spoke from every part of the room, from the elegant settees and chairs to the glass cabinet full of crystal. Carol did not keep them waiting.

"Good morning," she said stiffly.

Diana left them.

"Hello, Mrs Ewing. I'm Sergeant Salma Din. Sorry to trouble you at this terrible time. My colleague PC Selby would like to talk to your three children while PC Price and I talk with you. Where will he find them?"

"They'll be in the family room, across the hall. They've got the TV on. That will lead him to the correct room."

Frank left. He found the family room, knocked and on being told to come in, he entered and found Ian and John ensconced on the settee and Diana on a large pouffe at their feet. The TV was showing a quiz programme which Frank did not recognise. One of the boys rose and switched it off.

"I'm PC Selby," said Frank, showing his identity card. "I want to ask you a few questions about your Dad."

"OK," said one of the boys.

"Are you John or Ian?" asked Frank.

"I'm John."

"John, can you tell me if you know of anyone who might have disliked your Dad enough to kill him?"

"Apart from Mum?" laughed John.

"John!" said Diana, horrified.

"Well, it's the truth. Mum's hated him since she found out that he'd been having an affair for two years."

Frank took out his notebook.

"Do you by any chance know who he was having this affair with, John?"

"Yes. His receptionist, Wendy."

"How do you know all this?"

"It wasn't difficult," said Ian, quietly. "Mum gets very loud when she's angry."

"Mum wouldn't have killed Dad," said Diana. "Wouldn't she have done if before now if she'd wanted to?"

"Was your Mum wanting a divorce?" asked Frank.

"No but Dad was. Mum stupidly thought we'd be upset and she made him pay in other ways."

"John. Stop telling him all our private things," said Diana.

"Nothing is private in a murder enquiry Miss Ewing," said Frank. "What other ways, John?"

"She got more money from him and she denied him her 'favours'," said John, sounding like a hardened man of the world.

"How do you know this?" asked Frank.

"Well only yesterday he tried to hug her and she said he could stop that as it was 'off limits' and he had his floosy for that sort of thing."

"So the affair with Wendy was still going on."

"I imagine so."

Diana started to sob and Ian put his arm round her,

"Is that all, constable?" he asked Frank.

"Yes, thank you for your honesty, John and sorry to have upset you, Diana."

Frank left the room and re-entered the sitting room.

Salma was just thanking Carol Ewing for her time and her honesty. She and Penny rose and the three of them were shown to the door by Carol.

"I would try to get your doctor to see your daughter, Mrs Ewing. She's very upset," said Frank.

Carol agreed to do this and they made their way to the car.

"What did she tell you?" asked Frank.

"She was very open. She told us that Brian had been having an affair with his receptionist for about four years and that she had stayed with him for the sake of the three children."

"Did she intend to leave him?"

"I don't think so," said Penny. "I think she enjoyed her life style. She said that life was going to be very hard without Brian as she didn't work and the boys were at university and Diana was at private school."

"So she didn't have a motive for killing him?"

"Apparently not, if she was being honest." said Salma.

"She said that Brian had told her recently that the affair with his receptionist was over," said Penny.

"Did she believe him?"

"She said she didn't care one way or the other. It was over between her and her husband anyway."

"What did you get from the kids?" asked Penny.

"Much the same," said Frank. "They knew all about the affair and one of the boys said that his mother would not have sex with his Dad and got more money from him than she had before."

"Were they not upset?" asked Salma.

"The girl, Diana was. She must have been fonder of her father than the boys were but I suppose it's natural for boys to side with their mother and girls with their father. One of the boys said the affair was still going on."

Knowing that their DCI and DS would by now be having lunch, Salma suggested that they too, gave the work canteen a body swerve and had lunch somewhere nicer. They were almost at Rouken Glen so Penny suggested they go there, to Boaters by the pond. They all decided on toasties with various toppings, followed by a cream cake each, then they got back in the car and headed for the station. They had started on their reports when Davenport and Macdonald arrived back.

"I'll finish off my typing of the statements I took last night," said Fiona.

"OK and I'll hear what these reprobates have to say," said Davenport, smiling at his three young folk.

It did not take long for them to bring him up to speed with Brian Ewing's four year old affair and Carol Ewing's treatment of him.

"So she had no motive for getting him out of the way."

"Seems like it, Sir," said Salma.

"Well, you can all go home now. Christmas day tomorrow but I want us all here for the morning at least. We need to sort out who we need to interview now."

"Santa, Sir?" laughed Penny.

"If only," Davenport laughed back and Frank felt a small stab of resentment. If he had made this comment, the boss would probably have reprimanded him.

Salma noticed his look and smiled at him. Never one to be moody for long, he grinned back.

"Bye then Sir," they chorused. "See you in the morning."

Christmas was not going to be, for them, a season of good news and joy.

CHAPTER 17

She lay in the darkness. Like last night, her ears pricked up at any sound but her bedroom door stayed shut. She knew that he would not come tonight. She touched her breasts under her nightie and felt the nipples harden. She had never touched herself before. This was not unpleasant. Her orgasm when it came was wonderful. Suddenly she wanted more. She got up and put on her dressing gown.

As she crept across the landing, she was careful not to stand on any squeaky boards as he had done on those previous nights. Reaching her targeted room, she raised her hand and knocked very gently. No reply. She knocked again, slightly louder this time but not loud enough to waken the rest of the house.

This time she was successful. A light came on under the door and she heard him call out;

"Who is it? Come in."

She opened the door quietly and stepped inside, saying, "I want you."

Earlier that same evening, Sandra Rogerson rang Derek. She had had a tiring day with Jim who was full of childish pleasure about the approaching Christmas Day. He had made a big fuss of her not seeing the present he was wrapping for her, though she knew what it would be, a large box of chocolates, perfume and some expensive lingerie. Why he continued to buy the latter she did not know as he hadn't seen her in her underwear for ages. She brightened at the thought that it would soon be seen by Derek, but how soon? That was why she was phoning him now.

"Hi Derek, it's Sandra."

"Hello darling. How are you and when can we meet again?"

"I'm fine but missing you terribly .What are you doing tonight?"

"Tonight! Won't Jim miss you on Christmas Eve?"

"He goes to church about ten o'clock to check that everything's ready for the Watchnight Service and he'll be there till about one o'clock as they have mulled wine and mince pies after the service."

"But don't you go?"

"Usually but I can plead a migraine and he'll go without me."

"You beauty! Will you come here or will I come to you?"

"I'll come to you. I've taken a real liking to your dining room table."

He laughed.

"I'm sure we can add some other furniture to your 'like' list," he said in a deep sexy voice and she shivered pleasantly in anticipation.

"Have to go. Jim's coming upstairs."

"Who were you phoning San?" asked her husband as he came into the bedroom.

"Just Derek to thank him for last night," she replied truthfully.

"Did you have a good time?"

"Well let's just say it had the edge on Ralph and Sally's party!"

"Yes, poor Sally."

"Sally. Don't you mean Carol?"

"Carol will cope. She never struck me as being in love with Brian though she'll miss his money. Sally on the other hand is very fragile after her anxiety attacks. I hope it doesn't put her back. Ralph must be feeling murderous......well you know what I mean."

Sandra rubbed her forehead.

Jim was instantly concerned.

"Are you OK darling?"

"Feel a bit of a headache. Think I'll take a migraine pill just in case."

"Will you be OK for the service tonight?"

"I hope so."

Sandra put some emphasise on 'hope'.

"I have to go shortly to open the church and get things ready."

"I know. I do hope I'll be OK but if I'm not there, come in quietly as I might be asleep."

"I won't wait for the mulled wine and mince pies."

"Oh Jim, don't be silly. You know how much you enjoy that part of the evening. Just stay but I'll probably be there anyway."

Looking happier, Jim let himself out of the front door. He could walk to his church in Newlands and usually did. It was a crisp, clear night, the moon shining brightly and looking enormous in the velvety black sky and he enjoyed his walk. He unpadlocked the church gates and then unlocked the door. Good, the heating had come on. That had been his main worry as it had been temperamental of late. He switched on the main lights. He would switch them off nearer the time of the service as the church was only lit by one or two lights on this evening. He checked the advent candles, four red ones with the white one for Christmas Day in the middle. The matches were sitting ready.

Moving off to the halls, he put out the cups for the mulled wine and put on the large kettle for tea for those who would not drink wine. The mince pies would be brought by the president of the Women's Guild and all he had to do was put on the oven at a low heat. They had a church officer but he went to stay with his daughter in Perth over the festive season and Jim always took it upon himself to do all these duties.

Ralph had been worried about Sally all day, not because she was upset but because she was, he felt, too calm and had even suggested going to the church at 11.30pm.

"I think we should give it a miss this year, Sal," he said now.

"I think we need the message of Christmas even more this year," she replied quietly. "And we promised Hazel that she could go this year. Imagine how she'll feel if she doesn't go and Pippa goes to *her* church!"

"What will Carol and the kids think?"

"They won't know. They don't come to our church anyway."

There was no dissuading her so Ralph had to content himself by pouring them both a stiff drink.

Also in Newlands, Arthur Mackie was puzzled. Something was playing at the back of his mind but, try as he might, he could not bring it forward. He had arranged to go with Jean to the church service at her small church in Shawlands and he hoped that this annoying niggle would have resolved itself before they went.

In Eaglesham, Carol was wondering what to do about Christmas. Should she try to keep things as normal as possible or give up any pretence of this being a normal Christmas Eve? She asked her sons who thought they should definitely not go to church this evening but who thought that they should exchange presents tomorrow and have their usual dinner as most of the preparations had been made before their Dad died. Diana, unusually quiet, had no opinion to give and seemed happy to go along with whatever her brothers and mother decided. She stayed close to Ian all day.

Colin and Aimee, along with Colin's Mum and Dad, were going to their church in Newton Mearns. Aimee wanted to see a service in the church she would be married in. She wanted to concentrate on thoughts of her wedding. She hoped that Colin had not seen Brian Ewing pat her on the bottom last night as she had not protested, in fact she had found herself strangely attracted to the man. Although she would not have wished him dead, she was glad that he was out of her life as he could have made things complicated.

Going to the same church would be Charles Davenport and Pippa. This would be her first

Watchnight service and she was excited about being allowed to stay up so late. Charles, fond though he was of Fiona Macdonald, had not invited her, wanting his daughter's first Christmas Eve service to be with him alone. Her mother had come up from England to stay with her parents over Christmas and Pippa would spend the holiday with them. He had phoned his wife to ask her to pick the wee girl up from her Aunt Linda's and he had arranged to pick up his young daughter from her gran's at 11.30pm. It was lucky that this had all been arranged some weeks before, given that Charles would now have to be at work on Christmas morning and for some time to come. He had asked Fiona, whose Christmas plans had had to be cancelled, to join him for Christmas dinner in the evening. She was on her own as he was and he had told his team that they would only be working during the morning.

It was a changed Christmas that would greet them all tomorrow.

CHAPTER 18

Sandra was with Derek. She had gone to his house as soon as Jim had left for church and had been welcomed literally with open arms. She had felt very special as he had taken her into his lounge this time and given her a glass of champagne. She had told him about the murder of Brian Ewing but she felt strangely distanced from last night's events and they had progressed from his cream leather settee to his white fur rug where they had sat and eaten oysters, holding each one for the other person to eat. After this, they had had strawberries and whipped cream and somehow the cream had got onto faces and had to be licked off. She didn't remember afterwards who had suggested getting the rest of the cream from the fridge, undressing each other and putting the cream over each other's bodies. Licking this off had made them both horny and the sex on the rug was the most marvellous Sandra had ever had. She had refused more champagne, knowing that she would have to drive home.

They had lain on the rug and talked about their lives. Derek had divorced his wife some years ago and he had two grown-up children. He had had a few brief relationships since then but nothing serious. He told Sandra that he had admired her since she first joined his team. He found her fashion articles cleverly done and soon he found her body exciting to watch, though from a distance as he knew that she was married.

She in turn, told him of her marriage to Jim, her first love. She had had no affairs till this one although there had been opportunities. She told Derek that she had admired him from a safe distance and only recently had realised that he liked her too.

They moved to the bedroom. She was startled to see black silk sheets on his bed and he told her that he had bought them only that day. She felt turned on at the sight of them and when she felt the silky smoothness, she almost climaxed. Derek was slow this time. He teased her to the brink of orgasm then stopped, then began again till she was almost pleading with him to let her finish. They climaxed together for the first time.

All she wanted to do now was fall asleep in his arms and wake still there but she noticed the time, almost midnight. Telling him that she would try to get away to meet him again soon, she got up and retrieved her clothes which were strewn over the lounge floor.

She arrived home and had just got into bed when she heard the front door open and close. When Jim came into the bedroom, she feigned sleep as she could not bear to talk to him and wanted to fall asleep thinking of Derek and their evening together. About twenty minutes later, Jim climbed in beside her, turned over onto his side and was asleep in minutes as usual. She lay awake for a long while that night.

In another house on the South side, she lay alone. She knew after the last time that she was not welcome in his room. He had explained to her why they could not be in bed together. He had been angry but not with her. She felt confused, lay awake till about 2 am, then fell asleep with a worried furrow on her brow.

Sally took a Valium as well as her anti-depressant pills as she knew she needed help that night. Ralph watched her and felt so despondent that he almost asked her for a tablet for himself. How could he face another bout of depression for Sally? He loved her so much and felt so helpless. Sally, with the help of medication, fell asleep quickly. Ralph lay awake worrying till almost 4 o'clock.

Arthur Mackie sat in front of his real coal fire staring into the glowing embers, thinking about the service he had just been too. He had enjoyed his first Watchnight service for some years. He smiled as he remembered how comfortable he had been with Jean beside him. Then his smile faded and he wondered once again what it was that was puzzling him. He gave a sigh and drank down the last of his Glenfiddich. He banked up the fire and slowly climbed the stairs to his bedroom, followed by his cat Esmeralda. It was not until he was combing his thick, white hair that he realised what it was. He could do nothing about it now or on Christmas Day but on Boxing Day he would be asking some questions. He pondered this for some time, getting up to remake his bed after getting it in an untidy mess with his tossing and turning.

Fiona lay in her single bed and thought of the day ahead. Had she been wise to agree to spending the day with Charles without Pippa there? What did she hope for from this relationship? It had gone well since they first met and they were now firm friends, playing both golf and bridge together, and good workmates. She valued his friendship. Would he try to take things one step further when they were alone together and did she want him to? Her physical relationship with her boss in her last station had been wonderful while it lasted but she had been almost the last to know when he had strayed and she had been unable to remain at the station with everyone knowing what had happened. Could she risk this again? She enjoyed where she was now and liked her sergeant and her two constables, even Frank who could annoy her at times.

Should she fake an illness tomorrow? She fell asleep eventually with her problem still unresolved.

It would have comforted her to know that, lying in his big double bed, Charles Davenport was worrying too. He knew that he wanted more from his relationship with Fiona Macdonald but knew that working together might then be difficult, especially if things fell apart. He knew that he could not put Fiona through another change of job so would have to move himself and that meant uprooting his daughter yet again.

Should he keep everything on a friendly footing tomorrow or was she expecting and hoping for more? Although he tossed and turned for some hours, he was no further forward when in the small hours he at last slept.

Santa Claus, should he have arrived at any of these houses, would have found the occupants too awake for his visit.

CHAPTER 19

The sound of sobbing woke Ralph. He turned over in the bed and took Sally in his arms, murmuring soothing words and glad that she was able to cry. An expert at bottling things up, Sally always soldiered on. The psychiatrist who had diagnosed her problem had also, through letting her talk freely to him, discovered that two years prior to her panic attack, she had faced the closure of her first and only school. He said that for her, this had been like a bereavement as she loved the place, the staff and the pupils - well most of them. She had coped really well, going off to a new school and learning the ropes all over again, getting to know new classes and new colleagues. The psychiatrist had said that if she had coped less well, she would probably have avoided the mental breakdown which had started on holiday. She had coped too with the breakdown, never once missing a day at work and gradually with the help of medication she had come out of the cycle of anxiety and depression. Her second school was also in danger of closing but she was not so attached to it so would probably face it, if it happened, with less stress. The murder of his brother however would not be so easy to face.

"Please cry, Sal. It'll do you good, my love," he said tenderly.

"Who could have wanted to kill Brian?" she hiccupped.

"Apart from Carol, you mean?" he said jokingly.

"Oh Ralph, how can you joke about it?"

"Sorry love. That was uncalled for. I apologise. Look, I'll go downstairs and make us both a cup of tea. Hazel's too old to be getting up early to see what Santa's left her, so we should get some peace for a while. It's only just after seven o'clock."

Sally had shuddered at the word 'Santa' and now she said, "I'll never be able to see Santa again without thinking of Brian's murder. Who could it have been, Ralph? Surely not someone we know."

Ralph swung his legs over the edge of the bed and got up, pulling his black, silk dressing gown from the bedside chair where he had thrown it last night.

"Well, someone hated Brian, that's for sure. I hope it wasn't someone we know but let's face it; it could have been someone at our party."

"But we'd have missed someone surely?"

"Not with seventeen of us milling about."

Ralph, pulling the belt of his dressing gown tightly about his middle, went off downstairs and returned shortly with two mugs of steaming hot tea.

They drank in silence then Sally spoke:

"How on earth are Carol and the kids going to get through today? Should we go up to Eaglesham or invite them here?"

"I think it'd be better if we went up to them. I'm afraid that our house will have bad memories for them."

"And for us. How can we ever go into the study without imagining Brian lying there covered in blood?"

Sally shivered, though the room with its central heating was warm and cosy.

Ralph heard his daughter's bedroom open and gratefully called out to her to come and join them. Hazel was still excited and showed it.

"Dad, who do you think killed Uncle Brian? Was it Santa Claus? We never saw him after Auntie Carol found the body."

"Pet, let's try to talk of something else. Your Mum's upset. Let's all get dressed and go downstairs and open our presents."

Hazel was only too delighted to do that and was thrilled with her presents. She and Pippa were becoming fashion conscious although only ten years old and she loved the boots and CD her gran had bought her. Gran was Sally's mother who lived in Stirling. When she went to the phone to ring her gran, Ralph felt a minute's relief that his parents were dead and he did not have to break the news of their son's murder to them.

They had bought Hazel a much - wanted bicycle and hoped for everyone's sake that Charles Davenport had bought the same for his daughter. Hazel wheeled it round the house wearing her bright blue crash helmet and had to be restrained from phoning her friend.

"Pippa's with her Mum I think, love. You'll have to wait till she's back with her dad or till she phones you," said Sally.

Ralph expressed delight at the brightly coloured tie and socks from Hazel and thanked his wife for the beige sweater which was her present to him. Sally, in turn, thanked him for her gold bracelet and Hazel for her driving gloves. Ralph must have helped her here as he knew she needed new ones. They did not lavish presents on each other or their daughter, instead sending money to their favourite charities. Hazel this year had asked to send money to the Donkey Sanctuary so that they could sponsor a donkey and had her certificate for Danny in pride of place on her bedroom wall, along with her picture of Girls Aloud.

"Will we see Auntie Carol and the others today as usual?" asked Hazel now.

"Daddy and I were just wondering about that," said Sally.

"I think we should go over there. I wish they lived nearer and I could take my bike."

"Just take the CD gran gave you," Ralph said. "Did you get a present from Pippa?"

"No," she replied solemnly. "We wanted to send money to Barnardos instead. We had a talk about them in school. Remember I told you about it."

"Yes, I remember," said Sally. "How are you going to send the money?"

"Oh, Mr Davenport wrote us a cheque. We had both saved from our pocket money and gave him five pounds each."

Sally felt a lump rising in her throat at the generosity of the two young ones. They could surely teach some adults a thing or two.

"Well done, you two," said Ralph feeling proud of his daughter and her friend. "Right, I think I'll phone Carol and suggest that we come over."

He went out into the hall and they heard his voice. Minutes later he came back into the lounge.

"I got Carol. They'll be delighted to see us. Come on, coats on and get their presents, Hazel."

It took about fifteen minutes to get to Eaglesham as the roads were eerily quiet. Carol was quick to answer their ring. She looked tired and quite unlike her usual immaculate self. She was wearing navy track suit bottoms with a sweatshirt, not her usual newly - bought Christmas outfit.

"I'm so glad you came as usual. We haven't known what to do. It seemed callous to open presents. Hazel, you'll find Diana and the boys in the den. They'll give you your present."

Hazel went off to where her cousins were watching an old film on TV. She handed over their gifts and was handed one in return. She was delighted with her book token. Diana had a blouse from Top Shop and was delighted to get something modern. The boys, always difficult to buy for, showed their appreciation of their tokens for the HMV shop by giving Hazel a big hug each. She settled down with them to watch TV. She did not know what to say to them about their Dad so just kept quiet.

Back in the lounge, the adults were discussing Brian's death.

"Whoever would want Brian dead?" Carol said. "I mean he and I were forever arguing but I would never have killed him."

"Of course you wouldn't," said Sally. "What about his girlfriend? What was her name again?"

"Wendy," supplied Carol. "He told me that was all off but he never made any overtures to me in bed and Brian is......was… highly sexed so he must have been getting some action somewhere. I just thought he was lying. Still, the police asked for the address of the dental practice so I guess they'll see her soon and will find out for themselves."

"Yes, they'll soon find out," said Ralph. "Let's try to talk of something else. Are we having dinner with you as usual or have you not been able to think about food?"

"I've been up since six o'clock. I couldn't sleep so I got the meal ready and we'd be delighted if you three would share with us as you always do. I don't imagine you have a Christmas meal ready Sally."

"No," smiled Sally. "I haven't, though we could manage on what was left from the party. No one ate much, understandably, except the kids and Colin and Aimee who seemed quite calm about it all."

"Young and in love," laughed Ralph. "What's on TV Carol? Put it on and let's watch some easy-to-follow Christmas programme."

This they did.

CHAPTER 20

Aimee was thrilled when she woke to find a Santa stocking at the foot of her bed. The rustle it had made had reminded her of childhood Christmas Days. She sat up and switched on the bedside lamp. It was only just after seven o'clock and the family never rose till after eight. This suited her as she was not an early riser herself. She pulled the large stocking up the bed and began opening the presents it contained. They were what Colin had called, "wee" presents, the kind that Santa had always brought many years ago.

Thinking of Santa brought back the death of Brian Ewing. She had been attracted to him as soon as she met him one day in the shopping centre at Mearns. Colin had introduced him, having met him at an earlier Christmas party. The kiss he had stolen from her when they had gone from one room to another during charades had excited her and when he had whispered, "Let's meet some time soon," she had whispered back,

"OK." They had sprung apart when they heard a room door opening but it was only one of the twins leaving the dining room on his way to the lounge. Aimee and Ralph had gone in to act out their part of the word 'witchdoctoring' and apart from a pat on her bottom later in the evening, they had had no contact.

Aimee had had many lovers during her short life and really saw nothing wrong with a fling with Brian. Colin was loveable, not sexy, the kind of man you married but did not have an affair with. She thought he would be unforgiving of any straying on her part but she would have made sure that he did not find out.

However, she shrugged; it was not to have been. Someone had murdered Brian.

She did not waste any more time thinking of what might have been but felt into the stocking for the first present which turned out to be a writing pad, envelopes and a book of second class stamps. She made a little moue of disappointment. She never wrote letters.

The second present was better, a small container holding eye make-up, the correct shades for her colouring. Next came a lipstick, also welcome. Why, she wondered, were there an apple and an orange in the stocking. They were not real presents surely; it must be some quaint Scottish custom. After opening the last two presents, a notebook which would be quite useful for wedding plans and a packet of shortbread, she decided to get up and shower. Colin's parents' house was an old one and none of the rooms had en suite bathrooms which meant all of them using the same bathroom along the hallway. She thought that Colin's Dad had been annoyed at the length of time she had taken to shower the day before and decided to get in early this time.

Colin was lying awake at the other end of the hall. He had not even considered asking his mother if he and Aimee could share a room, knowing how his mother would have felt. He too had woken to the rustle of his Christmas stocking and hoped that Aimee, if she had one, would appreciate the effort his mother always went to with these wee presents. Aimee loved the word "wee", he thought, smiling to himself. He pulled the stocking toward him and withdrew his first present, a Christmas tie with Santas on it. He too thought about the murder on Friday night. Someone had hated Brian Ewing enough to kill him, brutally. Colin felt sorry for the young Ewings but not for either Brian or Carol. Carol had not hidden her disgust for her husband, referring often to his 'floosy' while in company and Colin had never liked Brian who had always fawned over any attractive woman, even Sally, his sister-in-law. Colin had seen the pat on the bottom which Brian had given Aimee and had been going to remonstrate with him had not the announcement of supper and Brian's ensuing murder taken place.

Colin opened five more presents as well as taking out the apple and orange. It was a silly habit to give fruit, he thought, as he simply put the pieces back in the fruit bowl without his mother seeing him. He also had a pair of Christmas socks to match the tie, a small photograph album which would be useful for holding the photographs he had taken of Aimee and his parents recently, after shave, a small shaving mirror for travelling and a bar of his favourite Galaxy chocolate.

He heard a bedroom door close and the bathroom door close and realised that someone had beaten him this morning so he lay back in his bed and thought of the day to come.

Mr and Mrs Ferguson were discussing Aimee. Lying together in the large bedroom facing the front of the house, they were admitting to not being a hundred percent sure that Aimee was the right woman for their son.

"She's very pretty, I'll grant you that," said Mrs Ferguson, although her husband had never mentioned Aimee's prettiness. "I don't know why I'm doubtful. I just think she's impressed by Colin's job and prospects rather than by his lovely nature."

"Well, she's not had a very stable life, my dear. Security must be very important to her."

"I know. I just want Colin to be happy and I'm worried that he won't be modern enough for her."

"He is a bit old-fashioned, like me," smiled her husband.

They too heard the doors along the corridor opening and closing. Mr Ferguson, deciding to shave later, got up and dressed, deciding to go downstairs and get the table set for breakfast. He usually did this at night but they had been late back from the Watchnight Service because Colin had wanted to introduce Aimee to all his church and BB friends. Maybe his wife was correct, he thought, as he went downstairs. Colin was quite old fashioned with his love of the BB and his regular church attendance. He was an officer in the BB and a Sunday school teacher and would expect his wife to join in with his friends from these organisations. The minister had also asked him to become an elder and he knew that Colin was going to accept this post. Aimee had struck Mr Ferguson as a party animal and hoped that the wedding might be put off till later the next year to give the young people time to get to know one another better. However they had seen the minister and, if they could find a suitable hotel, the wedding was to be in Spring.

"Oh well," he thought. "It's none of my business."

He got out the Christmas table-cloth and red napkins, thinking how cheerful they made the dining room. He hoped that the two young folk would not think too much about the horrific event at the Christmas party, an event which they had told them of when they got home early. He also hoped that the police would not come to see them on Christmas Day.

Aimee, coming down next, smiled sweetly at him and asked if she could do anything to help. Christmas Day had begun.

CHAPTER 21

At the police station, the team was in the Incident Room. They were the only ones in the large building, apart from two officers manning the desk this Christmas Day. A large photograph of Brian Ewing lying spread-eagled on the study floor, had pride of place on a white board and written underneath was a list of the partygoers plus the cryptic, A N Other.

"It seems likely that Brian Ewing was murdered by one of the people at the party but it is possible that a stranger, known of course to Mr Ewing, entered the house dressed as Santa Claus and left immediately after the murder, stopping only to wash the knife and stuff the Santa suit into the large, brown, garden refuse bin."

"Seems unlikely, Sir that a stranger would look for a knife. Would he not bring his own? And if he did take a knife from the kitchen would he bother putting the knife back in the cutlery drawer. Would he or she not have got rid of it somewhere else, even in the same bin as the Santa outfit?"

"Yes Fiona, that is my opinion but it might have been done to throw us off the scent."

"But Sir, in that case would the killer not have simply left the suit lying on the study floor?" This from Penny, eyes bright as usual.

"They would have wanted the protection of the suit until they were away from the crime scene, surely?" said Salma.

"Yes, Salma, I agree," said Davenport. "If Santa was seen going into the kitchen, no one would be at all suspicious especially Ralph and Sally who each thought the other had arranged for this person and could have told him or her to help themselves to a drink of water. It gets hot under the beard I would imagine. I imagine he or she would keep the suit on till it was safe to shed it."

"It seems unlikely that it would be a woman," said Frank. "Santa is always a man."

"So what a good disguise for a woman then," rejoined Penny.

"Wouldn't it be risky for a stranger to come in as Santa? What if Ralph and Sally Ewing had both gone to the door and neither had asked for Santa to come?" Fiona had thought this last night.

The team were quiet as they assimilated this.

"Look at the position of the body," said Davenport. "Martin says Brian Ewing was stabbed once in the chest by someone standing in front of him. He went down face first and the assailant must have had to step back smartly to avoid being landed on."

"So, Santa must have stood up. What reason would he have had to do this without alerting Mr Ewing?"

"He might have been coming to the door with him. Had Brian been given his present?" Salma wondered if this was important.

"Yes, Salma. Good point. I saw a parcel, unwrapped, lying a few feet from his outstretched right arm. I gave it to the SOC team to test for fingerprints but the only ones on the paper were those of Brian Ewing, suspicious in itself, as you would have expected to find the fingerprints of the person who wrapped the present on it."

"Did Santa wear gloves?" asked Fiona. "I didn't think to ask that. How stupid of me!"

"Well you got the fact that he wore black shoes, not boots as Santa normally does," said Davenport. "We can ask that question when we interview each of them."

"Why shoes?" queried Frank.

"Probably to make it easier to escape unnoticed, Frank," said his boss. "Which makes me suspect a guest as he or she would have looked odd in boots and it would have been awkward to dispose of boots and don shoes once again."

"If there was an unwrapped present lying, then Santa must have got up to show Brian to the door," Salma went back to what her boss had said earlier.

"Yes and just continued on out of the door and out of the back door after having committed the murder."

"And come back in if it was one of the guests," put in Fiona.

"We can ask the guests if Santa wore gloves," said Penny.

"Yes, Penny but not till tomorrow. We can hardly intrude on them on Christmas Day."

"What a pity it hadn't snowed on that night, Sir," said Salma. "We might have seen footprints either going from the house or returning from the bin to the house."

"Frank, was there any interesting conversation among the people who came into the wee sitting room after we'd questioned them?" asked Davenport.

"The young ones were quite talkative. Diana Ewing was very upset and kept saying, 'My Dad's been killed. My Dad's been killed. Hazel - is that her cousin Sir?"

"Yes."

"Hazel was excited and in between trying to comfort Diana, was saying that it was really exciting being involved in a murder. Diana said she was cruel and Hazel apologised then she couldn't contain herself and asked her cousin who could have done it. Diana burst into tears and then one of the twin boys came in and Diana ran to him and he hugged her and told her everything would be OK."

"Did the twins talk much when the other one came in?" Davenport wanted to know.

"Not much when they saw how upset their sister was. One mentioned wondering if it was his mum or dad who had arranged for Santa to come then they just sat on the settee one on either side of their sister and when Hazel tried to talk about the murder, they told her to be quiet and she shut up. Not long after that, you came along Sir and told Hazel she should go upstairs and get ready for bed."

"Did anyone else join them?"

"Just the French girl, Aimee."

"Was anything said then?"

"She was quite calm and she said she was sorry to the Ewing kids. She asked if they'd been questioned about Santa's shoes and they said yes but that they hadn't noticed his feet. Then a young man came and took her away. Said you'd okayed it, Sir."

"So you heard nothing interesting?"

"An older man came in then with someone whom I think was his wife. An odd thing with her, she was half smiling as she came in, though the smile left her face when she saw how upset Diana was. She went over to her and hugged her. Those were the only folk I saw because you asked me to join the DS and Penny in the dining room after I'd called for Dr Mackie to come along."

"Thanks, Frank. Anyone know why Sandra Rogerson would be smiling?"

"No, Sir but she was half smiling when I was questioning her as if she was thinking of something other than the murder," said Fiona.

"I'll see her after Christmas Day and ask her."

Davenport left the room. The rest crowded round the photograph of Brian Ewing. Penny was amazed at how much blood was surrounding it and recounted how little blood there had been at a recent murder where the man had also been stabbed.

"I think this is more normal Penny," said Salma. "Isn't it ma'am?"

"Yes Salma, the stabbing of the Reverent Gentle produced remarkably little blood." Fiona referred to the murder last summer of a local minister. She looked round at the others, thinking what a good team they were. Even the slapdash Frank had come in willingly on Christmas Day. They pulled well together.

Davenport re-entered the room, carrying a tray with five glasses and a bottle of champagne.

"Can't have you drinking much but I'm sure half a glass will be OK. Let's drink to what's left of Christmas day and to the success of our investigations."

They each took a glass which he half-filled for them. They all raised their glasses.

"To success," they chorused.

CHAPTER 22

Charles Davenport was enjoying a quiet afternoon. He had given Pippa her Christmas present, her first proper bicycle, the afternoon of the party. It was a collapsible one as she would want to ride with her friend Hazel who lived quite far from them in Newlands. He had debated for quite a while before choosing a school near his work rather than near his home and knew he had been thought odd to put in a placing request for what was seen as a poorer school. The one near his home in Newton Mearns was much sought after by parents but he knew that it would be easier to collect Pippa from the one in Shawlands. She had settled in quickly and made close friends with Hazel Ewing almost right away. She had also befriended the school bully who was in the year above her and Charles had had a worrying moment when Pippa had asked if he could come for a sleepover in the summer. Finding out that Ronald's parents had no objections, Charles had bought a tent and three sleeping bags and had asked Pippa to invite Hazel as well and the three had spent the night in the back garden, much to their delight. Ronald had departed for secondary school in August so the friendship had lapsed maybe to be renewed when Pippa went there.

He had put on the TV but after the Queen's speech, he had lost interest and decided to set the table in the dining room. Any meal Fiona had shared with him and Pippa had been an informal one at the kitchen table and he wondered if the formal ambience would set the mood for the evening.

He stood back and surveyed the table. He had found the Christmas table-cloth and green napkins and had remembered to buy crackers. He had polished the wine glasses, two each for red and white wine and also put out liqueur glasses. They had made no plans for her getting home and he wondered if she would bring her car and not drink or come by taxi.

It was now about four o'clock. Going into the kitchen, he took out the turkey which he had precooked the night before. It was sliced up and in a casserole along with the chipolata sausages. He placed it in the oven then started on the potatoes which he would parboil then roast. He wondered if Fiona liked Brussels sprouts. He did but he knew that some people did not and only had them at Christmas, out of tradition. He would put the vegetables in separate dishes and she could help herself. She had offered to bring a trifle for dessert so he only needed to get out plates now, for the main course and dessert, the prawn cocktail being already prepared in ramekin dishes. He rang his in-laws, spoke to them and his wife then said, "Merry Christmas" to Pippa and asked what presents she had received. She would be back with him on December 28th as her mother had to be back at work, down South, the following day.

Fiona was not coming till seven o'clock, so he had time for a nap before showering and dressing. Debating whether to lie down on his bed or on the settee, he opted for the settee and fell asleep, waking in the middle of the Christmas edition of "Deal or No Deal". The contestant had just been offered £12,000 and had turned it down, gambling on her box containing £35,000. He switched off the TV set and turned on the CD player which he had already loaded with a Christmas CD. As strains of "White Christmas" drifted into the room, he left to get washed and changed.

Fiona had changed her outfit three times. She was happiest in her smart suits but knew that that would not be suitable for Christmas Day. She had lost some weight recently and had bought a dress of pale blue Jersey wool but looking at herself in the mirror, she thought that it would be uncomfortable to be holding her stomach in all the time. Back it went into the wardrobe. Next to be discarded was the red wrap over top and black skirt with split up the side. It was too - she hesitated to use the word - sexy as she felt this could never describe her - too forward and might send the wrong signals to Charles. Finally, she opted for a cashmere sweater in pale pink and a brown A-line skirt. She had treated herself to the sweater for Christmas along with the dress. She applied some make up and brushed her fair hair till it shone.

She had taken so long deciding what to wear that she was in danger of being late, so grabbing the Christmas presents for Charles and Pippa and a bottle of wine, she ran down the stairs of the tenement building and got into her car. She had decided that taking her car gave her a choice of what to do later in the evening. She could drive home sober, get a taxi if she had drunk too much or stay if Charles wanted her to and if she felt that it was the right thing to do. Turning up in a taxi might send the wrong signals. She did not want to push him into something he was not ready for. She was just about to set off when she remembered the trifle so she did not reach Charles's house till after the arranged time which was unlike her as she was usually punctual.

Charles saw the car pull up outside and went out to meet her. He thought she looked flustered but said nothing. He took the trifle dish, leaving her to bring the carrier bag which he guessed had presents for him and for Pippa. He took her jacket and when he came back from hanging it up, she was seated on his settee, looking, he thought, a bit nervous which was how he felt. They had seldom been alone together, only once really, on their holiday last summer when they had been too busy golfing, walking and climbing to be aware of being alone and so tired that they fell into bed in separate rooms almost immediately after their evening meal.

"Drink Fiona?" he asked, thinking that whatever she said might set the tone for the evening ahead.

"When are we eating?" she asked.

""I've just got the potatoes to roast. Would 8pm suit you?"

"Fine. In that case I'll have a dry Martini please, with lemonade." She put her hand into her carrier bag and pulled out a bottle of white wine.

"I thought I'd get something a bit special. Here you are. It had better go in the fridge if there's room."

"Wow! Cloudy Bay! That *is* special. Thank you. I'll put the red wine out to breathe a bit."

He suited the action to the word, returning with her Martini, topped with a slice of lemon and his glass of Whyte and Mackay.

Once he was seated, she once more delved into her bag and produced a beautifully wrapped parcel which she gave to him and reaching behind the settee where he had put it, he gave her her present. She was delighted with the perfume. It was one she had never tried, called Poeme. He in turn was thrilled with the book which was the latest by his favourite author, Quintin Jardine. He had all his other books in hardback form and this completed the set.

He had taken a seat by the fireside and lay back, crossing his legs at the ankles. Fiona kicked off her shoes and drew her feet under her on the settee. She probably looked more relaxed than she felt, she thought, experiencing a little knot of anxiety in her stomach.

Charles threw across his copy of the Radio Times.

"Anything you want to watch on TV? Or would you rather listen to music?"

"Music please. Something Christmassy if you have it."

As it turned out, they heard little of the CD as they started talking about the current murder, Charles came across to sit with her on the settee and their nerves vanished. They ate their Christmas dinner, still chatting, moved on to a discussion of a possible summer holiday together, with Pippa of course, and ended up sitting on the rug in front of the fire with the laptop, touring travel sites. They had long been thinking of visiting Malaysia, Indonesia or even Borneo.

"Pippa would love to see the orang-utans in Borneo," said Fiona. "One of the hotels has a kind of nursery for ones rescued in the jungle and there's also a day trip by plane to see them in Sepalok. Look."

Charles looked at the pictures of The Rasa Ria Hotel in Kota Kinibalu.

"Pippa's easy to please on holiday as long as there's a swimming pool and she has plenty to read. She always makes friends with someone too and I'm left by myself. It would be great to have some adult company, Fiona. Would you think seriously about coming with us?"

They had discussed this before but he felt he had to give her another chance to back out.

"It'd be ideal for me as the friend I went with the last two summers has got engaged and is saving for her wedding but what about work? Can we both get time off together?"

"That's the beauty of being one unit in a larger station. Another DCI or DS will be put in charge of our section for the time we're away. I think we'd need three weeks if we're going so far away."

Fiona agreed and they spent the next part of the evening, narrowing their choice of holiday to either The Rasa Ria in Borneo or The Rasa Sayang in Penang.

Some time later, Charles went into the kitchen and came back with mince pies which he had heated up and some Christmas cake which he and

Pippa had made some weeks earlier and it was then that he said, "I don't know how our friendship will progress Fiona. I felt nervous about tonight but I think, though I may be wrong, that you'd be happy to keep it platonic for a while longer at least. I know you must be a bit wary about a station romance after what you told me and I don't want to rush things though I hope that in time we can be more than just friends."

The last part came out in a rush and he was quite pink in the face. Fiona felt a surge of feeling for him.

"Oh Charles, how good of you to put that into words! I couldn't have put it better myself. Can I have a hug please?"

He put his arm round her, feeling a rush of pleasure at their closeness yet relieved that he knew where he stood.

"So, a single room for you next summer, my love and then we'll go on from there."

Shortly afterwards, having decided to give Pippa the casting vote on the hotel, Fiona rose to go, asking Charles to call her a taxi.

"You can stay here; use Pippa's bed if you like."

"Won't the neighbours talk, seeing my car left outside?"

"Let them, my dear."

So it was that Fiona spent the night tucked up under Pippa's Jungle Book duvet, half wishing that she could have been tucked up beside Charles who on his part wondered if they had been too rational about things and took some time to get to sleep wishing that Fiona was beside him.

CHAPTER 23

His brother and sister-in-law found Arthur very quiet over Christmas. He had arrived just in time for them to watch the Queen's speech on TV and hardly seemed to notice his niece and nephew complaining about being expected to watch this programme. Usually he would have agreed with them - it was almost part of the Christmas Day routine after all, this argument - but he sat quietly watching this year.

Halfway through the meal, he had come out of his reverie and entered into the spirit of the day, putting on his paper hat, reading out his joke from the cracker and seeming to enjoy the meal. As always he had helped his sister-in-law wash the dishes and had apologised for his earlier quiet mood, telling her about what had happened on the evening of Ralph and Sally's party. He had not wanted to tell the youngsters so had waited till now to tell Martha. Neither she nor his brother knew Brian Ewing but they had met Sally and Ralph on a number of occasions and Martha knew that this might affect Sally Ewing whom she had liked when they had met.

"Have the police any idea who the murderer is?" she asked now.

"I don't see how they can have any idea if it wasn't obvious to the guests. I mean who would want to kill Brian Ewing?"

"What did he do? I mean what was his job?"

"He was a dentist, senior partner in a two - man practice in Newton Mearns. It was his private practice till he took on a partner last year."

"A dissatisfied patient perhaps?" suggested Martha

"It's hardly likely that someone would kill over a botched filling Martha!"

"Sorry. It's not a laughing matter." Martha was contrite.

"Don't worry about it. Will you tell Larry for me when the kids aren't around?"

Arthur wiped up the last saucepan and they returned to the living room where the rest were ensconced in front of the TV. Pleading tiredness after a restless night, Arthur left shortly afterwards. He had thought about telling his brother about what was worrying him but it seemed unfair to bring a problem to Larry on Christmas Day. He would do his own investigating tomorrow and come to Larry then if he was still puzzled.

Jim Rogerson had prepared the Christmas meal as he always did. He had suggested eating out this year but Sandra was not keen on this idea. She had offered to make the meal for a change but he, being a bit of a control freak at Christmas, said he preferred to do it himself. He had asked her if there was anyone she wanted to invite but she had said no. For one fleeting minute she had thought of Derek who always went to his sister's but she knew she would have found it hard to hide her feelings for him, from Jim.

The meal over, she went upstairs and in the bathroom rang Derek's mobile.

"Hello Sandra. It's OK for me to speak to you. I'm in the garden having a smoke and taking a break from the youngsters. How's Christmas been?"

"So boring and I'm missing you so much. I envy you the kids. I'm in the bathroom so can't stay long. Jim goes back to work on Thursday. I'll see you at work then too and maybe we can sneak off here at lunch time."

"Is it safe to go to your house?"

"Jim never comes home at lunchtime and I want to introduce you to some of my furniture."

He laughed, a deep throaty laugh which made her feet curl.

"Have to go Derek. Love you."

Jim was coming up the stairs as she came out of the bathroom.

"Were you talking to yourself, my love? They say it's the first step towards madness". He laughed and, not waiting for a reply, went into their bedroom. He joined her downstairs having changed into his slippers. Sandra looked at him, sitting comfortably in his usual chair, remote in his hand and thought how old he had become recently. He seemed totally content with his lifestyle, unlike herself. How she envied Derek his freedom though she would not want Jim to die like Derek's wife. She also envied Derek his Christmas Day surrounded by his nephews and niece. This was children's time and how she wished she had a child of her own. There was no reason why she could not get pregnant except that now it would be a miracle for a child to be Jim's. Derek had taken precautions when they had made love and she had been tempted to tell him not to but that would have been foolhardy until they knew where their relationship was going.

She would have been very surprised to have known Jim's thoughts as they sat together in front of the TV. In spite of his easy-going nature, Jim thought deeply about things and he had noticed a change in his wife. She had never been a flirt but she had flirted with Brian Ewing last summer when they had met in the street outside Ralph and Sally's house. Jim had felt then that Brian was not a person to flirt with safely but after that Sandra had seemed her usual self until recently when she seemed to have an inner ... excitement ...was the word which came to his mind. Sandra had been his only love and he would hate to lose her.

As soon as it was acceptable to go to bed, Sandra did, leaving her husband to watch TV. They seldom went to bed together these days and he was always up and about when she woke up.

So it was that, as Christmas Day ended, all the women who had been at the scene of the murder went to bed alone, even Sally Ewing who being an unselfish person had insisted on sleeping in the spare room to let Ralph get a good night's sleep without her tossing and turning.

CHAPTER 24

Boxing Day dawned, a foggy, cold morning. Charles and Fiona breakfasted together then went outside to scrape the ice from their cars. In spite of everything, both had eventually slept well and were refreshed and cheerful.

Penny, who walked from the bus stop today as her mum wanted their shared car, saw their cars coming from the same direction. This was unusual as the DCI turned left into the road the station was on and the DS turned right. It was very probably a coincidence but she thought that she must tell Frank who liked anything which even hinted at a relationship between his bosses. Even the night at a Scottish evening had not curbed his enthusiasm for a possible station romance.

Salma was already in the Incident Room and looked up as Penny entered. These two had become close friends over the last year and often visited each other's houses. Frank, still racist where anyone else but Salma was concerned, sometimes joined them on trips to cinemas and theatres but had never visited either girl in her home. During their last case together, Frank had heard Salma being vilified and called racist names and had been horrified as he had grown to like Salma but Penny knew that he was still racist himself and would not want to go to Salma's home so she did not invite him either to save them any embarrassment.

Nothing, it seemed, could get Frank to be always on time and in spite of lectures from both Davenport and Macdonald he tended to arrive breathless and late. Today however, he was uncharacteristically punctual, arriving minutes after Penny. The three were chatting about what had been left of their Christmas Day when Davenport and Fiona arrived in the Incident Room sharply at 8.30am.

"Right, folks. I want some interviews done. I want all the guests to be asked to describe their evening in as much detail as possible. Find out who left the room and if possible when they left and for how long. I know it's expecting miracles but someone may have noticed an absence and not realised its significance. Interview the folk separately. Penny, you go to the Rogersons; Frank, you visit Jean Hope and Arthur Mackie; Salma, you take Aimee and Colin. Fiona, I want you to go to see Ralph, Sally and Hazel Ewing and I'll see Carol and her family. Ask everyone to come in during the next few days to have their fingerprints taken. It's a slim chance but we may find some unaccounted for fingerprints though I'm sure that the murderer must have worn gloves. Ask them all about Santa's hands without suggesting gloves to them. Also ask about his shoes and the size of his feet. Ask where each person was when Carol screamed and see if that tallies with what Fiona and I told you. Are there any questions?"

There were none so they all departed to their separate interviews.

Fiona, Frank and Penny went in the same car to Newlands as Frank could easily go on by foot to Shawlands to visit Jean Hope after he had seen Dr Mackie who lived near the Ewings, Ralph, Sally and Hazel, and the Rogersons.

Salma left for Newton Mearns and Davenport drove off to Eaglesham.

Frank drew a blank at Arthur Mackie's, there being no reply when he rang the bell so he took himself off to Jean Hope's flat in Shawlands. Jean lived one floor up in Tassie Street and she opened the door almost as soon as he rang the bell.

"I was in the hall, constable," she explained. "Come through to the kitchen. It's warmer in there as it's where I usually sit and I don't have central heating."

When they were seated at either side of her electric fire, Frank asked her first if she had noticed Santa's hands at all, only to be told that neither she nor Arthur had been in to see Santa. Frank apologised for his mistake, a natural one as he had not been privy to this information and had not as yet read Penny's notes. He then asked Jean to go through the evening, telling him what she remembered.

"Anything at all, Mrs Hope, even if you don't think it's relevant."

Jean told of being introduced to everyone in the living room, of the treasure hunt, laughing at how badly she and her partner, Colin Ferguson had done. When asked about the other pairings, the only two couples she could remember were Carol Ewing and Charles Davenport and the winners, Fiona whose surname she had forgotten and Arthur.

"I felt sorry for the man having Mrs Ewing as of all the guests she seemed the least friendly."

She told him about playing charades which meant one group in the lounge and one in the dining room.

"Two people left my group to act out part of a word, then I went out with Pippa.....at least I think it was Pippa as we changed partners for each word and we did three words each. We'd already played a humming game and Pictionary. Sally wanted to have supper after Pictionary but one of the twins asked for charades first."

"Which twin?" asked Frank.

"I've no idea. They're so alike I'm afraid."

Jean had been coming out of the lounge with Arthur when they heard the screams. She thought that Colin and his girlfriend had been in front of them.

"I think I spoke to your DCI and his partner because it was the first time we had all been to one of Ralph and Sally's parties and we had all enjoyed it."

Frank thanked her and asked her to come to the station in the next couple of days to sign her statement and have her fingerprints taken.

"It's routine, Mrs Hope. Nothing to worry about," he said when she looked frightened.

He left her and took a bus back to the station where he met Penny who had been quite briefly at the Rogersons, who had briefly visited Santa. Jim thought that the man had worn gloves but Sandra thought he hadn't. They had told Penny of the various games but had not mentioned one of the boys asking for charades, a point which Penny noticed as she read Frank's notes. She often read and sorted out his notes for him before he typed them into the computer as in spite of being good with IT, he was hopeless at grammar and his spelling was not his strong point either.

Both Sandra and Jim had been in the hallway when Carol had screamed. Jim remembered looking ahead and seeing all the youngsters ahead of them in the dining room and said that Sally was just going in with a tray of something. Sandra was vague about who else was in the room and said she had been too busy looking at what was on the table. Neither had noticed who was behind them in the hall. Neither mentioned arguing about Jim's Mum though neither could have explained why they kept quiet about this.

Penny and Frank were both hard at work typing, when Fiona returned. She went straight to her own room to type up her notes then the three met to discuss their respective interviews.

Sally had said she thought it was Ian who had asked for charades but Ralph had thought it was John and Hazel said that it was she and Pippa who had wanted charades as they had read about it in books but never played it. Sally had just reached the dining room with a tray of sausage rolls, had placed them on a plate on the table and was about to return to the kitchen for more when her sister-in-law had screamed, causing her to drop the baking tray. She thought that most folk had been in the dining room but was not certain.

Before John had taken Santa to the study on his arrival, she had asked if she would send the guests in one at a time and he had said yes. His voice was quite hoarse.

Ralph had also been in the dining room and Hazel said she and Diana and Pippa had got there first, followed shortly by John and Ian. They already had full plates and only stopped on their way out when they saw the sausage rolls being brought in.

When asked, Hazel said that Santa had gloves on his hands but she could not remember any detail. Ralph and Sally had not visited Santa though Sally thought he had worn gloves when he had arrived. Nobody remembered his feet.

Salma was next to arrive having been to Newton Mearns to see Colin and Aimee. Aimee had been in to see Santa and could remember that he had not been as plump as she thought Santa should be. She repeated that he had been wearing black shoes and not the expected furry boots. She had no idea about gloves. Aimee was able to tell Salma about all the games but Colin seemed to have little memory of what had taken place and when pushed by Salma had admitted that having seen Brian pat Aimee's bottom early in the evening, he had been thinking about that.

"I was waiting to have chance to speak to him about it," he said, "but I never got the chance."

Aimee, when asked, said that this had indeed happened but claimed not to have been upset as in France this happened to her all the time.

Fiona looked thoughtful.

"Colin hardly took his eyes off Aimee the whole evening but she flirted a bit with all the men. I think, though I could be mistaken, that the love there is a bit one-sided."

"Do you think ma'am that Colin would have been jealous enough to kill Mr Ewing?" asked Salma.

"Even if he had been, this murder was premeditated so unless Colin had been given cause for jealousy before the party, it's unlikely to have been him," replied Fiona.

Salma sat down at a computer and began typing up her notes. Penny and Frank went off to the canteen for lunch, promising to bring back coffee and a roll and cheese for Salma and Fiona went back to her own room.

When Charles Davenport arrived back, all the reports were typed and on his desk. He was impressed and said so to Fiona. He preferred to type up his own notes rather than give them to his secretary as typing them seemed to help him commit them to memory, so he sat down in his own room and when he had finished, he suggested to Fiona that they meet briefly with the others in the Incident Room and then go to the local pub for lunch.

"I'll tell you what I got from my four first and see if it tallies with your information," he told his team. "I haven't read your reports yet but will do that later."

Carol had not seen Santa. She remembered coming second in the treasure hunt. She had not liked the humming game or Pictionary and had found charades boring. She said that people must have left the room to go to the toilet in the course of the evening. She herself had gone upstairs and met Jim Rogerson coming down. She had been relieved when Sally had gone to get supper ready and had offered to go to the study to speed the Santa visits. Brian had been gone much longer than anyone else, she said. The study door was shut. Sally had passed her with a tray of something. A couple of guests were behind her but veered off to the dining room while she went to the study. She could not remember who they were but thought that the youngsters had already gone into the dining room as they had got up very quickly when food was mentioned.

At first she had thought that Santa was on the floor as there was a lot of red on the beige carpet, then she realised that she was looking at a white shirt soaked in red and that it was Brian lying there. She had screamed and run out. John had put his arms round her and someone had run to the study, maybe two people. The red was blood. Brian was dead.

Diana had noticed the black shoes Santa had worn as she had expected furry boots. A shy girl, she had looked down rather than into his face. Asked about his hands she said that she thought that his hands were bare but could not be sure.

John said that Santa definitely had shoes on, not boots. Black shoes, he thought. John had also noticed that Santa had on gloves as he had fumbled with John's present and nearly dropped it.

"A CD is so thin. I think it slipped as he had on quite thick gloves," were John's words.

"I asked Aunt Sal for a game of charades," he said. "It was still quite early in the evening and my sister and Pippa had said they hoped to play that. It's good fun. I thought that after supper everyone would just sit and chat till it was time to go home so now was the time to play it."

John had been in the dining room with the three girls and Ian his brother when his Mum had screamed and he had grabbed his mother while Ian and, he thought, his Uncle Ralph and Mr Davenport had gone to the study.

Asked about seeing Santa for the first time at the front door, John said that the man was about the same height as himself and taller than his aunt. His Aunt Sally had smiled and let him take Santa into the study. He had heard his aunt speaking to Santa before they went.

Ian was not as sure as his twin with regard to the shoes but agreed that Santa had worn gloves, black woolly ones, he said. He, John and the girls had just heaped their plates with food when the scream came. John had run to his mother but he and his Uncle Ralph and Pippa's father had gone to the study.

"It was awful. Dad was lying in a pool of blood. Uncle Ralph pulled me back to the dining room and Pippa's father stayed in the study."

Asked about the possibility of anyone being able to act the part of Santa and not be missed, he said that during charades there had been a lot of coming and going.

The rest of the team said that none of their folk had mentioned this which meant that any other sortie from the two rooms could have been missed.

"It seems that Santa wore ordinary shoes, probably black ones and he wore gloves, possibly black woollen ones," Davenport summed up. "Anyone could have left the two rooms. I remember one of the twins coming in to sort our team out."

"Yes," said Fiona. You were being too helpful with your sketches. I don't think you realised that the point was to be as obtuse as possible. I think it was Ian who went to give advice but I don't know why I think that."

"The point is," said Davenport, "people came and went throughout the evening. I went to the toilet a couple of times."

"And I went once, to the one upstairs as the downstairs one was engaged," Fiona volunteered.

"We're assuming that the murderer was one of the guests but could it not have been someone else, someone who knew of the party and decided to bluff his way in as Santa?" asked Frank.

"You're absolutely right Selby. I suppose it's wishful thinking on my part, hoping to narrow the field of suspects. We'll need to enquire about possible enemies outside the family. Brian Ewing had had an affair with his receptionist. We'll have to see her, find out whether she had another man in her life who could have been jealous. If Brian was the ladies' man I suspect he was, then there might be other angry men out there."

He groaned.

"On that pessimistic note we'll finish for today. I'll ask Pippa what she remembers and add it to my report and tomorrow I'll have copies made of all our interviews. Come in promptly and get them read and we'll meet again to discuss our next move."

Davenport left for the reprographics room and the rest went to get their coats and jackets. When he came out, Fiona was waiting and together they went out to his car.

CHAPTER 25

After having lunch with Fiona, Charles drove home. While things were fresh in his mind, he rang Pippa at her gran's. She was excited by the fact that her Mum had taken her in to the Christmas sales in Glasgow that morning and had bought her a new digital camera in Jessops.

"Mum wasn't sure if I would like that so she only gave me wee things yesterday," she informed her Dad. "The one I liked best wasn't in the sale but when Mum said she would get it somewhere else they took some money off it."

She went on telling him about the other things her mum had bought.

"Mum's got a boyfriend, Dad. She wondered if you would mind but I said you had a girlfriend too. Fiona is your girlfriend isn't she Dad?"

Charles solemnly agreed that Fiona was indeed his girlfriend and then managed to get in a word to ask his daughter if she could tell him anything about Santa's hands.

"He had on gloves. Santa always does have gloves on to make you think he's been in the snow," his young daughter informed him.

He went on to ask her about where she was when Mrs Ewing had screamed and had been informed that she and Diana and Hazel had been about to leave the dining room with full plates when Hazel's mum had come in with sausage rolls so they had waited to take a few of them.

"Hazel's mum was all worried about stuff burning in the kitchen but she wasn't allowed to go back in," said Pippa.

Charles thanked his daughter and asked to speak to her mum. When Anita, his ex-wife, came on the phone, he thanked her for collecting Pippa from her aunt's house and asked if Pippa was any the worse for the incident at the Ewing's.

"Pippa! Not likely. She regaled us all with juicy accounts of blood and being annoyed at being removed from the scene before she could glean any more information."

Charles laughed and rang off.

Frank, being uncommonly dutiful, had returned to Arthur Mackie's house that afternoon, Arthur's house not being too far from his own in Shawlands where he lived with his parents and one sister.

He was to be disappointed once again as no one answered his knock on the door. There was little chance of not being heard as the door knocker was a heavy one and made a loud noise when he dropped it against the wooden door. He was walking back down the path when Jean Hope turned into the driveway. He stopped and told her she was on a wasted journey as Arthur was not at home.

"That's funny. I've been trying to phone him all morning and got no reply. He was definitely coming home from his brother's on Christmas night. He didn't want to leave his cat unattended for too long and he dotes on that cat."

Deciding to check more carefully, Frank told Jean that he would walk round to the back of the house. He asked her to try to see if she could see anything through the front windows of the house and they parted company.

Frank opened the gate leading to the back of the house. Arthur must be a keen gardener as even in winter the garden was immaculate. He found one disgruntled large cat on the back doorstep but when he looked through the kitchen window there was nothing untoward to see.

"Constable! Come quickly," he heard Jean call to him and he hurried back to the front of the house.

Jean was standing on tiptoe at one of the front windows.

"I can see a pair of feet at the room door," she said in distress. "Maybe Arthur fell and is unconscious. What will we do?"

Frank got onto his mobile and rang the station. The sergeant on duty at the desk said he would get in touch with the DCI and get back to him so he and Jean had to be content to wait. Jean banged on the door and the window in an effort to rouse Arthur but to no avail.

It seemed ages but was probably only minutes before Frank's mobile rang and Davenport gave him permission to break into the house.

Telling Jean to stand well back, Frank smashed the window deeming the door too heavy to break down. That done, he clambered onto the window-sill and lowered himself onto the room floor. He found himself in a masculine sitting- room; the walls yellowed with years of smoking and went immediately to the figure lying on the floor. He felt for a pulse and there was one, faint but present.

He ran to the door and opened it.

"Come in, Mrs Hope. Please don't touch anything. It *is* Arthur and he's still breathing but I'm afraid someone has hit him on the head as his head is bleeding. I'm going to ring for an ambulance. Would you see if you can find a blanket to cover him with?"

Jean, with a quick look at the prone figure of Arthur, ran to one of the upstairs' rooms and brought a duvet from the bed there. She ran back down and arranged the cover over the body, being careful not to touch it with her hands. Frank had finished his 999 call and another to his boss and together they stood and looked down at the body.

"Why would anyone want to hurt Arthur?" Jean asked.

Frank had his own idea about that but he was not about to share his thoughts with this woman so he remained silent.

The noise of the ambulance siren could be heard in the distance and soon there was a flurry of activity and the figure of Arthur Mackie was strapped on to a stretcher and whisked into the ambulance. Not knowing what was the best thing to do, Frank decided to let Jean go in the ambulance and he stayed in the house to await the arrival of his boss. He looked round the sitting room. The cat must have followed him into the house at some point and was ensconced in one of the easy chairs. A small table beside that chair held a book and a pipe lay beside an ashtray. There was also a half-filled glass on the table and, sniffing it, Frank recognised the smell of whisky.

A loud knock at the door heralded the arrival of his DCI and he went to open it.

"No sign of a visitor, Sir, at least not one who stayed. There's only one glass."

"The person who hit him could have wiped the other glass clean," Davenport replied. He looked round the room.

"Where was he lying?"

Frank showed him. Davenport noticed some stains at the spot.

"Was he on his face or on his back?"

"On his face, Sir. The back of his head was in a mess."

"Did you check the rest of the house, Frank?"

"No, Sir. Will I do it now?"

"Yes."

It did not take Frank long to have a quick look through the house. Nothing was disturbed. Valuable ornaments rested on many surfaces and a wallet lay on a work surface in the kitchen. Frank, using his handkerchief, picked it up. It was of black leather, old and creased. It was unfastened and the strap which should have closed it was hanging down like a long, twisted, liquorice allsort. This old 'friend' brought a lump to Frank's throat. He went back into the sitting room.

"Don't think there was a burglary, Sir."

He held up the wallet and they could both see the edges of credit cards and paper money peeking out at them.

"It seems a bit of a coincidence that Arthur Mackie was present at the last murder scene and now someone has tried to kill him, don't you think?" asked Davenport.

"That's what I thought, Sir. I hope it was OK to have him taken to hospital and have Mrs Hope go with him," Frank looked for his boss's approval and got it.

"Of course, Selby. You might have saved his life by coming back to see him this afternoon and in the unlikely event that Mrs Hope attacked him, she won't be alone with him at any time."

"No, Sir. A paramedic went into the ambulance with Mr Mackie and her."

"How did she come to be here?"

"She came as I was leaving and it was the fact that she was anxious that made us both try to see into the house. She saw his feet. She had been phoning him all morning, she said."

"Right, I'll get off to the hospital. With any luck he may be conscious and can tell us who attacked him. There's nothing much you can do here except get the window replaced to prevent robbery. Once you've seen that done, get along home and Selby..."

"...Sir?"

"Well done, lad."

Davenport got into his car and drove off to The Southern General Hospital, wishing that the old

Victoria Infirmary had still been at full strength as that would have made his journey quicker. As it was, he got snarled up in the home-going traffic and did not reach the hospital till nearly 6pm.

He pulled up outside and ran into Accident and Emergency. He need not have hurried.

Arthur Mackie had been dead on arrival.

CHAPTER 26

Davenport had got the telephone number of the dental practice from Carol Ewing and rang on Tuesday morning to make an appointment to talk with the receptionist. He had asked Carol if she had contacted either the receptionist or Brian's partner and she said that she had rung the latter.

It was about 10.30 when he and Frank arrived at the end-of-terrace building in Giffnock. He pressed the buzzer and a detached voice said, "Yes?"

"DCI Davenport and PC Selby here to see Mrs Hamilton."

The door buzzed open and they went in. There was a desk in front of them and a woman was rising from her seat behind the desk.

"Mrs Hamilton?"

"Yes, I'm Wendy Hamilton."

Davenport repeated his name and Frank's.

"Tony told me the news this morning. He didn't want to spoil my holiday by telling me on the phone."

"Is there anywhere we can talk privately?"

"I can't really leave the desk. We're quite busy today. Tony is even busier as he's having to see Brian's patients too. I'm happy to talk here if you don't mind."

"I'd rather we could all sit down, Mrs Hamilton."

"Just let me speak to Tony."

She pressed a button on her desk and spoke to someone.

"Tony, the police are here. They want to talk to me about Brian. Is there somewhere private I can take them and can someone man the desk?"

A door down the hallway opened and a man in a white coat came out.

"Hello. My name's Tony Blackwell. This is a terrible business."

He turned to his receptionist, "Why don't you take them to the kitchen? I'll get Maria to stay at the desk."

He raised his voice and called, "Maria!"

Another door opened and a young girl of about eleven appeared.

"What is it Dad?"

"Wendy has to leave the desk for a while. Would you sit here and show my next patient into the waiting room when he arrives. His name's Mr Fraser."

The girl looked pleased. Charles guessed that her mother must be working and that the dentist had had to bring her to work with him that morning. She was probably bored and would welcome this task.

He and Frank followed Wendy Hamilton. She ushered them into a room which was kitted out as a kitchen but which had some comfortable chairs in it.

Wendy caught Davenport's glance round the room.

"We use this as a kitchen and makeshift sitting room where we take our breaks and lunch."

They sat down.

"There's no easy way to say this, Mrs Hamilton, so I'll be blunt. You've been having an affair with Brian Ewing?"

The woman flushed to the roots of her blonde hair. She was small, plumpish and fresh-faced and Davenport could see that she might be a refreshing change from the immaculate, cool Carol for someone as reputedly ardent as Brian Ewing.

"Yes I had an affair with Brian. He told his wife about it in the hope that she would divorce him but she wouldn't."

"What about your own husband Mrs Hamilton?"

"Keith left me when he found out."

"When was that?"

"About a year ago."

Her terse reply suggested that she did not want to discuss this and Davenport wondered if she had been so sure of Brian that she had not hidden her affair from this Keith. He would not delve any further right now but if he needed to know the ins and outs he would ask her later.

"Mrs Ewing told us that her husband said the affair with you had ended some time ago. Is this true?"

"Yes, I finished with him some months ago."

"Why?"

"He had promised that he would leave Carol and ride out the scandal but he didn't and I was going to have to spend another Christmas without him and..."

"And what, Mrs Hamilton?"

"I think he had found someone else."

"What made you think that?"

She blushed again. Being an observant man, he could see a few beads of sweat on her forehead.

"Well Brian was very physical if you know what I mean...he..." Suddenly the words came out in a rush. "He wanted a lot of sex and then suddenly he didn't."

"Where did you meet?"

"Here usually. Sometimes in a hotel. Once at his house when Carol was away visiting her mother and the kids were away at school and university, once or twice at my house when Keith was away on business."

"What about your children? Was there no danger of them finding you at home?"

"I don't have any chidden."

"When did this happen, this not wanting you so often and how often was often?"

"At least once a day during the week," she said with a touch of defiance.

"And this stopped when?"

"As I said, some months ago."

"Can you be more precise?"

"It was after the summer holidays, round about the middle of September."

"Did you question him about it?"

"Yes."

"What did he say?"

He was evasive. He said I was imagining things.

"Are you sure you weren't?"

"I followed him after work one evening. He never left early. He wasn't ever in a hurry to get home but he left at 5 o'clock one day."

"And...?"

"He went to our hotel."

"Which was?"

"The Busby Hotel in Kingspark."

"You followed him there, then what?"

"I waited in the car park for about an hour then they came out. They got into his car and drove off."

"Did you recognise the woman?"

"No."

"Can you describe her?"

"Only that she was slim and nearly as tall as Brian. She was wearing a headscarf."

"Did you ever follow him again?"

"He never left early again."

"But your affair didn't restart?"

"It didn't completely stop. It just happened less often. I stopped it in the end. I had to keep some pride."

She was crying softly and Davenport gave her time to wipe her eyes before continuing.

"Is there any chance that your husband might have wanted revenge on Brian Ewing?"

The red tide which had risen in her cheeks, ebbed swiftly leaving her cheeks white.

"Keith wouldn't kill him. He wouldn't. He couldn't kill someone."

"Oh no?" thought Frank, "then why are you so scared?"

"Can you give me his current address, Mrs Hamilton?"

"Yes. We still correspond about legal matters."

She got to her feet and left the room, coming back with a capacious handbag from which she pulled an address book.

Davenport thanked her for the address.

"Mrs Hamilton. I have to ask you where you were on the night of Friday 23 rd. December."

"I was at home. By myself."

The two men thanked her for her time and left.

Once in the car, Frank was quick to comment on the fact that Wendy Hamilton had been very scared when asked if her husband could have wanted revenge on Brian Ewing.

"Yes, she protested a bit too much, didn't she?"

"She hasn't got an alibi herself either, Sir," added Frank.

"I think she's too small and plump for Santa. Everyone seemed to think that Santa was reasonably tall and didn't someone say he was thin? I think it was the French girl, Aimee."

"Her husband would have the best motive, wouldn't he?"

"Yes, but how would he know about the Christmas party?"

"Brian might have mentioned it to Wendy Hamilton and she might have told her husband."

"I suppose it's possible. We'll need to pay him a visit tomorrow."

They drove in silence and were almost at the station when Frank who was a pub quiz buff volunteered, "Wendy was a name invented by Barrie when he wrote Peter Pan," and on that light-hearted note they went up the steps of the large building.

Charles was not feeling so light-hearted half an hour later. He had heard a rumour that the chief constable, Grant Knox was back from a winter holiday in Tenerife and he had just received a phone call from the man's secretary asking him to come upstairs as soon as he got back to the station.

"So, onto murder two, Davenport. I go away for two weeks and I come back to your usual incompetence. Can you never solve a murder before another one takes place?"

The man was obnoxious, Charles thought. He must have had a triple charisma by-pass.

"Sorry Sir."

"And I believe you were actually at the party where the first murder took place! A box office seat and still no results."

Charles remained silent.

"Who handled the press?"

"Mr Fairchild, Sir."

Knox grunted.

"He always seems to get away with telling them nothing."

Unlike him, Charles thought. Knox always told them that an arrest would be made soon and was made to look foolish when this did not happen.

"Right, Davenport. Get on with your job and get some results. Fast."

Dismissed, Charles went back downstairs.

CHAPTER 27

Charles Davenport called a staff meeting that afternoon after lunch and 2.00 pm saw them all seated in the Incident Room. He had only managed to tell Fiona about the murder of Arthur Mackie before leaving with Frank for the dental practice but he knew that she would have told the rest of the team so there were no gasps of surprise when he pinned up a photograph of the second victim beside that of the first.

"Arthur Mackie died before the ambulance arrived at The Southern General. He was unconscious when Selby found him but I'll let him tell you what happened. Selby, take my place out here."

Davenport changed places with Frank who rose looking decidedly pink in the face. He had never been given the chance to do anything like this before and looked very nervous. Penny gave him a supportive smile. He cleared his throat.

"I hadn't found Mr Mackie in yesterday morning, so I went back in the afternoon. There was still so answer to my knock and I was leaving when Mrs Hope arrived. She'd been trying to contact Mr Mackie all day and was worried as he hadn't said anything about going out. She looked in the living room window and saw part of his body half in and out of the door. I broke the window, got in and let her in by the door. Mr Mackie was injured but conscious so I called an ambulance and informed the DCI."

"Could it have been a burglar, Frank?" asked Salma.

"Don't think so as when I went through the house, nothing seemed to have been taken, nothing obvious that is. His TV and video were still there and money and his credit cards were in his wallet and that was lying out on the kitchen work surface. There was no sign of a break-in. Mrs Hope went in the ambulance with Mr Mackie."

Frank looked at his boss who got to his feet.

"Thanks Frank. Very well put. I'll take over now."

Thankfully, Frank sat down. Penny patted his arm and gave him a stealthy thumbs-up sign and he grinned back at her.

"I went to the hospital but Arthur Mackie was dead on arrival. Jean Hope was extremely upset as she had been in the ambulance with him and a paramedic and knew her friend was dead.

I'm having his house tested for fingerprints but I'm not hopeful. This murderer isn't careless."

"Sir, are the two murders connected, do you think?" asked Penny.

"I think so Penny. It seems too much of a coincidence that another person from the party has been killed. Maybe Arthur saw something that night and challenged the murderer."

"He couldn't have done it that night, Sir as the guests were never left alone," remarked Fiona. "He must have contacted the murderer the next day or sometime in the days that followed."

"I wish he had contacted us instead," sighed Davenport. "Why do people always think they can go it alone?"

He stretched his arms over his head and flexed his shoulders which were aching.

"I want you, Salma and Penny, to go round to see Jean Hope tomorrow. I know she'll be upset but we need to find out what Arthur saw or heard that night and she would have been with him a lot of the time. He might even have told her what he suspected.

Frank, you tell Ralph and Sally Ewing. Arthur was their family doctor. This will be another burden for poor Sally Ewing to bear. I hope Dr Mackie gave her some medication to help her. She'll need it more than ever now. Ask if they noticed Arthur looking distracted before he left.

Go next door and tell the Rogersons. He was their doctor too. While you're there, see if you can find out from Sandra Rogerson what Brian Ewing was like. I guess they must have met apart from the Christmas parties. He seems to have been quite a ladies' man. She might have something to add to what we already know of him. Oh and ask Sally if she heard any noise outside when she let Santa in. If he was dropped off, she might have heard a car moving away but don't suggest that to her please."

"Right, Sir."

"Fiona, I'd like you to go to see Carol Ewing and give her the news. If John is around, ask him about any noise he might have heard at the door. I think that's all folks."

"What about Colin and Aimee?" This from Penny who always wanted all the 't's to be crossed and the 'i' s dotted.

"They don't need to be told yet. Arthur wasn't their doctor, at least I don't think so as Colin lived in Eaglesham and Aimee is a newcomer. I'll be seeing Aimee myself later on to ask her opinion of Brian Ewing. I've been wondering if the pat on the bottom was the first time he'd come on to her. She's a beautiful girl and he seems to have been a man with an eye for the women."

"I think we'll find that the murderer was a jealous man," said Fiona.

"Me too, Ma'am," said Penny eagerly.

"Does anyone have anything to ask or say before I tell you what happened when I visited the dental practice owned by Brian Ewing?"

No one had.

"Wendy Hamilton, his receptionist, had been having an affair with Brian Ewing for a few years. She said that recently he had cooled off which suggested to her that he had found a new partner. She said he was highly sexed and that they had had sex at least once every day, sometimes at the surgery, sometimes at The Busby Hotel and once or twice at each other's homes."

"Was that not risky, Sir?" asked Penny before he could continue.

"Her husband had left her and she has no children so her home would be safe. With Diana at boarding school and the boys at University in Stirling, Brian would just have needed to be sure of Carol being away from home."

"When did you find out about Diana being at boarding school?" asked Fiona, to whom this came as a surprise.

"The night of the party. I asked her what school she was at and she told me. She came home every weekend and had Wednesday afternoon off so Brian often collected her at midday and took her back on Thursday morning. That was when I heard that the boys were at Stirling University."

"Sorry. I interrupted. Go on, Sir."

"Please anyone, do interrupt if you're puzzled about anything," Charles replied.

"Wendy followed Brian one evening as she suspected that he'd found someone else and saw him go into what she described as 'their hotel', the Busby Hotel. She waited in her car till he came out with a woman wearing a headscarf, a tallish, slim woman."

"When was this, Sir?" asked Salma.

"Some time in the autumn. Wendy finished with him a few months ago as he'd stopped making love to her as often as usual, round about the middle of August. He still had sex with her occasionally after the summer but she knew there was someone else and ended the affair herself."

"What about her husband?" asked Fiona.

"He found out about Brian and left her, about a year ago."

"He could be a suspect, couldn't he, Sir," put in Frank. "Another man who wanted revenge?"

"Yes. Though how he would have found out about the party, goodness knows. I'll be going to see him tomorrow morning while you're all busy. I phoned and arranged to see him at his work."

There was silence.

"No other questions then. Penny, completely satisfied?"

"Yes thank you, Sir." With the ebullience of her youth and enthusiasm Penny saw no sarcasm in Davenport's words and looked puzzled when the others laughed.

CHAPTER 28

On Wednesday morning, early, Ralph Ewing rang Davenport and after commenting on the tragedy of Arthur's death, he asked if Pippa could come down to Newlands to cycle round the quiet streets with Hazel.

"I'll be with them all the time," he assured Charles. "Hazel has been asking me to invite Pippa since Christmas Day but I knew you'd be very busy with the murder. I'm only asking now in the hope that you might be able to bring her down if you're going to be in the area. With Arthur's death also taking place here, it might be suitable for you and if it isn't, perhaps I could come up and get Pippa and her bike."

There was a silence.

Ralph did not wait but rushed on, "Of course I might be a murder suspect and you won't want Pippa to be near me."

Charles Davenport was in a quandary. True, everyone was a possible suspect but it was also true that Pippa would be incensed if kept away from her best friend. He made a quick decision.

"I was just wondering what my plans were for the day, Ralph, and I'm coming down to interview someone in Pollokshields so I can fold the bike and put it and Pippa into the car. Would you just make very sure that the bike is securely put up? I'd rather have bought her a more sturdy bike but I knew there was every chance that she would want to come down to Hazel, or to school with it at some time."

"No problems." Ralph sounded relieved. He had been wondering how he would explain to his daughter that she couldn't see Pippa until the murder was solved.

"I bought Hazel a folding bicycle too in case she came up to visit Pippa, so I know your worries about them collapsing and I'll make sure all the nuts and bolts are secure."

Charles rang off and went to tell Pippa who was ecstatic. She found her helmet and gloves and wrapped herself up in an old anorak and by the time her dad had picked up the bike, she was waiting at the door of the garage.

It only took him fifteen minutes to get to the Ewing house, the roads being comparatively quiet during the holidays. Hazel was in the garden, dressed ready for their ride and waved excitedly at her friend. Ralph, hearing the car, joined her in the garden.

"We'll keep Pippa for lunch if that will make things easy for you. Sally can have a sleep while we cycle and then the girls will be good company for her."

As the girls fell on each other, comparing helmets and bicycles, he whispered to Davenport, "Sally was even more upset about Arthur dying than she was about Brian. She never really liked my brother but Arthur has been her doctor since she was very young and it was he who delivered Hazel, at home. He was a father-figure I suppose."

"Why did Sally not like Brian?"

"He was a bit of a ladies' man and flirted with her as he did with most women. She didn't like it. My Sally's as straight as a die."

"How's she been?"

"Arthur gave her some Valium and I've made her take them. They make her sleepy so she's been dozing a lot over the last few days. No bad thing."

Charles saw the girls heading towards them wheeling their new bikes.

"Well, Ralph I'll leave you to the mercy of these two. Almost glad I've got work to do," he laughed. "Can I phone you when I'm on the way home? If you don't mind keeping Pippa for lunch, I can go to the station after I've been to Pollokshields."

He said goodbye to his daughter, warned her to do what Hazel's Dad told her and getting into his car, drove off to Pollokshields in search of Keith Hamilton.

Keith lived two stairs up in a tenement building on Shields Road. The door to his flat was needing attention as the red paint was peeling off. He answered the door immediately.

"Mr Keith Hamilton?"

"Yes. You must be Detective Inspector Davenport. Come in."

He took Davenport into his living room, a sparsely furnished room, ill-decorated and lacking in warmth both in colour scheme and in temperature.

"Sorry about the room. I'm renting the place so no incentive to decorate. What can I do for you? You mentioned when you rang, a recent murder, that of Brian Ewing."

"Yes, Sir. Brian Ewing was killed on Friday 23 December. Can I ask where you were that night?"

"I take it that you've talked with Wendy, my wife and know that he wasn't really my favourite man. To be frank, I hated the man. He took my wife from me or as good as took her. When I found out about the affair they were having, I left."

"How did you find out, Sir?"

"Wendy told me. She said he was leaving his wife for her. That was enough for me. I cleared out right away, went to stay with a mate until I found this place."

"You haven't answered my question Mr Hamilton. Where were you on the evening of the 23rd December?"

"I was here, alone unfortunately."

"I have to ask you then, Sir, did you kill Mr Ewing?"

"No I didn't but I'm glad he's dead. Incidentally, I haven't got a car and Newton Mearns is far from here."

"Thank you Sir. I need you to come into the station on Aikenhead Road and give us your statement. I can give you a lift now if you like."

"That would be fine. I'll get my jacket."

On the way, Keith Hamilton was very quiet. It was not till Davenport was turning into the car park that he asked hesitantly, "You've met my wife, Mr Davenport. How is she? Is she very upset about Brian?"

"All I can say, Sir is that she had broken up with him a few months ago and didn't seem grief-stricken to me."

For a man who could be accused of murder, Keith Hamilton looked almost happy as they went up the station steps. It took about half an hour for his statement to be typed up and signed. He refused the offer of a lift home and Davenport would not have been surprised to learn that he had taken a bus to the dental surgery.

All his team were absent on their various duties so he poured himself a cup of coffee using his own percolator and sat back in the chair to think over what Keith Hamilton had said. Unless he was bluffing, he had assumed that the murder had taken place in Brian's house in Newton Mearns and he certainly would not have made himself obvious by taking a bus wearing the Santa outfit and how on earth could he have known where to find the outfit in the first place? Could he and Wendy have planned this together? Brian might have told her about the party and where it was to be held but would she have known about the Santa outfit being in the church hall cupboard?

It was unlikely.

Coffee cup drained, he decided to read over the reports while he waited for the others to arrive back.

CHAPTER 29

Salma and Penny had set off for Shawlands about 11am to see Jean Hope. They were never short of conversation and spent the short journey talking about their proposed visit into Glasgow the coming weekend, to choose an outfit for Penny to wear at her Mum's wedding in the spring. Penny thought that Salma had good taste and wanted her input for this special day.

"Thank goodness Mum didn't want me as a bridesmaid, just as a witness," she said.

They arrived at Jean's tenement building and rang the controlled entry bell. Soon they were seated in her kitchen, a comfortable room, warm and obviously where Jean usually sat as there was a magazine lying on the floor by one of the armchairs.

"I was brought up to think of the living room as the 'good' room," she told them, half apologetically, so I only use it on formal occasions.

Maybe this is a formal occasion. I'm sorry but I need comfort right now."

Both girls hurried to assure her that they were happy where they were.

"I'm sorry to question you when you're upset, Mrs Hope but we think that Dr Mackie must have seen or heard something on the night of the party and as you were his partner maybe you saw or heard the same thing."

"I've been wracking my brain," Jean said. "I'd realised that he had to have noticed something and been killed for that but I can't think of one thing that might have been suspicious to him. Certainly there was nothing suspicious to me but then I didn't know everyone as well as he did. It's horrible to think that he might have known well the person who killed him."

She shuddered.

"Will you tell us," asked Penny, "who he knew well that night. That might give us a clue."

"Well he obviously knew the folk who were hosting the party, Ralph and Sally Ewing. He knew Brian and Carol Ewing, from previous parties I assume, though, wait a minute, I think he said he had been their doctor before they moved to Eaglesham. He didn't like either of them. He saw Brian pat the French girl's bottom and made a comment about him liking the ladies and he found Carol quite stand-offish. He knew the neighbours,

Jim and his wife - I've forgotten her name. I think he was their doctor as well as Ralph and Sally's. Of course he knew the children too, Hazel very well as he'd been her doctor since birth he told me. He probably knew the other Ewing kids too, unless they'd moved before the children were born."

"Thanks, Mrs Hope. Is that all?" asked Salma, grateful with Penny for having asked the question.

"I don't think he knew Mr Davenport, Fiona and his daughter or Colin and Aimee as Colin was Ralph's colleague, not his neighbour.""

"Did Doctor Mackie seem preoccupied that night?"

"No but he was a bit on Christmas Eve. We went to the church service together and a number of times I had to repeat myself as he didn't seem to have been listening to me."

"So," mused Penny, "he must have contacted someone between then and Boxing Day." She saw Jean looking upset and mentally kicked herself for being so insensitive.

"Arthur was going to his brother's on Christmas Day. Maybe he said something to him," said Jean.

Salma got to her feet, signalling the end of the interview and Penny rose too. They thanked Jean for her help.

Once back in the car, Salma reassured Penny who was feeling guilty about not taking Jean's feelings into consideration.

"You didn't mean it, Penny. Anyway I think we've narrowed the field a bit, don't you?"

"What? Do you mean that the boss and the DS aren't suspects now?" laughed Penny who never stayed glum for long.

Salma laughed too.

"No I meant Colin and his fiancée."

"That's true, unless they had met Brian somewhere before. Brian did pat Aimee's bottom at the party, so someone said. Did that show familiarity or was he always that forward with women he didn't know?"

"Bother, I guess we can't rule them out till we know for sure that they were strangers till that night." Salma look despondent and it was Penny's turn to cheer up her friend.

They reached the station, reported to the DCI that they were back and went to the canteen for lunch, having been told to come to the Incident Room at 2pm.

Frank joined them about half an hour later.

He had been to see Sandra and Jim Rogerson and Ralph and Sally in that order, so had not seen his boss dropping off Pippa for her cycle expedition and had unfortunately woken up Sally who came to the door rubbing her eyes and wearing her dressing gown. He asked her if she had heard anything when she let Santa in but she had not. He had not stayed long, promising to return in the afternoon to see her husband.

"Sandra Rogerson didn't like Brian Ewing. He had flirted with her at a past party. She said he did this to most women and she wasn't sure if it was done in fun or in the hope of a positive response. She felt uncomfortable being alone with him."

Frank ate a hurried snack of pie, chips and beans and left once more for the Ewing house asking the girls to tell Davenport he would back as soon as possible.

By the time Salma and Penny reached the Incident Room, Fiona and Davenport were already there and Salma explained where Frank was.

"Did you have time for coffee, girls?" Charles asked and on finding out that they had not, he went back to his room and brought his coffee percolator always primed ready for such occasions, and three cups.

"Fiona you haven't even had lunch. This might sustain you for a wee while."

They had their coffee and the talk turned to other station concerns.

It was about three o'clock when Frank returned. Davenport asked him to tell them about this interview while it was still fresh in his mind.

"Mr Ewing didn't notice Dr Mackie being anything other than light-hearted. He said that his wife had been really upset when they were told the news. He had delivered Hazel and had been Sally's doctor since she was young herself. Sally hadn't heard anything when she had let Santa in. Sandra Rogerson didn't like Brian, Frank continued, telling the others what he had told Penny and Salma earlier.

Penny and Salma reported what they had learned and the DCI said they would have to find out whether or not Colin and Aimee had met Brian Ewing before the party. Also someone should interview Arthur Mackie's family about how he had been when with them on Christmas Day.

Penny, irrepressible as ever, informed her bosses that they were cleared of the murder, having never met Brian and his family before.

Davenport laughed and Frank thought again that Penny got away with saying things he could never have said.

Then it was Fiona Macdonald's turn.

"I informed Carol about Arthur's death. She was shocked. I asked if she had noticed Dr Mackie being preoccupied on the night of the party and she said no. Carol Ewing struck me as someone who was only ever concerned with how she was feeling," added Fiona and Charles agreed. Having been her partner at the treasure hunt, he had found her aloof and disappointed at being beaten by another couple.

"Did you see John Ewing?"

"Yes. He opened the door when I arrived. He said he didn't hear anything when he and his aunt let Santa in."

"Sally didn't hear anything either," Frank reminded them.

"Right, folks. Get your reports written up and then get off home. Before I pick up Pippa, I'm going to pay a visit to Arthur Mackie's brother. DS MacDonald, would you ring Mrs Hope and get the address. Hopefully she'll know it."

The youngsters made for the door, Frank coming last so he heard Davenport tell Fiona that he was going to collect Pippa from Newlands and ask her to come with them both for a Chinese meal in Shawlands.

Salma and Penny were treated to a verse of "Over the Sea to Skye" as the three of them went down the corridor to collect their jackets and hats.

CHAPTER 30

As soon as Pippa and Hazel got back from their cycling with Ralph, Hazel whisked her friend up to her bedroom. As usual they sat on the bed.

"I've been dying to see you, Pippa. Nobody will talk to me about Uncle Brian's murder and it's the most exciting thing that's ever happened!"

"I know, Dad won't talk about it either. He asked me about Santa wearing gloves but that was all."

"He did wear gloves didn't he?"

"Yes."

"Why don't we try to find out who did it?"

"That'd be brilliant!"

Pippa grasped Hazel's arm in her excitement and the pair were silent for a moment relishing this great idea then Hazel broke free and getting up went to her desk and brought back to the bed a paperback book.

"I got this from Mum's bookcase. It's by her favourite author, Agatha Christie. I've been reading it over the last few days and the detective who's called...look... there's his name."

She had opened the book and Pippa read the name, Hercule Poirot.

"How do you say his name, Hazel?"

"I don't know but it doesn't matter. He talks about using his little grey cells, that's his brain and his friend Mr Hastings writes things down in a notebook. I haven't finished the book yet but I think we should do that ... write things down I mean. I got two jotters from Mum - she always has some spare ones - and I thought we could write things down together now and then when we aren't together we can add anything we think of."

"Brilliant."

Pippa was full of admiration for her friend.

"Let's start right away."

"Before we do, Pippa, I think we should promise to keep our jotters a secret from the grown- ups."

"Oh yes, lets. We won't tell anyone, not even Ronald if we meet him." Ronald, their friend from last year had been kept down a class that year but on the request of his parents had been allowed to go up to the secondary school, Bradford High in August.

The two youngsters knelt together on the bed, held hands and solemnly chanted, "We promise not to let any adults read our jotters."

Hazel went to her desk, sat down and pulling one jotter towards her wrote on the cover, in capital letters: DETECTIVE HAZEL EWING then she gave her seat to Pippa who sat and wrote: DETECTIVE PHILIPPA DAVENPORT on the other jotter.

"Right now, let's think of how to start," said Hazel.

Pippa, anxious to make up for not having had this idea in the first place, suggested that they put everyone's name at the top of a separate page. Hazel agreed and they sat on the bed, jotters on their laps and did this, making sure that they had the same names in the same order.

"Now what?" asked Pippa.

"Well in the book, Mr Hastings writes down if the person had a reason to kill the dead person."

"Right, who's first?" Pippa turned to page one and read out, "Aunt Carol."

"Well Uncle Brian didn't love her any more. I heard Mum and Dad talking once about them and Dad said Uncle Brian wanted a divorce but Aunt Carol wouldn't give him one."

"So why would she kill him?"

"Don't know. Maybe she hated him for not loving her."

They solemnly wrote: "She hated him because he didn't love her any more."

"Next."

"Mr Rogerson."

"Well Uncle Brian liked other women and…"

"How do you know that?" demanded Pippa.

"I heard Ian and John talking about him once. They called him a ladies' man and Diana asked them what they meant and they said that their Dad fancied most women."

"Right," said Pippa anxious to contribute, "so your Uncle Brian fancied Mrs Rogerson and Mr Rogerson was jealous and killed him."

They scribbled away again.

"Mrs Rogerson."

"She loved Mr Rogerson and didn't like Uncle Brian fancying her," offered Hazel.

"Colin… what's his name?"

"Don't know. I just wrote Colin."

"So did I. Same reason?"

"Yes and he's just got engaged so he would be really angry at Uncle Brian fancying Aimee."

"Aimee?" asked Pippa then she remembered something she'd seen that night. "Your Uncle Brian patted her bottom at the party and she didn't seem to mind."

"What will we write then?" asked her friend.

"No reason."

"OK."

"Dr Mackie."

"It couldn't have been him because he's dead."

"How ?"

"Don't know but Dad told us he was. He died on Boxing Day I think."

Pippa felt that she had missed out with living in Newton Mearns and decided to ask her Dad what Dr Mackie had died of.

"Dr Mackie's friend?"

"Jean," said Pippa.

"Yes, Jean."

Hazel scribbled in her jotter.

"This is getting hard. Why would Jean want to kill Uncle Brian. He wouldn't fancy her. She's too old."

"So, 'No reason' again then?"

"Who else?"

"Your Mum and Dad."

Hazel was indignant.

"My Mum and Dad wouldn't kill anyone, Pippa Davenport."

Reluctantly, Pippa agreed, mentally deciding to think about their possible reasons once she got home.

"How about your Dad and Fiona?" queried Hazel.

"My Dad's a police inspector. He solves murders; he doesn't do them. You can write their names down if you like but they wouldn't have a reason."

Hazel wrote Mr Davenport's name at the top of a page and Fiona at the top of the next one. Pippa did the same feeling very adult about including them. She hastily added Sally and Ralph to the tops of two pages.

"Well, OK you can put Mum and Dad's names down too then ," said Hazel and Pippa pretended to write in names she had already written down.

"Any reason?"

Hazel defied her to find one.

"What about your Uncle Brian fancying your Mum and your Dad being angry?"

"Fancying Mum? Don't be daft!"

"Is there anybody else we've forgotten?" Pippa said hurriedly.

"Yes. Us and Diana and John and Ian."

They wrote their own names and those of Hazel's cousins, one page to each name.

"Any reasons?" asked Pippa.

"Diana for him buying her that ghastly dress," said Hazel and they both laughed.

"Why Ian or John?" asked Hazel

"No idea. No reason, again."

Hazel wrote, and then laughingly said, "What about you?"

"Well I wouldn't have killed him. I liked him," said Pippa. "He said I looked beautiful that night."

Hazel pretended to be sick into the waste paper basket and Pippa pushed her off the bed. Soon they were rolling about the floor together, their attempts at amateur detecting forgotten.

They were brought to their senses when Hazel's Dad shouted up the stairs that lunch was ready. They stood up. Hazel shoved the jotters into her desk drawer.

"I'll come up and get yours when you're going home," she said. "Have you got something to put it in?"

"I'll put it into the inside pocket of my anorak," promised Pippa. "Let's write in anything we think and I'll get Dad to ask you up to our house soon and we can read each other's jotters."

"I'll ask Mum if you can have one of her murder books and then you can read it. You're a quick reader. See if you get any ideas. And I didn't kill him either so you can write that in later."

They went downstairs and were soon tucking into lunch. They stayed downstairs watching one of Hazel's Christmas DVDs until Fiona and Pippa's Dad came to pick her up.

CHAPTER 31

Sandra was delighted to get back to work on the 29th. She knew that as editor, Derek had gone in the day before just to keep things ticking over but she had thought that it would look very suspicious to Jim if she had gone back to work a day early. She dressed carefully in her best underwear but in her usual casual denims and tee-shirt and, with a spring in her step, went out to her car. Jim came out behind her. Some months ago he had noticed that she was getting morose but recently she had cheered up in spite of being present at a murder.

"Glad to see you looking so cheerful, my love," he said, coming up to her car and watching as she got in. She had beautiful legs as he was always telling her and the tight denims accentuated these legs.

"Yes. Don't know why I'd got so depressed recently. Sorry. I must have been awful to live with."

As she drove off down the driveway, she made a mental note to try to hide her new delight in life or

Jim might get suspicious. He was a mild-mannered man and had taken with good part Brian Ewing's flirting with her when they'd met some weeks ago at The Avenue at Mearns but all men just laughed at Brian Ewing's attempts at gallantry. She had felt sorry for Carol Ewing. It must be awful to be married to someone who thought himself a lady-killer. Now the man was dead. Maybe it would be a relief for Carol. Sally had hinted to her neighbour that things were not right with her brother-in-law and his wife.

She was kept very busy all morning and did not even talk to Derek till 12.30pm when the rest of the staff left to have lunch. There was no canteen so most folk either brought lunch or ate it at a nearby snack bar. Most must have been fed up with leftovers as no one had brought sandwiches. She managed to get out of lunch with her closest friend, Jilly, by pleading a headache. Derek overheard her.

"A headache, Mrs Rogerson," he teased her when they were alone.

Lunch time was a short one as they were all very busy after the holiday getting the next edition of the magazine up and running so they made do with a chat, a few passionate kisses and an arrangement to meet up at his house at the weekend.

"I'd better not miss visiting my mother-in-law again," said Sandra, "but Jim will probably play golf on Saturday morning so I can come across then."

She had changed her mind about inviting Derek to come to her house as they lived right next door to Sally and Ralph and they might notice the strange man arriving or leaving and in all innocence mention it to Jim.

During lunch time they had discussed the possibility of them getting away together. She was often away on fashion assignments and as editor he could contrive a meeting abroad, leaving his assistant to man the office.

"We might have to put that on hold, Derek," she mourned. "I don't imagine I'll be allowed to leave the country until this murder is solved. Isn't that what happens in murder mysteries?"

Derek said he was a non-fiction reader and did not know the protocol for a person who had been present at a murder but he knew she was making sense. They would have to make do with snatched meetings and be very careful in case she was under scrutiny.

"Who do you think did do it?" he asked her now, hearing the sounds of people arriving back from lunch and getting off her desk.

"Not a clue. Brian was a nuisance, well to women he was but I wouldn't think anyone would be so annoyed that they would want rid of him permanently."

The others coming in caught the last part of the sentence and were eager for her to tell them what had happened the night of the party. Sandra had not been taking much of an interest after her time with Derek and she saw him grinning as she tried to remember the events in any detail.

"Santa did it," she told them, "and I never got in to see him, so I wasn't much use to the police. I was in the dining room ..."

Derek choked and turned it into a cough and she made a face at him unseen by the others.

"I was in the dining room when Carol, the dead man's wife, screamed. She found him, poor woman."

"How did you know it was Santa?" asked Derek, who knew all this already but thought he'd better appear interested like the others.

"One of the guests turned out to be a DCI and his partner was a Detective Sergeant. They found out it was Santa who had committed the murder and asked us all questions about the person who had played the part."

They all went back to their desks, chattering excitedly. Their magazine did not cover news, being a periodical, so the story was of no use to them professionally but it was exciting to be working with someone who had been present at a murder.

Sandra found it very hard to concentrate on her work. It was in her interest to have the murderer discovered as then she and Derek could have their few days away but she could not help the police in any way. Adding to her excitement was the thought of another liaison with Derek at the weekend. She wondered how she could contain herself throughout the next day's work and the boring visit to Jim's demanding mother who had been insufferable at Christmas over her missing out a visit on the night of the party.

However, Sandra Rogerson was no longer bored.

CHAPTER 32

There was a strange hushed atmosphere when Davenport woke the next morning and looking out of his bedroom window he saw that heavy snow had fallen during the night. An almost eerie glow from the snow -covered garden came into the room and he quickly got into his warm dressing gown. He looked in on Pippa, pulling her duvet up round her shoulders and tucking it in. He would have to take her to his sister's before going to work but she could stay asleep for a while longer. She loved the school holidays when she could lie in bed late.

He switched on the radio and was enjoying Terry Wogan's repartee when his daughter ran into the kitchen.

"Dad, it's been snowing. Can we make a snowman?"

"I promise we can do it when we come home pet but there's not time right now and anyway it's still quite dark. Go and get washed and dressed. Maybe you can make one at Aunt Linda's."

"I want to make it with you," she pouted.

"You could have a practice so that ours will be perfect," he smiled at her.

"So I could," she agreed, smiling back before she whirled away to get ready. He smiled after her. His daughter was never moody for long.

He made her porridge and toast. As he got out the knife to butter the toast he thought of the murder weapon. The large kitchen knife with which Brian Ewing had been stabbed had been found by SOC in Sally's kitchen drawer. Obviously the killer had not had time to go outside and throw it away but then the Santa suit had not been well-hidden either. Funny how that made it look like an unpremeditated murder yet the Santa suit had to have been planned.

After breakfast, Charles drove down to his sister's house which was quite near Pippa's school then drove back up to Newton Mearns. He still had to drive very carefully as the roads were very wet and slushy but they were much clearer of snow than they had been when he had driven down. Even forty minutes had made a difference and he hoped for Pippa's sake that there would still be some snow lying in the garden when she got home.

He got to Colin's house about midday.

"Come in Sir," Colin welcomed him. "What can we do for you this time?"

He led the way into a comfortable sitting room where an older man was sitting reading a newspaper. He rose and shook hands with the DCI.

"I'm George Ferguson. Nasty business this murder. I'll leave you both. Mary could probably do with some help in the kitchen."

Mr Ferguson left.

"Colin, one thing only at the moment. Had you met Brian Ewing before the party?"

"Yes, met him once about a fortnight before Christmas in the shopping centre here. He was with Ralph, I think or maybe Sally. I can't remember now but one of them introduced us."

"Was Aimee with you?"

"Yes. Why?"

"Well we have to find out who knew the man."

"I don't imagine meeting him once meant that we knew him Inspector." Colin sounded rather annoyed.

"By all accounts he was a ladies' man. How was he with Aimee?"

"How any man would be faced with a beautiful woman," Colin answered. Davenport could see that the young man was getting angry and wondered if he had touched on a raw nerve.

At that moment Aimee herself came into the room. She really was a beautiful young woman.

Davenport explained why he was there and asked her about meeting Brian Ewing a few weeks ago.

"I did not meet him!" she denied abruptly.

"Yes you did, darling," Colin reminded her, "at the shopping centre, remember?"

"Oh...yes..I had forgotten." Aimee looked relieved, Davenport thought.

"What did you think of him Miss..."

"Aimee, please."

"What did you think of him, Aimee?"

"What relevance does this have Inspector?" Colin asked brusquely.

"It's important for us to know as much as possible about the dead man, Sir."

Aimee thought for a second or two then said that she had found Brian friendly but his wife not so friendly either that day or at the party.

"But then women don't seem to like me very much," she smiled contentedly, confident in her own beauty.

Thanking them for their help, Charles left. He thought about the conversations he had just had. Aimee had been on the defensive when she had denied ever meeting Brian before the party and Colin had seemed ready to pour cold water on any suggestion that Brian had been especially attracted to his fiancée. This could mean anything or nothing and Brian was not here to tell what had happened when they had met.

It took him about half an hour to get to the station and the snow was falling again as he went up the steps.

Penny and Frank were out dealing with some minor problems and only Fiona and Salma were present so he told them about his talk with Colin and Aimee.

"Do you think Aimee could have been the one Wendy Hamilton saw at the hotel that evening?" asked Fiona.

"It wondered that myself. I think that young man will have his work cut out to keep her to himself," replied Davenport.

"Would he have killed anyone who tried to make out with Aimee?" asked Salma.

"He's the quiet, respectable type who smoulders underneath then explodes, I would imagine. So the answer is yes, I think he might have but I don't know if he would have got anyone else to do the job for him and surely it would have been noticed if he left the party."

"He went in to see Santa, Sir," Salma reminded him.

"That's right so if he was responsible then he hired or got someone else to do the killing."

"Sounds too much like an American gangster film," laughed Fiona.

"Could he have left the house while charades was being played and not returned to the lounge at the end of the game?" Davenport mused aloud.

"I suppose so," said Fiona. "At a party you're too busy socialising to count who's there and who's not. Did you see him after charades?"

"I can't remember. I suppose that's true of nearly everyone though I do remember talking to you and Arthur and Jean just before Santa was announced."

"And I remember the kids getting up and running out to be first to get to the food."

"Anyone we met in the hallway could just have come from the study."

"True."

"This is getting us nowhere."

At that moment they heard voices and Frank and Penny arrived back.

"Unless fresh evidence comes in before tomorrow, you can take the day off folks to make up for Christmas Day. Oh, by the way, Arthur Mackie's brother said that Arthur was very quiet all day on Christmas Day but he never confided in any of them and went home early."

Charles left to write up his notes on his interview with Colin and Aimee and left the station about an hour later to pick up his daughter and get home before it got very dark so that the promised snowman could be made.

CHAPTER 33

"San, would you like to have a meal out after seeing my mother?" Jim asked. "Maybe cheer you up a bit."

"No I wouldn't."

"Are you OK?"

"I'm fine."

"No you are not fine, my love. You've got a face that would scare off a mad gorilla."

"Very funny."

"Are you feeling ill?"

"No!"

"Is it that time of the month?"

"No it isn't!"

Jim sighed and walked away from her into the lounge where he picked up the book he was reading. Sandra sighed too. The heavy snow had put paid to Jim's game of golf the next morning with Ralph and she would have to ring Derek to cancel their meeting. To add insult to injury, she would have to visit Mrs Rogerson that evening and that lady had still not forgiven her for missing out her visit last Friday.

"Jim, I'm going out for a walk," she called, shrugging herself into a warm coat.

"Do you want me to come with you?"

He knew the answer before it came.

"No... thanks."

It was more the polite 'thanks' than the 'no' which hit Jim harder. Sandra had turned overnight into a stranger, one who tried to be polite but was obviously not happy. And yet...she had been almost unnaturally happy last Friday at the party, for no reason.

What were mood swings a sign of, he wondered and being a gynaecologist he thought he had the answer. She was starting to go through the menopause. He knew how much she had wanted a baby and this would signal the end of her fertile years. He would have liked a child too but was content with his life alone with Sandra and his rewarding job. Would she go on HRT he wondered. He recommended it to a lot of women but could not really prescribe for his wife. She would have gone to Arthur Mackie but that was not possible now.

His mind skipped to Arthur's death. He had been killed in his own home and his murder would be connected to the murder of Brian Ewing as two killings not linked would be too much of a coincidence. Jim had never liked Brian Ewing, not since he had come on to Sandra at a dance they had been to together with both Ewing brothers and their wives.

They had attended Ralph's firm's annual dinner dance two years ago. Ralph had wanted him and Sandra to accompany them so that Sally would have some friends round her.

Sandra had gone off to the ladies' room and had been some time so he had gone to look for her and had seen her pushing Brian away from her. Brian had laughed it off by saying he had drunk too much but Sandra had looked frazzled and Jim had wondered if this had happened before. He knew of Brian's reputation with women but had never thought that Sandra would be his target.

Even the thought of Sandra in the arms of Brian or in the arms of any man come to that, made Jim feel almost light-headed with panic.

Unaware of the upset she had caused, Sandra walked to the park. The scene which met her was a bare one, like a black and white photograph, the tree branches reaching like skeletal fingers towards the grey sky, the snow sparkling white on the ground and peppering the bushes. The greyness of the sky matched her mood which had swung from anger with Jim for just being there instead of Derek, to one of despair. The affair with

Derek was exhilarating while she was with him but when she was alone she could see no future in it. More than anything else she wanted a baby and she could not see that happening with either Jim or Derek. What should she do?

Should she try to persuade Jim to see a specialist about his poor sex drive?

Should she leave Jim and try for a family with Derek?

Would Derek want another family?

She cleared some snow off one of the old wooden benches and sat down to watch two children playing with a new puppy. It was a blur of honey-coloured fur as it rolled over and over in the snow down the slight incline across from her seat, the children squealing with delight as they chased it. The man with them laughed and picked up the puppy.

"Come on you two, time to get her home. She's had enough for today."

The family walked off.

Sandra felt tears stinging her eyes and she brushed them away with her gloved hand and gave herself a mental shake. For all she knew, Derek only wanted a brief fling. He maybe did not want her on a permanent basis, never mind having children with her. And what about Jim? Would he stand by and willingly let her go off with another man? He valued loyalty and as a Christian he thought marriage was for life. She sighed and her breath appeared before her, held suspended in the cold air.

Her thoughts turned to the two murders.

Who would want rid of Brian? He had been a likeable man, if a bit of a nuisance always trying to flirt with her when Jim was not around. Maybe he had gone too far with some man's wife. But whose? The only women at the party were Sally, Carol, Aimee, Jean Hope and herself. Could Ralph or Arthur or Colin have seen Brian as a threat? Not Arthur because he too had been killed and anyway Jean although being a lovely woman would surely be too old for Brian. That left Colin and Ralph... and Jim.

Jim had no reason for being jealous of Brian so that left the two others. Surely Brian would not have tried to take Sally away from his brother and Aimee had just got engaged to Colin and would surely not have encouraged Brian's advances.

It was getting cold sitting still on this bench so she rose to her feet and set off for home. She had no answers to anything, she thought smiling weakly. She was almost home before she remembered to phone Derek.

"Derek, Sandra here. I won't be able to come tomorrow morning."

"Yes, I thought that with the snow there would be no golf for Jim."

She listened to her lover's voice and felt her mood lifting a little. She heard herself promising to miss church on Sunday morning. That would give them about an hour and a half together and all she needed to do now was think of an excuse for not accompanying Jim to church.

"Jim, let's go out for that meal. Sorry to be such a moody bitch," were her first words to her husband who decided to bring up the subject of HRT that evening after they had seen his mother and were enjoying a meal together.

Mrs Rogerson was sitting asleep in her chair in the lounge when they went into the nursing home. Jim shook her gently.

"Mum. Wake up."

Her rheumy eyes opened and she peered up at him.

"What kept you?"

"It's only 7 o'clock, Mum. That's when we always come. Do you want to stay here or do you want me to help you up and we can go into your room?"

"I'm not staying here for these nosy parkers to listen to our conversation."

"Who're you calling nosy?" demanded the woman on her left while the one on her right looked vacantly at them all.

Jim hurriedly offered his arm to his mother and she got slowly to her feet while Sandra spoke pleasantly to the annoyed woman.

Once settled in her own small room with Sandra in the other chair and Jim perched on the bed, Mrs Rogerson started her diatribe about the meals.

"Mince again, Jim, and ice cream for sweet."

"You like ice cream Mum,"

"Not every day!"

Sandra surreptitiously put her wrist up to her nose in the hope that the perfume she had remembered to put on would mask the smell of urine in the room. Mrs Rogerson refused to let the carers put her into incontinence pads, declaring that she did not need them but she did need them at night and in spite of the bed being changed regularly there was always a smell in the room which was stuffy at the best of times having one small window which her mother-in-law always kept closed, winter and summer alike.

It seemed an interminable length of time before they were rising to leave, promising to come again on New Year's Day.

"Do you still have some Advocaat left Mum?" asked Sandra.

"Don't know," she answered ungraciously.

"We'll bring some more in so that you can toast the New Year," Jim said patiently.

Sandra was pleasant to Jim for the rest of the evening and he forgot to mention HRT till they were having coffee. He was surprised when she said that she had no symptoms of the menopause, so sweats, no hot flushes, and no vaginal dryness. As she said this, she smiled and he wondered why. Seeing his look of puzzlement, she hastened to assure him that she had read up about the menopause and knew the symptoms.

"I could still get pregnant, Jim. Would you see about your...problem?"

Jim looked embarrassed then gave her a pretend leer and said to wait till they got home and he would show her that he had no problem.

True to his word, he made love to her that night. It was not a memorable event and she went to sleep even more confused about what she should do.

CHAPTER 34

"Great, a girly day out" exclaimed Penny, meeting Salma as arranged at Marks and Spencer's in Argyll Street.

"I've got a list of things to get."

Her cheeks, rosy from the cold and looking very vibrant in her cherry red jacket and red beret, Penny hugged Salma who was also looking colourful in a royal blue coat. She was hatless, her beautiful black, shiny hair gleaming in the watery sunlight.

"Oh I knew you'd have our day all planned," smiled Salma. "Can I fit in getting a present for my Mum's birthday?"

"When is it?"

"January the second."

Laughing and arm in arm, they made their way to Debenhams and rode up the escalator to the second floor where Penny hoped to find an outfit to wear at her Mum's wedding to Jack in March. She tried on a number of things but could not find anything which would be suitable for the registry office ceremony and also the reception afterwards.

It was Salma who found the cream and brown dress in a floaty chiffon which looked stunning on Penny with her rosy cheeks and dark brown curls. They found a bolero in cream which matched it perfectly and shoes and a handbag which complemented the outfit. Penny was delighted, though the dress, at £110, was more expensive than she would have liked.

They made their way back to Marks and Spencer's and went to the cafeteria. The place was thronging with customers who had had the same idea and they were lucky to find a table for two where they sat and enjoyed a latte and a muffin each.

"Now I've got to think of a wedding present for them."

"Something useful or something they wouldn't buy themselves?" asked Salma.

"Well with both of them having a house there's not much they need, so something they wouldn't buy themselves."

It was Salma who suggested trying a gallery in one of the lanes off Buchanan Street. They browsed the pictures and Penny, to her delight, found the very thing for her Mum and Jack.

"Salma, look, it's a picture of The Brig O' Doon in Alloway where Jack proposed to Mum. Wonder how much it is. Where's an assistant?"

Salma grabbed her arm as she was about to fly off looking for someone.

"Penny, calm down. The price is written in the bottom right-hand corner."

It was and it was less than Penny had intended spending so when Salma bought her Mum some perfume in Boots in the St Enoch Centre, Penny bought perfume for her Mum and after shave for Jack.

By now it was time for lunch and they opted for D'Arcy's in Princes Square. Again it was busy. They had noticed that some shops already had sale notices up, not waiting till January and there were obviously lots of folk taking the chance of getting a bargain on Hogmanay.

Salma was vegetarian so she had a vegetable lasagne and Penny chose the meat variety. Neither girl was driving, so they had glass of wine to wash it down. It still surprised Penny that Salma would on occasion have an alcoholic drink. Frank had been amazed. He was hidebound by his racial and religious prejudices and was sexist into the bargain though Penny was trying hard to change him and in spite of his dislike of Salma who had got the promotion he himself had gone for, he got on quite well with her now.

"What are you doing tonight, Salma?" Penny asked.

"Nothing. We never do anything at Hogmanay. Just wait up till 12, watch some TV and then go to bed. What about you?"

"I'm going out with some of my church friends. We take it in turns to go to each other's houses. It was my turn last year. It's Alec's this year. He's just bought a new flat in Newlands and is looking for a lodger. I'm half thinking about it for myself as I want to move out when Jack moves in."

Penny got on really well with Jack, her Mum's fiancé. She could not remember her Dad very well and was really glad that her Mum had found someone else to share her life with. She knew that she could stay at home but felt that it was time she branched out on her own anyway. She liked Alec with whom she had been friends through Sunday school and Bible Class. She suspected that he was homosexual as he had never had a girlfriend but that did not worry her. On the contrary it made sharing a house with him easier.

"The last time you mentioned moving out, you said you were going to use your half of the money from the house to buy your own flat," Salma reminded her. Penny's Mum had had the flat she shared with her daughter valued and had promised her daughter her share when she married Jack and he moved in.

"I know I did but I keep changing my mind and maybe sharing for a while will help me make a decision. If I buy, I'll have to take in a lodger anyway to help pay the mortgage." Penny would have loved to share with Salma but knew that she would not leave her Mum, especially as her elder brother had left to live in London.

"Will you always stay at home, Salma?"

"Probably. Mum would love me to be married but I don't want an arranged marriage at least not to someone I don't know at all."

"I thought that arranged marriages usually worked well," said Penny, interested.

"Yes most do, probably because each person has to work at making it work, unlike a marriage where two folk fall in love and think that love will see them through everything."

"D'you think that Frank will ever marry?" Penny asked, sitting back and sipping her white wine thoughtfully.

"As long as he can find someone, Catholic and white who can cook like his Mum," laughed Salma.

"And doesn't want to drive his car," Penny added another stipulation to the list. She looked at her watch.

"Well it's nearly three o'clock. Will we make a move?"

"Before we go, what about this murder? Have you any ideas who the murderer might be?" asked Salma.

"I think it's going to be one of the men who were at the party. It'd be too hard for someone from outside to plan the Santa scenario, don't you think?"

"Yes I agree and I think it'll be a jealous husband."

"Who?"

"Well, there is only Ralph Ewing, the guy Rogerson..."

"Jim Rogerson."

"Yes, him and Colin Ferguson."

"So Brian Ewing was having an affair with either Sally Ewing, Sandra Rogerson or Aimee whatever her name is?"

"Yes."

"I agree," said Salma.

Penny looked at her watch again

"It's after half past three. We'd better get going. You'll have to come up some night next week."

They picked up their purchases and made their way to Union Street where Salma waited with Penny until a 38 bus came along before walking to her own stop to catch her own bus.

CHAPTER 35

"A piece of coal and black bun? Why?" Pippa looked at her Dad with a puzzled frown.

"I suppose it came from the days when houses were cold and folk didn't have much to eat. These were symbols - signs - of hoping the person you gave them to had enough heat and food for the rest of the year."

"We haven't got coal or black bun to take to Auntie Linda," she pointed out.

"I know. I'll just take chocolates instead. We won't be their first foot anyway."

This of course led to him telling her what 'first foot' meant and he wished he had got this over with earlier as he figured that they were now going to be late at his sister's. Not that Linda would mind. She was a slapdash sort of person and seldom on time herself. He loved his sister dearly and she was such a help with Pippa, especially when he had to work odd hours and weekends but he knew her faults and unpunctuality was one of them.

This was to be Pippa's first experience of Hogmanay and staying up till after midnight, as she had gone down to her Mum the last two years and she was really excited. She would be the youngest at Linda's tonight as her cousin Alice was eighteen. She would probably only be with them for a short time as she would no doubt be meeting up with her friends later on. He hoped that Pippa would not be disappointed with the evening.

They had an enjoyable time. Alice was not going out till later and was happy to entertain her young cousin. They spent time in Alice's bedroom listening to music and Pippa told her about the Agatha Christie book she was reading. Alice was impressed as Pippa was only ten years old but Pippa did not tell her why she had started reading these adult books. She thought Alice might laugh at her.

"It's called "The ABC Murders" and the detective is a man called Hercule Poirot," said Pippa now, saying 'rot' at the end as if it rhymed with 'cot'. Her cousin laughingly corrected her pronunciation of the Belgian detective's name and Pippa made a mental note to tell Hazel that they had got it wrong. She was really enjoying the book but would not give up her Chalet School books as she wanted to read the whole series.

Alice left at 11pm and Pippa joined the adults in the lounge. She was beginning to feel tired but would not of course admit this to anyone. Hazel was staying up late again this year. She had done it last year and Pippa felt that she had stolen a march on her as down in England her Mum and her friends did not celebrate Hogmanay and she had not been allowed to stay up.

At two minutes to midnight, her Dad went outside with his box of chocolates and as midnight was chiming on TV, he knocked at the door and was invited in much to his daughter's amusement. Everyone raised their glasses and said, "Happy new year" and then there were kisses all round. Aunt Linda brought out mince pies and Madeira cake and they all sat down again to eat. Charles did not wait long after that, taking the chance to leave with Pippa when the doorbell announced the arrival of some neighbours. She was asleep in the car by the time they were half way home and Charles had to half carry her into the house and up to her bedroom where she got undressed and got straight into bed. He thought she was asleep till a small voice asked, "Dad. How did Dr Mackie die?"

"He was killed, pet."

"OK."

With the brain of a child, she seemed to accept this without further explanation, for the present anyway, he thought.

He was in bed and asleep not long after her.

Fiona Macdonald was hoping that she was going to enjoy her evening as she was spending it with her newly engaged friend Jill and her fiancé. She did not want to be a gooseberry and half wished that she had declined Jill's invitation. She was even more unsure when she got there to find that another guest had been invited, a single man named Robert. So Jill was matchmaking was she? Robert was a handsome young man but knew it and he became boring as all he wanted to talk about was himself and his new job.

"Well, how do you like him?" asked Jill when they were in the kitchen getting the supper ready.

"Well he might improve with time," laughed Fiona, "but at the moment I'm getting fed up listening to him going on about his job. He hasn't even asked me what I do."

"Maybe just as well," said Jill. "Don't you think men get put off when you tell them?"

"If they do then they're not worth getting to know," retorted Fiona, quite sharply, thinking how Charles seemed to value her opinion and treated her as an equal partner at work.

"Oh, Fiona," said Jill. "I meant to ask you, did you see the article in The Herald about the death of that man you talked about a while back, the one who seemed to be a bit of a sex fiend and was involved with the widow of the murdered school teacher?"

Fiona looked puzzled then her expression changed.

"James Buchanan?"

"Yes, I'm sure that was the name. The Herald said he was a lawyer."

"That must be him! Did it say how he died?"

"I think it said a massive heart attack, a sudden death anyway, in his church at Newlands. I'm sure of that. There was a photo of his distraught mother."

"Couldn't have happened to a nicer man," said Fiona, making up her mind to tell Caroline Gibson, the widow who had got involved with the man.

She spent the rest of the evening comparing Robert unfavourably with Charles and was quite relieved when 'the bells' had passed and she could get off home. Robert offered to take her home but she declined his offer. Jill looked disappointed and Fiona made a mental note to tell her friend that she had a man friend, without actually telling her who that friend was, as she knew that Jill would warn her against another station romance.

Aimee had been looking forward to a Scottish Hogmanay but she was disappointed. Colin had taken her to a party at a friend's house and she had met a lot of his church friends. They did drink; well the men did, but not enough to make them let their hair down. She noticed that all the wives drank only non- alcoholic drinks - they were obviously driving home - and they were a serious, sober bunch, some of them church elders like their husbands and speaking of serious affairs such as the trouble in the Middle East.

Aimee stood in the circle of women and tried to listen in to what the men were talking about. They were certainly laughing more than the women. She caught the eye of one rather handsome man and smiled flirtingly at him. He blushed and turned back to the group.

Supper over, they all sat round the TV and watched a programme about the goings on in George Square. Aimee wished she could have been there as it all looked much more alive than where she was. She whispered to Colin, "Darling, could we not go there, to that place on the television? It looks so exciting."

Colin frowned. He had seen the look she had given his friend Tom. He was beginning to suspect that his fiancée only really enjoyed male company. She made a much greater effort to be charming to his father than to his mother and he sensed that his mother did not really approve of her. He tried to keep irritation out of his voice.

"Aimee, we can't leave the party. It would be so rude. Try to enjoy yourself darling."

Aimee pouted and stayed very quiet for the rest of the evening.

Sandra and Jim watched TV. He had asked her if she wanted to invite anyone in but she thought that Sally and Ralph might come in as usual and that was enough for her. She was already looking forward to seeing Derek on Sunday morning and had spent some time ruminating over how she was going to get out of going to church. The headache excuse could not really be used twice.

As if fate was being good to her, about halfway through the evening she felt a dryness in her throat and realised that she had the start of a cold.

"I've got a cold coming on, Jim," she said.

"Take some paracetamol. Do you want me to phone the Ewings and put them off?"

"No, don't do that. They'll want something to take their minds off the murders."

At 10.30 the doorbell rang. Jim opened the door to their neighbours and got them drinks, even Hazel who was delighted when her dad said she could have a very mild martini and lemonade. She hoped that Pippa had only been allowed lemonade.

They were laughing as the clock hands moved towards midnight and then Ralph moved towards the door to get himself outside in time to come back in as their first foot. They heard him speak as he crossed the threshold and as midnight struck on TV, he came back in, accompanying another man.

It was Derek.

"Sorry if I'm intruding, Sandra," he said. "You said that you weren't having a get together so with having no one to share the bells with I thought I'd pop over and first foot you."

Jim shook his hand and wished him a happy new year before turning to kiss his wife.

Sandra turned to Derek and kissed him chastely, and then the three of them kissed and shook hands with the Ewing family. Jim liked Derek, having met him a number of times at Sandra's work's parties, and Ralph was pleased to have a stranger with them as they would not be tempted to talk about the murders. Sally had been doing very well after the initial shock and he wanted to keep her that way.

Hazel was delighted as she foresaw that with another person joining them it might be some time before her Mum and Dad suggested going home. She wanted to stay up later than her friend and she had her wish as they did not get home till just after 2am.

Diana found it very difficult to say the words, "Happy New Year" as the bells rang out on TV and could not understand how her brothers and her mother could appear so calm. She wanted to shout at them, "It won't be a happy New Year. Dad's dead!" but she managed not to, thinking that the others were only really putting a brave face on things. She wanted the holidays to be over so that she could get back to school and a life that was normal. As soon as she could, without showing that she was upset, she went off to bed. She thought about her Dad and how she had not thanked him for the dress he had bought her. How she wished he was still here and that she could show him she loved him. It was difficult to love Mum. She was so perfect, so calm even in the face of the tragedy. She felt that she was a disappointment to her Mum, with her plump figure and flyaway hair. She loved her brothers, Ian more than John she thought now but they would be leaving soon to go back to Stirling, that is if police solved the murders and let them all get back to what passed for normal.

The only person as sad as Diana, was Jean Hope. Although she had not expected a romance with Arthur Mackie, she had begun to work her life round her games of bridge and golf with him. They had begun to spend some evenings together in their respective houses and it was going to be difficult to go back to being alone again. Hogmanay only emphasised her future loneliness and she poured herself a gin and tonic at 11.50, drank it slowly while the TV entertainers did the lead up to midnight and went to bed once the drink was finished. As she lay in bed listening to the sound of revellers outside in the street, she wondered for the umpteenth time who could have killed Arthur.

As each of the folk involved in the murders drifted off to sleep, the New Year came inexorably in bringing with it much sadness and puzzlement.

CHAPTER 36

Somewhere between sleeping and being fully awake, Jean remembered something that she thought might be important in the murder case. It was January 1st and she figured that the police on the case would not be at work but she was not going to repeat Arthur's fatal mistake and tell someone else so it would have to keep till the next day.

Davenport received a phone call early on the Monday, a phone call which sent him straight off to see Jean, pausing only to tell DS Macdonald where he was going.

"When I come back we'll all meet to discuss our next moves. Make sure all reports have been typed up."

"And after that?"

"You can all have a quiet reading time to make sure you have all the angles of the case firmly in your heads."

It took him about ten minutes to reach Tassie Street. He had not realised how close Jean lived to Fiona. Maybe they could invite Jean to the occasional bridge game if they were short of a player at any time and they were playing at Fiona's house.

He spoke into the intercom and she buzzed the door open for him. When he arrived at her flat, the door was open and she shook his hand and stood aside for him to enter.

"I hope I've not brought you out on a wild goose chase, Inspector." Her quiet voice pleasant on the ear, reminded him of his mother and he asked Jean where she came from.

"Tarbert, Loch Fyne."

"My mother came from Campbelltown. You sound just like her."

By this time they were sitting across from each other in her living room cum kitchen.

"Now Mrs Hope, you said on the phone that you thought that one of the guests was missing from the group at one time. Who was it and when was it?"

"Please call me Jean. I'd better start at the beginning. Arthur asked Jim the neighbour if he'd be taking a video of the party as he used to do."

"Yes, I was there when Arthur asked him."

"He told me later, Arthur that is, that it was a perfect nuisance having the camera poked into everything that went on and when he discovered that Jim had forgotten it he wished he'd kept quiet. Well, this morning in bed I suddenly remembered that Jim had the camera later.

He must have left the house to get the camera at some stage...but he seemed such a nice man and..."

"Even nice people have committed murder Mrs Hope... sorry... Jean. So Jim didn't have the camera at the beginning of the party but he had it later."

"Why would he want to kill Brian his neighbour?"

"That's the big question, Jean. We can't think of why anyone would want to kill Mr Ewing but someone obviously did. Have you mentioned this to anyone else but me?"

"No. I thought of what happened to poor Arthur. Do you think he remembered this and went to Jim instead of coming to you?"

"I don't know. He didn't necessarily go to the person who killed him - the person came to him but it could have been their second meeting I suppose, though it would have been risky letting Arthur have time to tell someone else or inform us."

"What now, Inspector?"

"If I'm to call you Jean you must call me Charles," said Davenport who was as sure as he could be that this lovely little woman was not, and never would be, a suspect. "I'll go over to Newlands and have a chat with Mr Rogerson. Hopefully he won't be back at work yet. Please don't mention what you've told me to anyone else. Promise?"

"I promise."

Thanking her for her help, Davenport went back to his car. The snow had by now turned to a grey slushy mess and he got his feet soaked when he stepped into the gutter to cross the road to his car. Shaking his foot to get rid of some of the cold, wet mass round his ankle, he leant into the car and pulled the in-car phone towards him. The reception was usually better outside the car. The police constable at the desk put him through to his DS and he told her where he was going.

"I'll not go into any details now, Fiona but I'll be later back than I thought. Tell the others to have lunch - you go too if you can stand the canteen cooking. If not, wait till after the meeting and I'll take us somewhere better."

He laughed at her reply, replaced the phone and gave his leg another quick shake before getting into the car and heading for Newlands and the Rogersons' detached house next door but one to Ralph and Sally Ewing.

He was out of luck as no one came to answer his ring. Both must be back at work already. He racked his brain but could not remember what they worked at or where they worked, in fact he could not even recall having been told.

He had more success at the Ewing's. Ralph was back at work but the schools did not reopen till next Monday so Sally and Hazel were in.

"Hi Hazel," he said to that young lady who came to the door. "Is your Mum in?"

"Hi, Mr Davenport. Yes she's in. Mum!" she called.

Sally came to the door and invited him in, wiping her hands on her apron as she led him into the kitchen.

"Hope you don't mind sitting here," she said, pulling out a high stool for him to sit on, "I'm in the middle of making tonight's meal" and she took a large knife and continued slicing carrots.

Davenport thought she looked a lot better but decided not to comment. Instead, he asked Hazel if she would leave her Mum and him alone. Looking extremely disappointed, she left and Davenport shut the kitchen door before perching on the high stool.

"Sally. Can you remember when Jim Rogerson had his camera with him the night of the party?"

"Not when he arrived but I think I saw him with it later but not exactly when, I'm afraid. I remember being delighted when he didn't seem to have it with him."

"So he must have gone home for it at some time."

"I suppose he must have done."

"Round about the time when Santa arrived?"

"You surely don't think that Jim could have murdered Brian! Why would he do it?"

"I don't know. I've been to see him but there's no one in."

"Jim's a consultant at the Southern General and Sandra's a journalist. They would both have to be back at work today, like Ralph. Only lazy teachers like me have an extra week off."

He laughed with her.

"Please don't mention this to anyone else, Mrs Ewing, not even your husband and certainly not Jim or Sandra. I don't want to frighten you but Arthur Mackie spoke to someone and either he spoke to the murderer or he spoke to someone who told the murderer and look what happened to him."

She looked frightened and assured him that she would tell no one.

When Davenport moved out of the kitchen and was on his way to the front door, Hazel appeared from the sitting room and asked him if Pippa had been allowed to stay up till midnight the night before.

"Yes she was."

Hazel looked disappointed and Charles smiled inwardly. He could remember the days when such things were very important and he realised that Hazel had been hoping to steal a march on Pippa.

"I'll get her to invite you up some time this week," he told her. "You can compare notes then."

"Notes? What notes?"

He wondered why she sounded almost guilty but Sally was talking.

"Would tomorrow or Wednesday be suitable Mr Davenport? I want to go into school one day to get things ready for Monday."

Davenport thought for a minute then told her that Wednesday would be better as he was going to have to take Pippa into the station with him the next day as Linda was too busy to look after her but he was sure that his sister would not object to coming to his house to chaperone the two young girls the following day.

"Could I not come to the station tomorrow too?" asked Hazel excitedly.

"Hazel! Mr Davenport doesn't want two pests getting in his way at work," remonstrated her mother and Davenport said he was sorry but there was not enough to keep two of them busy all day.

"Maybe you can come in another time to see where I work," he said and with this she had to be content.

It was nearly 1.30 by the time he got back to the station and there was only Fiona present in their area. However, he had hardly got his coat off when noise along the corridor heralded the arrival of the other three. The five of them congregated in the Incident Room and Davenport told them of the most recent development.

"I'm going to stick my neck out and say it must have been a man who committed the murder of Brian Ewing and therefore either a man or an accomplice who killed Arthur Mackie, possibly because Arthur knew that that person could have played the part of Santa."

"So what do we do now Sir?" asked Penny, never prepared to wait even a second to find out what she wanted to know.

"I can understand why you weren't called Patience," said Davenport, smiling at her.

He wrote on the white board, one below the other the names of all the men present at the party:

Ralph Ewing
Colin Ferguson
Jim Rogerson

He paused then added,

John Ewing
Ian Ewing

"Surely the boys would have no reason to kill their own father," protested Salma.

"We don't know any reason for anyone doing it yet, Salma but I want them included too until we can dismiss them."

"So, Ralph Ewing," said Fiona. "Could he have done it and why would he do it?"

"Sally came in to tell us about Santa. Was Ralph in the room at that time?"

Fiona thought for a moment.

"I couldn't swear to it but I don't think so. Sally looked round the room when she told us. She could have been looking for Ralph."

"Why would he want to kill his brother?" asked Frank.

Silence.

"Next," said Davenport looking at the board. "Colin."

"I really can't remember if he was in the room then," said Fiona this time. "Can you?"

"I do remember Aimee squealing with delight but it was Sandra Rogerson who was sitting beside her, I think."

"Why would he kill Brian Ewing?" asked Salma.

"Maybe Brian had come on to Aimee before the party somewhere. OK," Davenport put up his hands in mock surrender. "I know it's flimsy. Who's next?"

"Jim Rogerson?" said Penny quickly.

"I can't remember seeing him or not seeing him," Fiona looked dismayed. "Some police woman I am. Can't remember much."

"Me neither," said Davenport.

"Why would he kill Mr Ewing?" Salma asked the same question as before.

"No idea," said Davenport dejectedly.

"John let Santa in, so he couldn't have let himself in," said Frank.

"No but it might have been his twin Ian who let Santa in. Was he in the lounge when his Mum announced that Santa had arrived?" Penny had been quick to spot the problem with identical twins.

Once again they drew a blank, both Charles and Fiona having been busy chatting to Arthur Mackie and Jean about bridge to have been paying much attention. Fiona thought she had seen one of the twins in the lounge but it might have been later when he put on a CD.

"Right, we've got no clear idea of who was in the lounge when Sally announced that Santa had arrived though we think that Ralph was not there and we're not sure of Colin. Jim Rogerson went out at some point for his video camera and could have brought the Santa suit back with him too. We know that one of the twins took Santa to the study so one is in the clear but we're not sure which one and no one has a motive that we know of right now," Davenport summed up.

"So, what next, Sir?" Frank risked asking a Penny - type question. Davenport made a face, before replying that he thought that they needed to question everyone again in private to try to find out what Brian might have done to warrant being murdered.

"We'll interview the women first. Brian Ewing was a womaniser. We know that. He might have gone too far with someone's wife, someone who was jealous enough to kill."

"Do you want us to start this afternoon, Sir?" asked Fiona.

"No. We'll make a start bright and early tomorrow. Salma, I'd like you and Penny to visit Sally Ewing. Phone her first. I think she'll be at home as she's going into her school on Wednesday but better check in case she's going shopping. Then go to Colin Ferguson's house. He works with Ralph so will be at work but Aimee isn't working. She told us that at the party. Penny, phone the house now and make an appointment to see her later in the morning."

"I'll phone Sally Ewing now too, Sir," replied Salma and she and Penny left the room.

"Fiona, give Sandra Rogerson a ring tonight and arrange a time to go to her place of work, tomorrow. Take Frank with you."

"What about Jean Hope, Sir?" asked Frank.

"I'm discounting her as we were talking to both her and Arthur when Santa was announced and anyway Arthur didn't kill himself."

Frank reddened. He wished he had not asked what now appeared to be a silly question. Seeing his discomfiture, Davenport told him he had been right to mention Jean.

Penny coming back into the room asked if they were also to include the young females but Davenport said that there was no reason to involve Pippa, Hazel and Diana.

"Are we to interview Carol Ewing again too, Sir?" asked Salma who had just returned.

"Well her husband was killed so he couldn't have been jealous of another man."

Like Frank, Salma looked embarrassed, realising that she had asked a silly question. Frank smiled at her sympathetically.

All the arrangements having been made for the next day, the young ones went for their hats and jackets. Charles asked Fiona if she would mind if they collected Pippa from her Aunt's and all three went for a meal.

"Won't all restaurants still be closed on the second of January, Charles?"

"I imagine that the Chinese ones won't be," was the reply.

"In that case, phone Pippa at your sister's and let's get going. I'm starving."

There had indeed been someone in when Davenport had rung the bell at the Rogerson house. Sandra had been sound asleep, in a confused dream caused by her high temperature. The hoped-for cold which was to have been her passport to seeing Derek on New Year's Day had become instead a dose of the real flu. She had spent Sunday in bed hardly able to lift her head from the sweat-soaked pillow. Jim had been attentive, bringing her paracetamol and hot drinks and holding her up while she drank. Coming round from yet another bout of hallucinatory sleep, late in the afternoon, she heard, as if from a distance, Jim telling her that her boss had phoned to wish them once again a happy New Year.

It was not until evening that her fuzzy head cleared enough for her to remember that she had been going to call off going to church and go to Derek's instead.

"Did you tell Derek that I was ill, Jim?" she asked when he arrived with her next dose of pills.

"Yes I did and he said he hoped you'd be better soon. You've not to go back to work till you're completely well."

Sandra found herself feeling quite relieved that she had not had to see Derek after her confused feelings in the park and Jim making love to her the same evening. Maybe being away from work and her boss might give her time to assess the situation she was now in. She lay back against her pillow and sighed. Jim was instantly concerned.

"What's wrong San?"

"Nothing, love. Just feeling very sweaty again and I've got a bit of a headache now." Sandra recalled her mother telling her never to pretend to have an ailment as you would probably get it and she remembered lying about a headache in order to miss church last week in order to visit Derek. So she was being paid back for her lie! Jim went over to the dressing table and got a fresh nightie for her. He helped her into it and she lay back exhausted after the slight exertion.

CHAPTER 37

Tuesday the third of January was a wet day. Penny groaned when she woke up and opened her curtains. She knew that all over Glasgow, policemen and women would be experiencing the same reaction to the weather as this was the day of the Old Firm football match, Rangers versus Celtic at Parkhead. One of their DCIs was in charge of policing the event and he had asked for all personnel to be made available. Her boss could possibly have pleaded that he needed his staff right now but there was a definite lull in their murder investigations so he had had to agree to free all except Fiona Macdonald and himself for the football game.

Penny had looked out her spare uniform suit, her old one, the night before and had rung Salma to advise her to do the same, only to be told that Salma was an old hand at football policing and had had the same idea herself. Frank, an avid Celtic supporter, actually enjoyed being in the thick of the football crowd and hoped to be placed where he could get a good view of the game.

The three of them had agreed to meet at their own station first and go along together in the hope that they might be allocated the same area so that they could at least chat some times, so at the appointed hour they gathered on the steps prior to getting into a squad car and driving to Parkhead. Davenport had told them not to come in till later as the match was at midday as usual in the hope that less alcohol would be consumed before the start of the game.

Mounted police were in evidence. Penny loved the sight of these large, proud animals. They snorted their breaths into the damp air and pawed the ground impatiently, their white 'socks' looking like part of a smart uniform. They were ready for action and little knew that they would be kept standing around should no action be needed. Penny patted the nose of a dark brown, glossy - coated horse and saw that Salma and Frank were keeping well back. She laughed.

"It'll not eat you. Have you never patted a horse before?"

"No!" they chorused in unison and Frank added, "And I'm not likely to either."

The metal blinds were being wound up on the food outlets. The smells were tantalising. It was like passing a fish and chip shop or a bakery and desperately wanting to sample the food being produced. Frank especially hoped for a lenient officer in charge who would let them buy something to eat and drink. "Could Salma eat a mutton pie?" he wondered and asked her.

"It's pork I can't eat, Frank but I'm vegetarian anyway so no pie for me."

"Frank, do you notice nothing that goes on round you?" Penny was exasperated. "Salma always has the vegetarian option in the canteen."

Frank laughed good- naturedly.

"OK penny farthing, keep your wig on! Who is it that can't eat beef?"

"That's the Hindus," replied Salma. "I asked a Chinese colleague once what the Chinese ate and she said everything, including the table."

They were having a good laugh at that when an officer came over to them and allocated them their positions.

He looked Salma up and down and sneered, "You'll be about as much use as a wet paper bag if things get rough."

"Why?" Salma asked pleasantly.

"Probably against your religion to get involved in anything unpleasant."

Penny went for him verbally. She never thought first.

"How racist! Sergeant Din is a super policewoman."

Frank was annoyed too, yet was honest enough to realise that it was only because it was Salma who was being vilified that it angered him. He would probably have shared this officer's opinion had it been someone he did not know. He put his arms round Penny as if to hold her back from attacking the man who looked startled then furious. He asked Penny what station she came from and told her he would be reporting her.

"Go ahead. My DCI will understand."

"Penny, leave it," said Salma. "I'm used to these things remember."

The officer went off, muttering under his breath and Frank, Penny and Salma moved to their allocated positions.

As the interval whistle sounded, a sea of blue supporters waved towards the food outlet. Salma, looking across the pitch, saw a surge of green humanity moving foodwards too.

Supporters made their way back to their positions clutching polystyrene cups of Bovril, liberally seasoned with salt and pepper and tinfoil containers with pies covered in tomato ketchup. Microwave ovens were working overtime, churning out the heated specials. The pie and Bovril were synonymous with Scottish football games and Frank especially was hoping that there was some left over for the police force and they were in luck. The racist officer had been replaced by a friendly one who gave them permission to buy food for themselves. Penny and Frank availed themselves of the opportunity and bought a pie each. Frank picked up the ketchup and poured it liberally over his pie, Penny settling for vinegar. Salma took a cup of Bovril, sipped it, made a face and put it back down on the counter. Penny laughed and told her that Bovril had meat extract in it.

The score was nil-nil so the atmosphere was relaxed and friendly and the only sound coming from both sides of the park was laughter.

However, as the game progressed, Celtic scored from a penalty which the Rangers supporters thought was an unfair decision and the mood became ugly. Boos rose from the mass of blue scarfed men, women and children and cheers echoed back from the rows of green.

"We are the champions" rose from the other side and "Follow, follow, we will follow Rangers" was sung back, the tunes meeting in the middle, in no man's land, like two opposing armies.

Out on the pitch the teams were continuing with the game. A Rangers' player was given a yellow card for a foul and as if to beat that, a Celtic player was shown a red one and left the field to jeers from the opposing fans who settled down hoping that with one man short their team would score. This did not happen and soon the final whistle pierced the air.

The Rangers' supporters surged out of their seats, either to escape possible trouble or to cause it. Penny, being small, was almost knocked down as she tried to hold back the first wave. Salma came to help her but it took Frank added to their efforts, to stem the tide. The rush slowed where they were and they could see fellow policemen and women at work near them doing the same with their groups of supporters. The mounted police were using their proud steeds to keep the supporters in line, the horses looking regal compared to the humanity they were controlling.

It seemed to take hours but was probably only about twenty minutes before the stands were emptied, the masses moving outside the ground to hopefully go home quietly.

Grateful that they had been on duty inside and not outside where there was likely to be more trouble, Salma, Penny and Frank made their way back to the police car they had come in and were waved out in front of the supporters' buses by a fellow policeman on traffic duty. They arrived back at the station in mid- afternoon. Davenport, seeing how tired they looked, took pity on them and sent them off to the canteen for half an hour's break, telling them to report to the Incident Room afterwards.

In the canteen, Salma asked Penny how her Hogmanay party at Alec's had gone. She was surprised when Penny blushed. Frank noticed it too.

"Aha, you met someone there didn't you?" he said teasingly.

"Yes I did."

"Well tell us his name. Let's have some details. The three musketeers don't have secrets from one another," Frank was insistent. Salma glowed with delight at being included in this way.

Reluctantly Penny told them about Gordon Black whom she had met that night.

"Hey!" said Frank, delightedly. "If you marry him you'll be Penny Black. A rare stamp," he explained, seeing Salma's bewilderment.

"I've only just met him," Penny laughed.

"Are you seeing him again?" Salma asked.

"Yes. We're having a meal out on Friday. Now no more about it, please."

They had reached the Incident Room so they had to leave it there.

"Right, team." His familiar words met them. Had it been DS Macdonald she would have said, "OK folks." Davenport always called them his team and as always when worried he pulled at his left ear lobe.

"We know that Brian Ewing was stabbed by a kitchen knife which was put back in the drawer of Sally Ewing's kitchen. This tells us nothing as the cutlery drawer was where cutlery drawers often are in a kitchen, at the front of the sink so anyone would have known where to get a knife. It had been wiped clean but traces of blood and no fingerprints were found on it. The murderer would have no blood on him or her as the Santa suit would have covered all the assailant's clothes. We think that gloves were worn but none have been found. Any questions or comments?"

There were none so he continued:

"Arthur Mackie was hit over the head with something, we don't yet know what. There was not much blood from this wound so the murderer might have escaped being marked with it."

"And we are taking it that both murders were committed by the same person, Sir?" asked Fiona.

"I think so as it would be too much of a coincidence to have two people at the same party being killed within days of each other. I think we can assume that Arthur Mackie saw or heard something suspicious and told the murderer."

"Are we limiting the suspects to the people who were at the party, Sir?" queried Frank.

"For the moment, yes. It *is* possible that Wendy Hamilton's husband wanted revenge on Brian but it would have been almost impossible for him to know when to arrive at the Ewing house even if he did know about the party which was unlikely as he wasn't speaking to his wife at the time."

"Do you still think it was a man, Sir?" Penny wanted to know.

"Yes. Maybe wrongly, I'm ruling out Sally who had no motive, Carol who would surely have done it years ago and Aimee who I think saw him as lover material. No one in their right mind would suspect Hazel and my Pippa and I can't see Diana stabbing her father."

"So then we're left with Ralph Ewing, Jim Rogerson, Colin Ferguson and the twins." Fiona summed up who remained.

"And the twins are hardly likely, Sir, are they?" asked Penny.

"Less likely than the others I have to admit but they had the same opportunity as the other men though no motive that I can see."

"Ralph maybe found out about abuse of his wife," contributed Salma.

"Colin found out about a liaison Aimee had with Brian if she was the mysterious woman at the Busby Hotel," chipped in Salma.

"Jim Rogerson found out that he'd propositioned Sandra," Fiona added.

"Ok team that's the state of the parties summed up. Go home and think about it. Meet here tomorrow nine o'clock sharp."

Fiona had remembered something.

"Before you all go, I've got a bit of news for you. Do you remember that creep, James Buchanan, the one who sexually harassed Caroline Gibson after the murder of her husband?"

"Yes." Davenport replied and the rest nodded their heads.

"Well, a friend of mine read of his death the other day."

"A jealous husband stabbed him?" Penny sounded hopeful.

"'Fraid not, Penny."

Fiona laughed.

"He took a heart attack, my friend thought, at church. She couldn't find the newspaper for me to read."

Looking quite delighted, the young ones walked off down the corridor. Davenport went back to his own office and Fiona Macdonald to hers. On the way down the corridor Frank pulled his left earlobe with his left hand and said," Right team. Over the sea to Skye!"

Guffaws of laughter swept up the corridor.

CHAPTER 38

"What will I do today Dad?" asked Pippa. She was desperately hoping to find out some information about the murders so that she could tell Hazel when they met the next day so was delighted when he told her to go and sit in the main room where the rest of the crew hung out.

"You did bring your book with you didn't you?" Davenport asked now.

"Yes Dad."

"Is it the next Chalet School Book, Pippa?" asked Fiona, interested as they both shared a love of these books.

Pippa, looking a bit furtive, said that she was in the middle of, "Three Go to the Chalet School". She did not want Fiona or her Dad to know that she had been reading a murder mystery. They might ask why.

"I've had a report from Martin and the post mortem showed that Arthur was hit over the head with a heavy blunt instrument. We'll need to go back to his house and have a look round inside and out to see if we can find out what was used."

"Who do you want to do that?"

"All of us. We'll meet outside his house at say 10.30am and we can divide up the house and garden among us."

Davenport and Fiona with Pippa in tow, went into the main room where they found the others waiting to be told what to do today.

Having been told to meet at Arthur Mackie's house, they all went off.

Salma and Penny arrived at Dr Mackie's house just before 10.20. Their car was the only car in the driveway so they were first. They stayed in the car as it was a dank, misty day. A few minutes later their DCI arrived. He got out of his car and got into the back of theirs.

Their conversation was interrupted by his mobile phone. It was DS Macdonald ringing to say that she and Frank were on their way. She had been held up by a minor police matter.

"OK. We'll make a start inside. You and PC Selby search the garden when you do arrive."

Davenport opened the house door. The hall smelt musty and unlived-in as houses do if their owners have been on holiday. Telling the girls to look out for something that could have been used to hit Arthur over the head, Davenport went into the kitchen. Salma went into the dining room and Penny into the lounge. It was Penny who came up with a possibility.

"Sir," she called. "There's only one candlestick on the mantelpiece. Should there not be two?"

Davenport and Salma arrived together.

The mantelpiece had on it as a centre-piece one brass candlestick. On one side of this there was a clock and on the other two glass ornaments.

"Sir, that does look odd. Surely the clock would be in the middle," said Salma.

"Yes, Sir," added Penny. "It would be candlestick, ornament, clock, ornament, candlestick, wouldn't it?"

"I'm sure you're both right. So the murderer took time to rearrange things before leaving. I wonder where he or she put the other candlestick."

"I thought you were sure it was a man, Sir," Penny put in.

""Yes, for the first murder but the second could have been done by an accomplice who could have been a woman. It's possible and we'll have to keep an open mind. Now let's have a quick look for that other candlestick."

Not really expecting the weapon to be upstairs but going up just in case, he looked down and saw the arrival of the other police car. Opening the window, he called down, "DS Macdonald, we're looking for a candlestick. You and Frank get to work in the garden."

Nothing was found in the house or the garden but when they had asked for and received permission from the next door neighbours to search their gardens, the candlestick, its base encrusted with brown dried blood in which some grey hairs had become stuck, was found in some bushes near the front gate of the neighbour on the left. Carefully handling it by the top with a large handkerchief, Frank carried it to Davenport who put it in a large polythene bag which he had brought with him.

"Ok folks, search over."

He went next door, rang the bell and thanked the neighbour who looked agog with curiosity but was told nothing.

Back at the station, Charles dispatched the murder weapon to Vince Parker. He rang him and warned him of what was arriving and asked as usual if he could be as quick as possible with reporting his findings. He listened to what was being said at the other end.

In the Incident Room, he informed his colleagues that Vince Parker had been promoted. He would be leaving at the end of the month. He had sounded, for once, quite cheerful and had promised to send his findings on the candlestick as soon as possible.

"Right, before lunch, let's pool our findings from this morning's interviews of the women," he said.

"Salma, you first."

Penny looked disappointed but she had enough sense to know that, as her superior, Salma should be the one to make the report. She was aware that what Salma had to say was very interesting.

"Mrs Ewing was very reluctant to say anything about her brother-in-law, Sir. She said at first only that she wasn't terribly fond of him. He had told her to pull herself together when she had depression."

"What an idiot!" Fiona was disgusted at this old fashioned and totally unsympathetic reaction to mental illness.

"We asked her if she knew that he had been a womaniser and she just said yes but Penny pressed her. Mrs Ewing said she knew that he had had a lover but Sir, that didn't seem to be something she would want to hide so I asked her if he had ever tried it on with her..."

"...And she admitted that he had," Penny broke in.

"Did she give details?" Davenport asked.

"No, Sir. She wouldn't say anything else after that, I'm afraid."

Salma looked apologetic.

"She'll have to be told that nothing can be kept back in a murder enquiry," said the DCI,

"But don't worry, the DS or myself will take it from there. What about Aimee?"

"She was totally different, Sir, almost proud of the fact that Brian Ewing had found her attractive. She had met him in the shopping arcade when she was there with Colin some time ago. Colin had left them together while he went for an evening newspaper and Brian had asked her for her mobile phone number."

"Did she give it to him?"

"She said she didn't but I'm not sure she was telling the truth," Salma looked thoughtful.

"We asked if Colin knew and she said no. She told us that Colin was old fashioned and wouldn't have seen it as a compliment as she did."

"What about you?" Charles looked at Fiona Macdonald. "Did you have any luck with Sandra Rogerson?"

"She was probably in when you called, Sir. She has a real dose of flu and was still in bed today."

She turned to Frank

"You took the notes, Frank. You tell the DCI what she said."

"Well, Sir, she appears to have disliked the man intensely. He had made a pass at her at a dinner dance, actually asked if she would meet him somewhere. She told us that she said no. When we asked if Jim knew about this she said yes, he had seen it happen and he had been furious. He wanted to confront Brian but Sandra had persuaded him not to as it would make meeting him another time awkward and she didn't want Ralph to know in case it embarrassed him."

"So all the woman had been propositioned, except Sally and we're not even sure that she wasn't. Jim Rogerson knew, Colin might have found out and maybe even Ralph had something to hate his brother for."

"Does that mean we can narrow it down to those three men, Sir?" asked Fiona.

"No we'll have to keep an open mind. Wendy Hamilton's husband is still a possible suspect and although it seems unlikely, John and Ian Ewing might have had a reason for wanting their father dead."

"What, Sir?" asked Penny.

"I don't know but I just want us to keep them in the frame until we can rule them out."

"Could Carol Ewing have wanted rid of her husband and got someone else to murder him?" Frank asked.

"It's possible but unlikely. He'd wanted her to divorce him so she could have got rid of him easily and taken him to the cleaners financially so I don't see what she had to gain by refusing that and then taking the risk of having him murdered."

The phone rang in Davenport's room and he went along the corridor to answer it. He returned minutes later to inform them that Arthur's house phone had been checked and that he had rung Carol's house, Ralph's house and the Rogerson's on the day of his murder.

"I'm going along to get more from Sally Ewing and I'll ask her why Arthur Mackie rang her that day. Fiona, ring Carol Ewing and Salma, remember later to ring once Jim Rogerson gets home and ask them why Arthur contacted them. Better not disturb his wife if she's ill."

Stopping for a minute to check up on his daughter who looked a bit flushed, he left for the Ewing house in Newlands, promising Pippa that they would go home when he returned.

Some minutes later, Fiona asked Pippa if she wanted to go to the canteen with her. She caught the youngster scribbling in a jotter and wondered if she had to do another talk exercise in school. Pippa had already done talks on her favourite books and one on her day at the police station earlier in the year. Pippa hurriedly stuffed the jotter in her bag and they went to the canteen where over a muffin and orange juice, Pippa confided in Fiona that she had started reading Agatha Christie books.

"I haven't given up The Chalet School, Fiona but with being involved in a murder, Hazel and I thought we would read some murder books. I got this one from her Mum's bookshelf. She dived into her bag and produced "The ABC Murders".

Fiona laughed. "And was that why you were listening in to what your Dad was saying in the Incident Room?"

Pippa went red.

"Don't tell Dad, Fiona. I just want to know more than Hazel."

"Well that's fine but will you promise not to tell Hazel what you heard today, please?"

Pippa was disappointed but she promised.

"How did you know I was listening?"

"I saw you in the glass door. We should have shut the door but I guess we forgot you were there. I won't tell your Dad if you promise not to say anything."

Pippa, she knew, was sensible for her years and would do what she was told. She really should tell Charles but she was trying to establish a rapport with this young lady so decided to say nothing.

Davenport arrived back at the station to find his team busy with their reports. He called Fiona along from her room and told them all together that Sally Ewing's story was an unhappy, not uncommon one. Brian Ewing had sexually assaulted her in her own home where he had come to put up shelves for her. She had never told Ralph, fearing that he would think that she had led his brother on. She had been wearing her dressing gown when he arrived and felt that she should not have come downstairs like that, knowing his reputation. Fiona was saddened at yet another woman feeling guilty for something that was not her fault. She had come across this often in rape cases.

"I suppose the sixty-four thousand dollar question is, "Did Ralph somehow find out?" Davenport wondered aloud. "Sally admitted that she had told her psychiatrist as she was sure that this incident, not her school closure had caused her panic attack on holiday but has asked him not to tell her husband."

"Could he have found out all that time ago and done nothing?" asked Fiona.

"Maybe he only found out recently," Davenport replied.

Fiona told them all that she had rung Carol and asked why Arthur had phoned them on the day of his murder.

"She said that he had called to ask how they all were. John had assured him they were fine but he had asked to speak to Carol herself. She said he was a fussy old man."

Davenport told them that the doctor had phoned Sally and Ralph to thank them for the party in spite of the awful ending to that night. Sally said that Arthur was a dear soul.

Reminding Salma to contact the Rogersons, Charles went off to find his daughter and the others went back to their typing. What a lot they had learned that day.

CHAPTER 39

Thursday was a beautiful winter's day, crisp, cold and sunny. Fiona, driving to work, had to pass Queen's Park and, held up by traffic, she noticed tiny green shoots appearing in the soil just behind the park railings. Soon she knew, the snowdrops would be appearing, although as early as this, maybe frost and snow might hinder their growth. Arriving at the same time as Charles, she mentioned this to him but he reassured her that the sturdy little flowers thrived on those conditions. As they were quite early he invited her into his room for coffee where they continued their talk of flowers. His favourite flower was the daffodil, he told her.

"Mine is the rose, especially the yellow tea rose. Well, Charles, what next?"

"The next event will be the funerals of the two victims," Charles reminded her and as if on cue his phone rang and Fiona heard him thank someone for the information.

Cradling the receiver, he told her that that had been Carol Ewing telling him that Brian's funeral was to be on Monday at Eaglesham Cemetery.

"I'll give Jean Hope a ring and ask if there's any news of Arthur's funeral," he said.

Fiona walked down to the room where the rest of the team worked and Charles joined them all a few minutes later to tell them that Brian Ewing's funeral was to be a burial on Monday and that Arthur's was to be a cremation on the same day. It was unfortunate that both were on Monday but of course Brian's funeral had been held up with Christmas and New Year intervening. At least Arthur's was in the afternoon at 3.30pm and the burial of Brian Ewing was in the morning at 10am.

"Carol asked if it was OK for the boys and Diana to go back to university and school on the day after the funeral of their father. I said yes. We can always find them if we need them."

Davenport asked Salma how she had got on with the Rogersons the night before and she informed him that Arthur had rung them but in mistake for Sally and Ralph, the numbers being very similar.

"Sir," Salma continued. "I couldn't sleep last night wondering about the murders and it struck me that we don't know where the gloves which Santa wore got to. Is that important?"

"Well we're pretty sure that Santa, the murderer, wore gloves but they weren't with the Santa suit in the dustbin so I've assumed that the murderer disposed of them elsewhere, either burning them or throwing them somewhere far from the scene."

"Would the murderer risk hanging on to them that night, Sir?" asked Fiona.

"Probably not. Any ideas?"

"Woolly gloves could have been soaked to get rid of the blood and then put away with other gloves," said Frank.

"Or as you said, Sir, set fire to." Penny chipped in.

"He or she wouldn't have much time on the night," Fiona was quick to point out.

Davenport felt that they had made a big mistake not searching for these gloves on the night of the murder and suggested that they had better do some searching now. He dispatched Frank to the Ewing house in Newlands where that young man searched diligently, helped by Hazel whom he found impossible to shake off. They found nothing. A search through drawers produced a couple of pairs of woollen gloves but they were Hazel's and too small for an adult. Hazel turned up trumps however when she told him of the compost heap round the side of the house.

"Mum and Dad often throw rubbish on it and they set fire to it every so often."

Frank found the remains of a fire and when he asked Sally Ewing, she looked puzzled and said that they had not done any clearing up or gardening since the holidays started. Frank went back to the station and told Davenport the possible fate of the gloves.

"It would only have helped us if we'd found them somewhere incriminating. Thanks Frank. At least it makes me feel better as the gloves were probably set fire to very soon after the murder."

Charles pulled his left earlobe and thought for a minute.

"Fiona, you take Frank and go to the Lynn Crematorium on Monday. I'll go to the cemetery myself. It's near my house so I'll go there before work. I'll have time to deliver Pippa to school before going."

Sandra had rung Derek that afternoon at work. She felt that by ringing him there she could keep the conversation friendly without being too personal. She had come to the conclusion while she was lying ill in bed that she would have to end things with him even though she had enjoyed their liaison so much. Jim was her husband and had been her dearest friend for many years and she could not hurt him and continuing to see Derek would be leading nowhere and might eventually come to Jim's attention. She simply told her boss that she would be returning to work on Monday. He was obviously with someone and merely thanked her for letting him know and asked how she was.

Sally was wondering if she should tell Ralph about being raped by his brother. Now that the police knew, he might find out from someone else and that would be wrong. She had kept quiet, fearing that Ralph might blame her or that he might attack Brian, or both. She had been so nervous since the murder, worrying that Ralph had somehow found out and killed Brian. Ralph was a dear soul and so caring but he had another side. She recalled now the time when their dog, Rob, a Shetland collie had dirtied the pavement outside a neighbour's house and the neighbour had tried to hit Rob with a shovel. Ralph had grabbed the man and would have punched him had not Sally intervened. There had been one or two instances of his temper during their married life but never with her or Hazel. She knew that Ralph was putting her recent anxiety down to her being upset over Brian's death but in reality she had been relieved that he was gone though, naturally, had been horrified by the manner of his death.

Now that she had told Davenport of Brian's attack on her, she knew that her husband had come into the frame for the murder, had he not already been in it. She really must have an honest talk with him, tonight if possible, she told herself.

Aimee had taken a phone call early that afternoon on her mobile from an ex- boyfriend who had come across from France. He asked her to meet him and she agreed. It was easy with Colin working to say she was going into Glasgow to shop. She asked Colin's mother for the number of a taxi firm and arranged to be picked up. Mrs Ferguson, who would always have got the bus into town, thought her extravagant but was delighted not to have to entertain her son's fiancée again so said nothing.

The three women whose men were the top three suspects in the murder enquiry spent a worrying afternoon, Sally hoping that Ralph had not found out about the abuse she had suffered at the hands of Brian, Sandra anxious about what to do about her relationship with two men and Aimee wondering if she had perhaps made the wrong decision to marry Colin.

CHAPTER 40

Sally had decided to tell Ralph everything but waited until Hazel had been in bed for some time as she did not want to be interrupted. Ralph had been watching the highlights of a football match but it had just finished. She put down her Sudoku with which she had not been having much success and said, "Ralph I've got something very serious to tell you."

Ralph looking at his wife's strained face, instantly thought that she had had another anxiety attack. He came to sit beside her on the settee.

"What is it my love?"

"This is going to be very hard Ralph but please hear me out without speaking."

He nodded.

Sally stared straight ahead.

"Do you remember the time some years ago when Brian came to put up shelves in our kitchen?"

"Yes."

"When the bell rang that day I was still in bed. It was the school holidays and Hazel had stayed the night with my Mum. You had gone to work earlier. I went downstairs still in my nightie and dressing gown and opened the door. It was Brian. He came in and hung his coat in the hall. I took him into the kitchen and he put his bag of tools on the floor and asked if he could have a cup of tea first. I told him to have a seat in the lounge but he said he would stay and watch me make it.

I got out two cups, filled the kettle and put it on and reached up to the top shelf to get a new packet of biscuits. They were chocolate digestives."

"Gosh, what a memory!" joked Ralph.

"Please Ralph, don't speak."

"Sorry love."

"As I stretched up, my dressing gown opened and I picked up the two ends of the cord to tie it up."

Sally felt rather than saw Ralph stiffen.

"He put his arms around my waist, pulled me round to face him and tugged the dressing gown down and off. I told him not to be silly, that you would be furious with him if he continued but he said he would tell you that I had opened my dressing gown in front of him."

"But Sal, I would have believed you," Ralph said.

"You've been so wonderful, so supportive of me through these last years that I know that now but at that moment I wasn't so sure."

Still staring ahead, she fumbled for his hand and he gripped hers tightly.

"What happened?"

Ralph felt sick as he waited for her reply.

Sally took a deep breath and continued.

"He took hold of the neck of my nightie and ripped it down the front. He pushed me backwards over the kitchen table and raped me, then he turned me over and took me from the back."

"He... sodomised you?" Ralph choked out the word.

"No, not that, thank goodness. I don't know how he managed to take me twice so quickly. I imagine it was the thrill of what he was doing. He was like an animal, Ralph. How different you both are...were. He had his tea...."

"He actually took tea after that!"

"Yes and he made the shelves too. I wondered at the time if he thought I owed him that for doing the shelves."

"Oh, my poor Sal. I wish you could have told me then."

"I spent the day having bath after bath, trying to get rid of him from my body.

I tried to tell you that night but I was so scared that you would believe him and then the time had passed and after that I thought it would look suspicious that I hadn't told you right away. I threw away the nightie and bought myself another dressing gown. He told me that Carol was frigid and that he knew I was a warm person and that he had known that sex with me would be wonderful. He said he envied you."

"Why are you telling me now? I mean I'm glad you are but why now?" Ralph asked.

"One of the police team, I can't remember who right now, asked me if I liked Brian and I found myself saying no, I didn't. I refused to say why but they must have told the DCI and he came to speak to me today. I had to tell him and I know that this will have made him suspect you. He'll think that you found out and killed him. He would have come to see you and he would have told you and I couldn't have someone else tell you."

"Sally, you're not thinking straight. Why would I not have killed Brian right away? Why would I wait years before doing it?"

"I thought about that. Brian might have boasted to you about it recently for some reason and you didn't tell me but killed him."

"Well, I didn't find out and I didn't kill him."

Ralph got up, crossed the room and picked up the telephone. Sally heard the one-sided conversation.

"Davenport? Ralph Ewing here, Sally has been telling me what happened to her with Brian years ago."

"No I didn't know and I didn't kill him"

"Maybe he did the same thing to someone else's wife or girlfriend."

"She's fine, thanks. I'll tell her."

He rang off and came to sit back on the settee.

"Well maybe he doesn't believe me but what is important is that you do."

"Oh, I do, Ralph."

"He says to tell you that he's glad you've got it off your chest and asked if you were OK. Do you think that this is what started your panic attacks, not the school closure?"

"I'm sure of it Ralph. I started feeling better after I had told the psychiatrist and I'm sure I'll be even better now."

"I love you so much, Sal."

"I love you too, Ralph."

Hazel passing the open lounge door on her way to the kitchen for a glass of milk looked in disgust at her elderly parents in a close embrace.

CHAPTER 41

Aimee arrived at The Busby Hotel at the same time as the taxi bearing Rene pulled up. She greeted him affectionately; he had been her lover for a few years and she had only broken off the relationship when she met Colin. Rene had phoned her saying he was in Glasgow and she had agreed to meet him.

They walked into the reception area and Aimee who had a better command of English, asked for a room and paid by credit card. When asked by the receptionist for the name she gave both her and Rene's surnames. Aimee was not ashamed of what she was doing - to her it came as naturally as eating and sleeping and she had not been very sexually active since coming to stay with Colin who was not happy to sleep with her in his parents' house and would never have dreamed of taking a hotel room as they were doing now.

"Aimee, I've missed you so much," Rene said once they were in the hotel room.

"And I've missed you, cheri."

Their kiss was long and passionate and it was only minutes before they were tearing each other's clothes off. Their coupling was feverish and they climaxed together and lay exhausted in each other's arms.

It was about an hour later when Aimee awoke. She lay deep in thought then, turning to Rene she began to stroke the inside of his thigh. He came awake slowly but was soon ready for her again.

This time they made love slowly and sensuously and, wrapped in each other's arms, they lay sated and happy.

"Rene. Would you take me back?" she asked.

"What do you mean? As my girlfriend or back to Paris?"

"Both."

"But you're engaged to this Colin, aren't you?"

"Yes but it was a mistake, Rene. He is so cold and boring. We 'ave made love only twice since I moved here."

"Of course I would take you back, to Paris and to my home."

They dressed quickly and Rene phoned and managed to change his flight and get a ticket for Aimee. Aimee rang for a taxi and gave Colin's address. She was delighted to find Mrs Ferguson on the point of leaving for the shops for something she had forgotten.

Rene waited in the taxi, keeping down until Mrs Ferguson was out of sight, and then he ran into the house and upstairs to help Aimee pack. She did not think twice about stealing Colin's suitcase from his room. She had no intention of leaving the new clothes he had bought her and left taking more than she had arrived with. Colin had given her her own new credit card that morning. She left it on the unmade bed and pausing only to write a short note to her fiancé, she went downstairs with Rene, got into the waiting taxi and left.

Mrs Ferguson was surprised to find no Aimee in the house when she arrived back ten minutes later. She remembered that the taxi had still been there when she passed by and wondered where the girl had gone now. More shopping? She had become more and more unhappy about her son's future wife and wished that he was not so generous, giving her a weekly allowance and today the credit card she had asked for.

There was still no sign of Aimee when Mr Ferguson came home from his indoor bowling club at 4.30pm and by this time Mrs Ferguson was getting concerned as Aimee had always been in to welcome Colin home every day.

Colin arrived home shortly after 5pm to find both his parents anxiously looking out of the window. He asked where Aimee was and his mother said, "She went into town dear, by taxi, early in the afternoon. She came back later, went into the house and must have left again by the same taxi which had waited for her. I was going out when she came home so didn't know she was leaving again or I'd have asked her where she was going."

"Did she leave a note Mum?"

"Not here dear, but maybe in her room. I didn't like to go in."

Colin took the stairs two at a time and went into Aimee's room. He saw the credit card and two envelopes lying on the rumpled sheets. With a feeling of apprehension, he picked up the one addressed to him and read:

"Sorry Colin. It was a mistake. I have gone back to Paris with a friend. Thanks for everything. Aimee."

Colin, an honest man, realised that mixed with feelings of dismay was one of...relief. He admitted to himself that he had been having doubts recently. Aimee encouraged other men to flatter her and pay attention to her and if she was doing this at an early stage in their relationship, what would it have been like further into married life?

He also experienced a hot surge of anger. He had given her so much, done so much for her in their short time together.

He picked up the other envelope which had 'Police' written on it

He opened the wardrobe. It was empty as were the drawers of the dressing table. His Mum had arrived in the doorway and looked at the empty wardrobe with relief, mixed with pity for Colin.

"Has she gone, son?"

"Yes. She has Mum."

"I'm so sorry."

"Don't be Mum. I don't think it was going to work. She flirted with every man she met and she was so expensive to keep in clothes and other things."

Mrs Ferguson was relieved at his reaction but still angry with Aimee. She glanced at the dressing table.

"Where are all the things that were on the dressing table?" she asked.

"In her suitcase I imagine," said Colin dryly. "I wonder if she's stolen anything else."

A quick search showed that the only other thing missing was his suitcase. They went downstairs and told Mr Ferguson who was seemed more upset than Colin and his wife.

Colin heard nothing more from Aimee and the next day he phoned Shawbank Police Station to inform Davenport of her departure. He felt embarrassed having to admit that he did not know where she had gone but Davenport was understanding. If necessary he could get Interpol to find her. Colin said that Aimee had left a note for the police and Davenport said that he would come over to collect it on his way home from work.

When his fiancée's new credit card statement came in a few weeks later, Colin found an item which explained something to him. His fiancée had spent some time at The Busby Hotel the day she left, presumably with the 'friend' she had gone back to France with and she had used the credit card to pay for her flight home. He had been made such a fool of!

CHAPTER 42

Penny's job made it difficult for her to date seriously as boys often suggested, naturally enough, that they go out on Saturday night and she could be on police work over the weekend. She had told Gordon of the possibility of her having to cancel their date but it was 6pm, she was at home and getting ready and nothing had gone wrong.

They were going to have a meal out at Chow in Byres Road. Penny had chosen this as she loved their sweet and sour prawn and Gordon had said he liked Chinese food too. It was a small restaurant and more cosy than the bigger Amber further up the street. She was going to meet Gordon outside as he lived in Milngavie.

She left home at 7.20pm, dressed casually in her best denims and yellow v necked sweater underneath a black leather jacket that had been her Mum's present to her last Christmas. She topped it off with a bright orange scarf which she wound twice round her neck. She didn't like the habit folk had nowadays of looping the scarf and pulling the end through the loop as the scarf had to be really long for that.

It took her about forty minutes to get to Byres Road and she was lucky to find a parking space on the road itself. Gordon was waiting outside though she was minutes early. He was a well-built young man of average height for a man, fair haired in a short back and sides' style. He was wearing denims too with a beige sweatshirt and no jacket.

Never one to be shy, Penny gave him a quick hug and a peck on the cheek before they went into the restaurant. They were given a table upstairs and climbed the rickety wooden steps in single file, Penny leading. They shared a combination starter, Penny delighted to find that Gordon did not like barbecued spare ribs which meant that she could eat them all. She in turn, gave him the sesame prawn toast.

They had not had time to talk much at the party but made up for that now. Gordon loved his job. He was a newly qualified vet and had been lucky to get a job in a practice in Pollokshaws. It was quite a journey every morning but worth the travel. He told Penny of operations he had helped with and the sadness he felt when an animal had to be put down. Penny in turn told him about her job and about the murders they were investigating right now. He told her that he played rugby which accounted for the bruise on his cheek, he said. She told him that when she had time she played tennis. Thus engaged, the time flew past and it was not till nearly 11pm that they left the restaurant. Gordon asked if she wanted to go on to a club but Penny was tired and had brought her car so apologised and said she would rather just get home. Gordon, laughing, said he was delighted as he was not a great clubber.

"I would have gone if you had wanted to Penny," he said now and she felt a frisson of pleasure at his unselfishness. Other men she had gone out with had done what they wanted and expected her to just go along with them. He walked her the short distance to her car and kissed her gently before handing her in to the driver's seat.

"Can I give you a ring tomorrow?" he asked.

"Yes please. I'm supposed to be off all day again but if I'm at work Mum will take a message and I'll get back to you. Thanks for a lovely evening, Gordon."

Penny drove home in a warm glow that had nothing to do with the car's heating system and was in time to see Jack before he left. They had spent the evening discussing their wedding plans. Jack had never been married before and wanted a church wedding which suited Penny's Mum who was quite a regular churchgoer as was Penny who tried to go when not at work. Having been married before, Margaret Price would be wearing a dress with a matching coat and hat rather than a bridal dress and Penny was to be a witness rather than a bridesmaid. Jack's brother was going to be his best man.

"Mum, if I'm still seeing Gordon can he come to your wedding?" Penny asked now.

"Of course, darling." Mrs Price was intrigued as Penny had always treated past boyfriends casually and this sounded more serious if she wanted to invite the new young man to a family wedding.

"Have you finalised the date you two?" Penny asked.

"Yes. Monday 17th March. It was the only day the Brig O Doon could give us as we've left it so late. They had a cancellation on that day and folk tend to want weekends. Will you get the day off OK Penny?"

"No problem Mum. I've already asked the DCI about a day off and he's said yes. I just hope this murder investigation is over by then." Penny was delighted at the venue for the reception as that would make her Mum and Jack even more delighted with her present of a picture of the same hotel which she had known was a favourite of theirs.

"Was the new minister OK with that date, Mum?" Penny asked now.

"Yes. He said that Monday was his day off but he'd just change it to Tuesday that week."

The church had recently got a new minister. Ministers were it seemed in short supply these days and it was only because the church was serving the community so well that it had been allowed to call a new one in spite of small numbers. Penny and Mrs Price had been to quite a few of his services and found him easy to listen to. The last minister, a hell fire and damnation sort of preacher had been murdered in his manse the previous year and Penny had been part of the investigation team.

The talk turned to the new murders and Margaret and Jack listened intently as Penny told them how the investigation was proceeding.

"Oh, Penny, I meant to say that Salma phoned just before you got back but she said she'll call again tomorrow afternoon. I've invited her to the wedding and she hopes to come if your Mr Davenport can spare you both at the same time."

On that note, Jack left, kissing his bride-to be and telling her he'd pick her up tomorrow and they would drive down to Alloway to have afternoon tea at their reception hotel. He asked Penny if she'd like to come too but that young lady was hoping to meet Salma and tell her all about her date with Gordon so she thanked him but declined.

Tired and very happy the Price women went to bed.

CHAPTER 43

"**A**shes to ashes, dust to dust," intoned the minister. She was, thought Davenport, a mere slip of a girl but by the greying of her dark hair at the temples, he knew that she must be in her forties at least. The service had been a lovely one and he hoped that the family, especially the distraught Diana, had taken some comfort from the analogy drawn between Brian's dying and a boat leaving port for foreign shores where others would be waiting to greet it. He had heard this at another funeral and thought it a clever way to describe death.

Diana had stopped crying at that point and Ian had taken his arm from round her shoulders where it had lain throughout the start of the funeral service. Carol, at the end of the family line, stood looking as ever cool and unmoved. John glanced at her once or twice. He was wishing that she would support Diana instead of leaving it to Ian. He wondered for the umpteenth time since his Dad's death if he or Ian or both should try to explain his father's reputation, try to put things into perspective for her. She was in danger of idolising the man for goodness sakc! He turned his thoughts to what was being said and realised that the rest of the immediate family had thrown their handfuls of earth onto the coffin and were waiting for him to do the same.

Diana burst into sobs again and Ian led her away to the waiting car. John followed with his mother who looked elegant as usual in a well-cut black suit and fascinator which set off her fair hair to perfection.

Davenport watching them from a distance, noticed that Diana was wearing the childish white dress which she had worn for the party, an odd choice for a funeral, he thought, unaware that Diana had almost made herself ill in an argument about this with her mother and brothers.

"I hated this dress - this frock," she used the word her father had used, "when Dad bought it for me but it's all I have left of him now." She had screamed this at her mother. Ian and John, called in to help, had met with the same almost hysterical reaction. They had all given in and not only would she insist on the dress, she refused to cover it up with a coat. Luckily the day was not one of winter's coldest but it was blustery and the wind must have been slicing through the thin material. She had lost weight since her father's death and the dress looked too big for her.

Ian and John were very smart in their dark suits and again Davenport wondered how anyone could tell them apart. He had commented on this to Hazel the day she had come to see Pippa and Hazel had said that they usually wore different clothes to make it easier to tell them apart though they had played tricks on their teachers at times, going into the wrong rooms and pretending to be the other twin.

Pippa had thought it would be great fun to be one of twins and even better to be one of triplets like Len, Con and Margot in her Chalet School books. They all looked different and had very different personalities just as Hazel said John and Ian had. John was quite lively and talkative while Ian was quieter and more thoughtful.

Hazel preferred John and said that Diana had too until recently when she had clung to Ian.

Davenport caught up with Carol and one of her sons, offered his condolences and was invited to the Redhurst Hotel for lunch. He shook hands with the twin who informed him he was John and made his way back to the road where he had left his car. It was only a fifteen minute drive to the hotel and he joined the other mourners in a lounge for sandwiches and sausage rolls.

The twins were going back to university the next day, one day late for the start of term and John confided in Davenport that they could not wait to get back to normality.

"It's so hard at home with Mum calm and collected and Diana in hysterics half the time. I hope when she gets back to school tomorrow, she'll calm down a bit."

"Fathers and daughters are often closer than fathers and sons," Davenport commented.

"That's true," John agreed.

He went off and Davenport was left on his own, drinking his coffee until Carol came over.

"I'll be glad when today's over and the kids are back at their studies," were her first words. "I can't get through to Diana at all. Brian's death has hit her unbelievably hard."

"Were they very close?" asked Davenport.

"Yes they were. He always collected her from school on Friday afternoon and this year he went up for her on Wednesday at lunch time and took her back on Thursday morning. I thought it was a bit silly as they had so many activities laid on for them on Wednesday afternoon half day."

"Was Brian close to John and Ian?"

"They used to play golf together a lot but this holiday I noticed that they refused his offer of a game. He was quite hurt."

"Perhaps they knew about his affair with Wendy Hamilton and felt sorry for you."

"Oh, they knew all right. They all knew. I was only too happy to let them know that their precious father was a cheat and womaniser."

"So did they feel sorry for you?" Davenport asked again.

"Maybe, but they never spoke of it to me and if anything, Diana got even closer to Brian."

It would be hard to speak about personal things to this ice queen, Davenport thought and, thanking her for her hospitality, he left and, getting back into his car, went down to the station hoping to take Fiona out for lunch locally.

She was busy with paperwork in her room but was delighted to have a break from it. They took his car across to Shawlands and had lunch in the '1901' on Haggs Road. They often went there. It was unpretentious and the food was cheap and tasty.

Over lunch Davenport told her about the funeral and Diana's distress.

"I wonder Charles, how she'll get on back at school."

"Well, she'll either get into the swing of things and start to feel better or it will be worse seeing everyone else normal," he replied.

They returned to the station where there was a message from Parker saying that the dried blood on the candlestick was, as they suspected, Arthur Mackie's. It was also no surprise to learn that there were no fingerprints on the candlestick.

Back at home after the funeral, the boys got ready for their journey to Stirling. Diana, on the way home, had asked her Mum for another few days at home and Carol had reluctantly agreed. Diana went straight to her bedroom and John and Ian, coming to say cheerio, found her sitting on the floor, still in her white, flowery dress, looking through a photograph album.

"Right, Diana. That's us off," John said briskly.

She stood up and gave him a quick hug before turning to Ian whom she hugged tightly.

"Remember to phone us every evening, Di," he said, sad to see how pinched her face still looked.

They all walked downstairs together. Carol was driving them to the station to catch their train and Diana had decided not to accompany them. They turned to wave as the car set off, knowing that the memory of her small, white face would stay with them for a while.

CHAPTER 44

Later that same day, Fiona and Frank attended Arthur Mackie's funeral at The Lynn Crematorium. Fiona always felt a bit sad when she went there as her Mum had been cremated there only a few years ago so she was quiet on the way over from the police station. Frank drove and kept his speed down, knowing from experience that his superior would not appreciate him breaking the law.

When they arrived at the gates of the crematorium, it was obvious that the previous funeral was still taking place as there were cars lining the driveway all the way down to the gates so Frank parked outside the gate and they waited. Fiona was still quiet so Frank broke the silence by saying that he had been lucky and still had all his family including four grandparents so the Lynn was not familiar to him.

They had been there for about five minutes when the cortege drew up, followed by a large black car containing the close relatives, Frank assumed.

Fiona motioned to Frank and he turned to the front and noticed that people were walking down the hill to their cars and cars from the car park were following the black limousine down to the gates. He drove carefully past the stationary cars and, on Fiona's advice, made his way to the car park which was emptying. Some people had obviously managed to get there sooner and a small queue of people was forming, waiting to enter. Frank and Fiona joined the queue and Jean Hope who had been waiting near the front came back to join them. Fiona looked at the bunches of flowers which were tied onto the benches in remembrance of loved ones. Some flowers were wilting and looked so sad.

"I don't know many people here," Jean said quietly to Frank. "Just a few from the golf club. I was going to sit with our bridge couple but they're not here yet."

Frank said she could go in with them if she liked and Fiona added her invitation.

The hearse pulled up. The wreath of white lilies was taken off the coffin and the mourners were signalled to go inside.

Leaving the front two seats at the right hand side for the close family, Fiona led Frank and Jean into the next row. Soon the chapel was filling up. Jean, looking round, saw her bridge friends come in. She smiled at them but stayed where she was.

The service was short but meaningful as the minister had obviously met the family and taken time to find out about Arthur's life. Afterwards, they shook hands with the man who said he was Arthur's brother and with his wife and children and in turn they told who they were and were invited to go back to the Busby Hotel for refreshments. Jean looked hopefully at Fiona.

"Are you going?"

Knowing that Charles always went to these wakes, Fiona assured her that they would indeed be going back and finding out that Jean did not drive and had come by taxi, offered to give her a lift. They were joined by Jean's bridge opponents who were introduced as David and Val and shortly after they set off for Busby. Once in the hotel, they shared a table with the couple and watched as other people came in. It was well -attended as the funeral had been and Fiona noticed Sally and Ralph and Jim Rogerson coming in together. They nodded across.

Arthur's brother made a short speech, thanked everyone for coming and then they sat and had sandwiches and biscuits with either tea or coffee. Frank would have preferred a drink but took care not to say so. He felt awkward here and was quite glad when the Ewings and Jim came across to speak to them.

"Any further forward DS Macdonald?" asked Ralph. It was, he knew, a silly thing to say as obviously he was not going to be told how things were going but he did not know what else to say to the woman who had only a few weeks ago been a guest at his party but was now a member of the investigation team. Fiona took pity on him.

"Narrowing down the suspects as always," she smiled.

"How is Mrs Rogerson?" she asked Jim.

"Oh a lot better thanks but still too weak to get out. She was hoping to go back to work today but the doctor has said to wait till nearer the end of the week."

"And how are you both?" she turned to Sally and Ralph.

"Fine thanks," Sally and Ralph spoke in unison and Fiona thought that Sally did indeed look well. She did not know that Sally had spoken to Ralph and had found out that he had never suspected his brother of coming on to, let alone abusing, his wife. He had been all concern for Sally, angry with the dead Brian and given not even a hint of blaming her for what had happened.

How she wished she had told him before and maybe escaped the agonies of anxiety and ensuing depression which had plagued her since and which had only lessened when she had confided in her psychiatrist.

Fiona, knowing none of this was puzzled at the demeanour of both Ewings who looked happier than they had been at their Christmas party. Deciding to tell this to Charles, she excused herself and she and Frank went over to Arthur's family and thanked them for their hospitality. Jean had decided to wait a while longer and would take a lift from her friends.

"I've been asked if I'll take Arthur's lovely cat, Esmeralda," she said, smiling. "It will be so nice to have her to remember Arthur by."

Fiona and Frank walked into the station to find their section deserted. The sergeant on duty at the desk informed them that the rest had gone home. Fiona offered Frank a lift home and he accepted gratefully as he had come to work that day on public transport.

"Thanks for coming with me Frank. Sorry not to be great company. The Lynn holds sad memories for me."

"No problem...ma'am,"

She smiled at the hesitation and he smiled back. Over the last few weeks it had become a kind of unspoken joke for Frank to hesitate very slightly before giving her her title, something which he had done before out of disrespect for his superior. He was coming to realise that Fiona was due his respect and this, plus his closer attention to his appearance, was giving him the makings of a better police officer. Penny was working on trying to show him that prejudice towards other races and religions as well as towards women was a case of prejudging them before he knew them as he had with his sergeant whom he now liked.

Fiona dropped him off near his home in Shawlands and went home herself to phone Charles and let him know how the day had gone. He in turn told her that SOC had reported that the candlestick was indeed the murder weapon. Charles apologised for not telling her of Sally confiding at last in Ralph.

Two deaths and two funerals had now taken place.

CHAPTER 45

The day after the two funerals, Charles was thoughtful as he drove Pippa to school. Fiona had told him about Ralph and Sally being happier than ever she had seen them. He knew that Sally had, as he had advised, told Ralph about what had happened between her and Brian some years before but he had not had a chance to tell the team any of this as they had all been off at the weekend and the funerals had taken up their time yesterday. He also had Aimee's note to tell them about. It had solved another mystery.

He let his daughter out of the car at the school gates. She was always early because of him having to be at work before her school started for the day but he knew she was allowed to go into her classroom and read so was not worried about her. Hazel never came in early as her dad did not have to be in his workplace till 9 and he dropped her off a few minutes before school started at 8.45am.

Today Pippa was anxious to see her best friend and naturally this would be the day when Hazel arrived on the bell, only having time to grin at Pippa before they went to their desks, in different groups. The class teacher, having no confidence in friendship groups, had separated friends instead.

Pippa usually behaved well in school, Hazel being the one likely to get into trouble but today Pippa could not concentrate on her lessons. It was OK for the first hour as it was the time for their project based on "The Silver Sword" by Ian Serrelier and she loved the book and the project involved. Today they had been asked to write a week's diary for Ruth, the oldest child in the family who had lost mother and father and home when the Nazis came.

Now however, it was time for Maths which was her weakest subject and her least favourite. She was a bright child and it frustrated her not to be able to do well in that subject. The problem in front of her had stumped her and her teacher was at another group helping a pupil there. She hastily scribbled a note, using one of the middle pages of her jotter and tearing out the other page too as it would only fall out later if left in. She wrote 'Hazel' on the folded-over missive and handed it across to the person nearest her in her friend's group.

Her teacher this year was a young woman called Ellen Jackson, a fresh-faced, rosy-cheeked woman who lived on a farm on the outskirts of Waterfoot. She had a number of young brothers and sisters and was well able to deal with her class of ten and eleven year olds. She was small but sturdy and stood no nonsense from her small charges and in spite of what Pippa had told her dad, she was only twenty five. She had come to this school from being a supply teacher since her one year of employment after leaving Jordanhill Teacher Training College or Strathclyde University as it was called now, having been taken under the university wing recently.

She looked up from the group she was helping just in time to see Pippa pass her note across the aisle.

"Pippa Davenport! Bring that to me!

Pippa, red-faced, picked up the note from Hazel's table and went over to her teacher. She had written, "Found out more. Take notebook out at the interval."

Miss Jackson read it, crumpled it up and walking to her desk, put the paper in the bin.

"Found out more about what Pippa?"

Pippa was silent.

"Oh so it's a secret is it?"

The teacher who was a good elder sister and knew when to let things go, took pity on the girl standing in front of her.

"Back you go and get on with your problem. Maybe if you try hard you'll find out more about Maths today."

The class laughed and so did Pippa who was very grateful that she had not written, "more about the murders" on the note. Hazel sent her a sympathetic look and was clever enough to realise what Pippa had meant.

It seemed to take ages till the interval came but come it did. Pippa and Hazel raced to the shelter where there was a bench seat. No one else would disturb them there as it was a beautiful day for January, sunny and quite warm, and the rest would want to be outside in the fresh air.

"I'm not supposed to be telling you this," were Pippa's opening words, "but we're detectives and they have to find things out and I did yesterday."

She felt bad about disobeying Fiona's order not to tell anyone but Hazel would never tell Fiona; she would be unlikely to ever see her again and the news was too good to keep to herself.

"Mrs Rogerson didn't like your Uncle Brian. What does "made a pass at her" mean Hazel?"

"Tried to get off with her," said that knowing little lady.

"But she was married to Mr Rogerson."

"I know but sometimes people who are married have affairs..."

Seeing Pippa's confusion, she added, "They go off with another person and their wife or husband doesn't know."

"So your Uncle Brian wanted to go off with Mrs Rogerson and she didn't want to go off with him?"

"That's right."

"So if Mr Rogerson found out or she told him he would hate your Uncle Brian?"

"Probably. Anything else?"

"They said that he had pro..pos..itioned all the women except your Mum."

"So he tried to get off with Aimee and Mrs Hope."

"Was Mrs Hope not too old for him?"

"I think so. Did you hear any more?"

"Well someone called Wendy Hamilton was mentioned. We don't have her in our notebooks."

"She's Uncle Brian's receptionist. Maybe he had had an affair with her too."

"And Dad said he couldn't say that John and Ian weren't guilty."

Hazel looked indignant so Pippa went on to tell her that her Aunt Carol wasn't suspected.

"Fiona...DS Macdonald... saw me listening behind the door. She said she wouldn't tell Dad but I had to promise not to tell anyone else so you're not to say anything to anybody. Promise!"

Hazel promised. She knew that Pippa would feel bad about breaking her promise to DS Macdonald and anyway she wanted them to have solved the crime before anyone else so she did not plan to give the game away.

The bell rang.

"There's no time to fill in our notebooks now, Hazel. I'll ask Dad if you can come up tonight or for a sleepover on Friday," said Pippa, as they hurried back into school.

Davenport had gone straight to the station where he called everyone involved into the Incident Room. He told them that he had advised Sally to tell her husband about her rape by Brian Ewing some years ago and that he had received a phone call from Ralph on Thursday night telling him that he now knew, that he had not known before and he had not murdered his brother. Ralph had suggested that maybe Brian had raped another woman who was married or had a boyfriend and that the husband or partner had killed him. Charles also read them the brief note from Aimee which said,

"I will write to Colin with my new address in case you need me but the only thing I kept from him and you was the fact that I met Brian Ewing at a hotel one evening some time ago and would probably have met him again. If possible don't tell Colin this as I have hurt him enough.

Aimee."

"Cool customer," exclaimed Frank almost admiringly. "Engaged to one man, having an affair with another and waltzes of with yet another."

"I pity the man who does marry her," was Davenport's response. "However, if Colin found out he could be our murderer."

"Have you ruled out Ralph, Sir?" asked Penny.

"Not entirely. For all we know, Brian boasted recently to him about what happened with Sally. So we're still no further forward. We still have Colin and Ralph in the frame and if he propositioned Aimee and raped Sally, he might have either had an affair with Sandra Rogerson or suggested one and she told her husband. Jim is the jovial kind who can harbour deep resentments, I would imagine."

"Do we need to interview Sandra Rogerson again then?" asked Fiona.

"I'm going to pick Pippa up from school and on the way home, I'll pop in and have a chat with Sandra."

"She was going back to work today, Sir," Fiona reminded him.

"Well I'll leave Pippa with a neighbour and go down after dinner. Or better still, Fiona, would you like to come over for dinner and stay with Pippa while I see Sandra?"

Fiona felt herself blushing. It was the first time that Charles had shown anything other than friendliness towards her in front of the others.

Charles, realising what he had done hurried on, "I told Pippa that you might be persuaded to come over one evening as she wants to ask you some things about your work for a school project."

"No problems, Sir," Fiona said grateful to him for this explanation which the others would understand as they had seen Pippa shadowing her a few months ago, for a talk assignment.

Pippa was delighted to see Fiona but it meant that she could not now ask if Hazel could come up. Never mind she would ask if she could have her friend for a sleepover that weekend instead and they would just have to wait till then to discuss what they had learned. Maybe she would have more to tell after tonight if she could eavesdrop on her dad and Fiona. Surely they would discuss the case at some time.

She had one sticky moment when her Dad had gone away after dinner and Fiona had asked her if she had kept quiet about what she had heard. Pippa did not lie easily and she was worried that Fiona might suspect that she had told her friend. Luckily for her, Fiona was having thoughts about their possible summer holiday in Malaysia or Borneo which they had discussed over their dinner of casseroled stew, carrots and potatoes and had hardly listened to the young girl's reply.

Davenport returned in about an hour, having driven over to Newlands to the Rogersons' house. Sandra had said that Brian had not sexually assaulted her but she knew he would have had an affair with her if she'd agreed.

"That sounds big-headed," she had said, embarrassed, "but women just know these things and he was known for his philandering ways. Can't say I totally blame him either. That wife of his is a stuck up ice maiden. I liked him better than her, by a long way."

"So," Charles told Fiona, "if she's telling the truth that rules out Jim Rogerson though he did have the chance to collect the Santa suit when he went back, ostensibly for his camera."

"I think Ralph is a better bet. He had a strong motive if he did find out about his wife's rape."

At this point Pippa came back into the lounge and they stopped talking about the murders. She had overheard the last sentence but had no intention of telling Hazel this. She did not know what rape was but it seemed that her friend's Dad was still a suspect and Hazel would not want to know this.

The rest of the evening was spent discussing the holiday. The three of them had decided to go to Penang where it seemed that there was a lot to see and Charles had been given the go-ahead for both himself and Fiona to have three weeks off in July. All it needed now was for them to make the booking and Fiona had offered to do that through Trailfinders in Sauchiehall Street.

CHAPTER 46

January 12th, Thursday, was the day for Diana to go back to school and she did not want to go. She had rung Ian at university on his mobile the day before and he had said that he and John were happy to be back at their studies.

"Are you coming home this weekend, Ian?" Diana had asked her big brother.

"No we're not. It's too soon after the holidays. You shouldn't go home either, Diana."

"I'm still at home," his sister admitted. "I asked Mum if I could stay for a few more days. I go back to school tomorrow and I still don't want to go."

"Why ever not?"

"I want to be close to Dad."

"He'll be near you wherever you go. Don't you believe that?" Ian did not believe in the afterlife himself but now was not the time to admit that to his sister who needed reassurance badly.

"I suppose so," Diana said. "It's just that I want to go up to the cemetery every day and I can't from school."

"Is Mum going with you every day?" asked Ian. He could hardly believe that his cool, often remote mother, who had not loved her husband when he was alive, would be paying daily visits to his grave now.

"No, Mum doesn't go and she doesn't know I'm going. I'm spending my Christmas money on taxis. It's not far and doesn't cost too much."

"Look, Di, I'll have to go. Give me a ring when you're back at school and please go tomorrow. John's here. Do you want a word with him?"

Diana spoke a few stiff words to her other brother then hung up. She had just gone to her room when her Mum came upstairs.

"Diana, time to get yourself packed for tomorrow."

"Mum, I don't want to go back. Can I not go to the school that Hazel and Pippa go to instead?"

"No you can't. You're at the best school money can buy. I'm not having you go to Bradford High. It hasn't got the best reputation and you're too old for Pippa and Hazel's school."

"But Mum you won't have so much money now. It would save money if I went to an ordinary school."

"No way, Diana."

"Dad would have let me move. If he'd known I was unhappy, he would have. I was going to ask him but he was..."

"Why are you suddenly unhappy there?"

"It was OK when Ian and John were still there but some of the girls bully me now."

"I'll have a word with the head teacher when I come up next."

"No, Mum, that'll only make things worse."

"Have it your own way but you're going back. Now get your case packed."

Carol turned on her expensively shod heel and went back downstairs. She was seeing the lawyer later in the day and would find out if she could afford Diana's private school and other luxuries. It would be dreadful if she had to work after all these years, mused Carol and shuddered at the thought.

Diana packed her case, putting a large framed photo of her Dad in at the top. It had been taken when he graduated and looked young and handsome, very like John and Ian.

That had all happened yesterday and now Diana was waiting for the taxi which was going to drive her to Perthshire. She had thought that Carol would take her as her father had always done but Carol had restarted her social life and was playing whist at the local golf club where one of her friends was a member. She was in good spirits as the lawyer had informed her that, apart from smallish sums to the children, Brian had left everything to her. If she could sell his part of the practice she would never need to work. In fact she could stay in the same large house and keep the same lifestyle if she made some economies. She had rung Tony Blackwell as soon as the lawyer had gone and asked him if he knew of anyone who would buy Brian's part of the business and he had said he might know someone and to leave it to him. He would get back to her as soon as possible.

Wendy had answered the phone and Carol had spoken briefly to her. She would have liked to have sacked Wendy but it wasn't something she could do although she had suggested it to Tony recently, telling him that Brian had been dissatisfied with the receptionist. Tony had shown surprise and told Carol that he was perfectly content with Wendy and Carol had to leave it at that. At least if Brian was to be believed, he had finished with Wendy around the summer. Carol wondered who had been Wendy's replacement in Brian's affections. She knew her husband well and knew that he would have needed to have some love, or rather sex, interest. Since the birth of Diana, Carol had slept in another bed, insisting that she had lost interest in sex. Brian had refused to allow different rooms. Carol knew that there had been many women replacing her over the years but did not want to know who they were and had not been happy to have been told about Wendy. Brian, desperate for a divorce, had flaunted the affair with Wendy in front of Carol. Carol was disinterested in having another man in her life and told Brian that she would never divorce him.

"Wouldn't have been surprised if Brian had murdered *me*," she thought now.

The peep of a car horn brought her back to the present and she went to the foot of the stairs and called to Diana to come down. The case was already in the hall.

"Will you come for me at the weekend, Mum?" Diana asked now.

"Oh Diana, no. It's only two days till then. I'll fetch you next weekend."

"But I always come home on Friday night and for Wednesday nights too. Dad always came for me. What will I do at school over the weekend?"

"I'm sure there will be plenty of activities. Now come along, the taxi's waiting."

There was nothing for it but to pick up her case and get into the taxi. Carol paid the man, gave Diana a quick peck on the cheek and stood back to wave.

Had she known what Diana thought of her, she would have been surprised. Diana at that moment would willingly have killed her mother.

CHAPTER 47

Sandra had managed to avoid a one-to-one confrontation with Derek as she had had to go away to Brighton where some fashion shoots were taking place. She had reached a conclusion when she was lying in bed ill. Jim had done nothing wrong to deserve being left. He had made love to her twice since she had been open with him about getting help for his low sex drive. Maybe he had just thought that she was not interested or maybe he had put himself on Viagra. She did not care what the reason was, she was just delighted that at least they were once again trying for a family. She had not mentioned the word baby to Jim but he knew she was not on the contraceptive pill and he had taken no precautions.

When she had thought of Derek, she had realised that although the sex was exciting, he had never once suggested that she leave her husband and she was also sensible enough to know that if she did leave Jim and marry Derek - all supposing he wanted to marry her - it was likely that the sex between them would become mundane once it was not illicit. Also he already had children and he was fifty so probably would not want any more.

The fashion event in Brighton had kept her very busy and as she had decided to drive down South, she used the drive North to think things over again. Derek had not phoned her while she was away. On the other hand, Jim had rung her at least once every day. She left Brighton very early on Thursday morning and had very quiet roads until she reached the outskirts of London where she needed all her concentration, especially on the M25. On the way down, she had nearly taken the wrong exit on the nightmare motorway and was determined not to do this on the way back. She wondered if she should have chosen the North Circular route but that was as bad as Jim and she had found out one year when they went down to Bexhill to visit her relations.

She stopped at one of the motorway service stations and had a breakfast cum lunch, wincing at the price but relishing the taste and while there she phoned Jim to let him know how far up the road she had travelled. He did not pick up his phone so she left a message and she was in the middle of a cup of coffee when he rang her back.

"Sorry, San. I popped outside for a breath of fresh air, switched on the mobile and discovered a message from you. I never have the phone switched on in the hospital unlike some folk I could name."

Sandra smiled to herself. Jim was so law abiding that he annoyed her at times but today she found herself liking him for that trait in his character.

"I'm almost at the border, Jim, so should be home around 4pm if nothing goes wrong."

"Well be careful and don't speed. See you at home."

Sandra made good time and was on the outskirts of Glasgow about an hour earlier than she had thought she would be. Never being one to avoid unpleasantness, she decided to use the extra time to go to the news office and speak to Derek.

She saw his grey head bent over his desk through the glass panel that separated him from the rest and felt a sudden rush of adrenalin course through her body.

"Whoa Sandra," she told herself. "It's not love, just plain lust."

She tapped on the door to his office and saw his face light up at the sight of her. She went in and carefully closed the door behind her.

His smile faded when he saw the serious look on her face.

"What's the matter, Sandra?"

"I think you know, Derek. I want us to stop meeting each other. You know what I mean."

"What's happened? Before New Year you wanted me as badly as I wanted you. What changed things?"

"I still want you, want sex with you. It was wonderful and I have never felt so special or so excited but it's no good. I can't keep cheating on Jim. He doesn't deserve that."

Derek gave a rueful smile.

"I didn't expect it to last but I didn't expect it to end so quickly. I love you Sandra."

"Enough to marry me and have a family with me, Derek?"

Derek looked taken aback. They had never discussed a future together, living only for the moment when they were together.

"I would have married you. I suppose....I don't mean that to sound condescending....I've just never thought of marriage but kids....no I'm too old to start being a dad all over again. Do you want children Sandra? You never said."

"In the throes of an orgasm, it didn't seem important but yes I do want children, very much in fact."

"Why have you never had any then?"

"I was on the pill for some years then it just didn't happen, then Jim seemed to lose interest in sex. That made me ripe for an affair with you I guess."

"So what happens now? We go back to boss and member of staff and you and Jim have a celibate old age?"

He sounded a bit bitter and she did not like the sarcastic edge to the last part.

"I hope we can still be friends, Derek and hopefully Jim and I can sort out our problem."

She felt no need to tell her boss that things had improved at home.

Derek smiled and apologised.

"Sorry Sandra. I suppose I should feel grateful for what we did have together. It was special to me..."

"...and to me. I'll never look at a dining room table the same way again."

They both laughed.

"Of course we can still be friends, Sandra. I think we're both adult enough for that."

Sandra gave him a chaste kiss on the cheek and left his office. On the way home to Newlands, she felt a mixture of relief and regret.

CHAPTER 48

Charles sat deep in thought. He had his section of the police station to himself as all his team were out on routine matters. Nothing new had come to light on the two murders and he was anxious now in case nothing did. He always hated a stagnant time in the middle of a case and it was even worse this time as he had actually been present when the first murder took place. The chief constable had been quite scathing about this once again.

"I'm being pressured Davenport, to get a result. It's over three weeks since the first murder. I mean man, you were there!"

"I didn't actually see the murderer, Sir." Davenport knew how Frank felt now as he said the 'Sir'. He felt small and foolish. "I mean, I must have seen the murderer before and after the killing but I didn't actually see him in his Santa Claus outfit."

"I've managed so far to keep the details from the press but when they find out that you're looking for Santa, they'll have a field day. Have you no idea who committed either murder?"

"There were seventeen people there. One was the first victim. We've ruled out three young children, DS Macdonald and myself, the hostess who let Santa in and one young man, one of her twin nephews, who was with her at the time. The second victim is obviously ruled out too as is his partner, so we are left with seven possible suspects."

Knox groaned. Davenport continued.

"Of those seven, the first victim's wife had no motive, in fact she will probably be less well-off now that he is dead. Aimee Levaux, the partner of one guest had no motive, having only just met the first deceased. One twin son of the dead man does not have an alibi so we're not ruling him out but think him unlikely to have killed his father. A female neighbour also seems unlikely as there is precious little reason for her to have killed the first victim. That leaves us with three possible candidates, the brother of the deceased whose wife was raped by the murdered man, the partner of the French girl who had a brief affair with the deceased..."

"Thought you said the French girl had no motive. She might have killed him to keep him quiet about the affair."

"We think it unlikely, Sir, having met her. She's too shallow to be worried about what her boyfriend found out and has in fact run off with someone else since."

"Who's the third suspect?"

"The husband of the female neighbour who might have been propositioned by Brian Ewing. The only motive for the second murder is the fact that the victim, Dr Mackie might have alerted the murderer that he suspected him or her so our likely suspects would be the same ones."

"Interview those three again, Davenport. I'm meeting the press later today and I'll tell them that you have three suspects and hope to make an arrest soon."

Grant Knox had been very mild for him and Davenport wondered if the assistant constable, Solomon Fairchild, had discussed the case with him and maybe tempered his attitude. He just hoped that, as often happened, Fairchild would be given the press to deal with as he never mentioned imminent arrests until they were indeed imminent.

Davenport fumed his way back to his department and was disappointed to find that Fiona Macdonald was still not available to unburden himself to.

What he was thinking now was that Knox was correct about one thing, namely that he should interview Ralph Ewing, Jim Rogerson and Colin Ferguson again. He heard footsteps in the corridor and went to his door. It was Penny and Frank, looking pleased with themselves. He felt angry with them for being happy when their case was dying on them and was about to bark at them when common sense prevailed. It was not their fault that they had not solved the two murders.

"Come in you two and tell me what's happened."

"Sir, the wee boy who'd gone missing since last night, turned up safe and sound. He'd been reading about a boy being kidnapped, some story where the kidnappers paid the parents to take the boy back because he was such a nuisance…"

" 'The Ransom of the Red Chief'," laughed Davenport. "I read it at school."

"That's it Sir," said Frank. "Well our wee fellow thought he'd hide and make his folks think he'd been kidnapped!"

"Where was he?"

"In one of his pal's garden shed. He fell asleep and when he woke up discovered that the door was locked. His friend's father had locked it without looking inside. It wasn't till they all came home the next night that they heard shouting and let him out."

"I don't think he'll ever do anything like that again, Sir," said Penny. "He was so frightened and hungry."

"Do you know where Sergeant Din and DS Macdonald are?" Davenport asked them.

"Salma was given permission to go to the dentist Sir. She was awake most of the night with toothache," Penny volunteered.

"And DS Macdonald?"

"Sorry, Sir, no idea," said Penny and Frank nodded in agreement.

Davenport went off to the front desk and found out that there had been a phone call from Pippa's school saying that Pippa had been sick and could her father come and take her home. The head teacher, a Mrs Hobson, had tried to get him on his mobile. DS Macdonald had gone to pick Pippa up.

Davenport took his mobile out of his pocket. He had, he remembered now, switched it off when summoned to the chief constable who had an almost pathological dislike of mobile phones and got incensed if one rang in his presence.

"When the DS gets back with Pippa, if she's well enough to wait a short while, we'll meet in the Incident Room," he told Frank and Penny. "Salma can be filled in when she gets back. Meanwhile come into my room and have a decent cup of coffee."

When Fiona arrived back with Pippa, that young lady was looking quite pale but insisted that she would be OK to wait for a short time before getting off home. She had been sick twice, she informed them all, quite proudly. No one else was ill so it could not have been the school dinner although that had been chicken and sometimes not everybody was affected if one bit was bad. Davenport decided to wait and see how she was later before phoning the doctor.

The team met in the Incident Room. Fiona closed the door carefully, remembering the little eavesdropper the last time they met here.

"I met with the chief constable while you were all away. As usual he wants results yesterday. I've been told to interview our main suspects, Colin Ferguson, Jim Rogerson and Ralph Ewing, again."

"When, Sir?" asked Fiona.

"Tomorrow morning. I'll phone them all this evening and arrange times. It will be awkward as they're all at work but too bad."

"Mr Rogerson's a doctor, Sir, in the Southern General," said his DS "Maybe he'll have operations scheduled."

"If he has, he'll have to come in the next day. I don't imagine he works on a Saturday."

As it turned out Jim was fully booked the next day and agreed to come in early on Saturday, at 8.30am. Ralph and Colin had more flexible jobs being accountants. Colin agreed to postpone a meeting with a client and Ralph had none till the late afternoon.

Charles made appointments with them for Friday morning. He took Pippa home. She had more colour in her cheeks by the time they left the station but he agreed to let her stay off the last day of the school week and rang Linda, his sister who agreed to come up to Newton Mearns and baby-sit though Pippa hated that word, declaring that she was an invalid not a baby.

Two more phone calls were made, to John, one of their regular bridge opponents and to Jean Hope who had agreed to stand in for John's partner Kim who was on holiday for two weeks. Both were willing to come up to Charles's house instead of Fiona's flat. Charles could tell Jean that Fiona would pick her up around 7.15pm. Jean lived in Tassie Street, just round the corner from Fiona. He had been going to take Pippa down to Shawlands with him as she liked Fiona's flat, in particular her bedroom with its bookshelves full of Chalet School books and other interesting things such as board games. Fiona had taught her some Patience games recently and she would have been quite happy to play them while they played bridge. However she was still a bit fragile, Charles thought, so he wanted her to be in her own home.

The evening went well. Charles had partnered Jean as she knew him slightly, leaving Fiona with John with whom she had never played either. All four were on their toes with different partners and even Jean lost her nervousness after successfully pulling off a difficult three no trump. Charles joked that they always played for a £1 a point and at the end of the evening when they added up the scores, Jean and he had scored 3,600 and Fiona and John, 3,640 so even had they been playing for money no one would have been bankrupt.

As John had no connection with the police or the case, the murders were never mentioned and it was only on the way home that Jean asked tentatively if they were making any progress.

Fiona told her nicely that she could not really discuss the case except to say that some people had been ruled out. Jean thanked her for the lift and an enjoyable evening and climbed the stairs to her own flat to be greeted by her new cat lodger who had not yet settled in and had literally caterwauled when Jean had left. She suspected that the moggy had settled down when she had no audience and made up her mind to ask her elderly neighbour if she had been disturbed at all.

Fiona, climbing the stairs to her own flat a street away, hoped that tomorrow the interviews would turn up some fresh facts.

CHAPTER 49

Salma Din had a secret; she was extremely superstitious, so much so that she was tempted to stay off work and remain in her bed on the Friday following her emergency dentist appointment. She had tried throwing salt over her right shoulder, making sure that none of family saw her, in an attempt to bring herself good luck on Friday the thirteenth. She was horrified, on arriving at the station, to see a window cleaner up a ladder in her path. To make matters worse, Frank arrived at the same time and walked unconcernedly under the ladder. He waited for Salma in the doorway but not even the thought of him ridiculing her would have made her risk danger by walking under that ladder and she sidestepped it and went the long way round.

"Sarge, are you superstitious?" Frank challenged her.

"Not at all. Just being careful. Don't want any water on my uniform," replied Salma.

Frank accepted that, knowing that she was fastidious about her appearance.

Davenport met them at the door to the Incident Room and gave them their instructions for the morning.

"Jim Rogerson has managed to get here after all. Salma, you and Frank use interview room one and question him. Remember we're trying to find out if he suspected Brian Ewing of either having a liaison with his wife or trying to have. Try to get him angry and on the defensive. Frank, you take the bad guy role and let Salma be nice to him."

Salma, aware of the date from the moment she had woken up, was sure that this was not going to go well but she could not refuse to do what her boss asked of her. She and Frank went into interview room one and Salma, taking a blank cassette from the window ledge, inserted it into the tape machine.

"You go and see if you can find Mr Rogerson," she told Frank. Bring him in here and start off with your aggressive tactic."

"OK, Sarge,"said Frank and went off to the waiting room where he found Ralph and Jim nervously discussing why they were there.

"Did they tell you why...." Jim was asking.

"Mr Rogerson, come with me please," Frank said without smiling. He led Jim, in silence, to the interview room.

Jim looked round the bare room, at the metal table and four hard-backed chairs, at the tape recorder and the sergeant sitting at the table. He had watched this scene many times on TV and had taken the seat across from Salma before she told him to do it.

Frank sat beside Salma and switched on the recorder.

"Friday 13th January. PC Frank Selby and Sergeant Salma Din in attendance with James Rogerson. The time is 8.40 am." Frank leaned across the table diagonally, resting his chin on his hands and looked searchingly at Jim who felt his hands go sweaty and managed not to wipe them down his trouser legs.

"Mr Rogerson, tell me about going back for your video camera, a fact that you omitted to mention when first questioned."

"I forgot to bring it with me. I always videoed the Ewing party. I went back to the house for it after Pictionary and before charades."

"Did you pick up the Santa suit at the same time?"

"No, I didn't pick it up at the same time, I..."

"Not at the same time, then when did you pick it up?"

"I didn't mean I picked it up at another time. I didn't have it at all."

"You saw Brian Ewing flirt with your wife at a recent event and you felt a murderous rage towards him!"

"No I didn't."

"Didn't what, see him flirt with her or feel a murderous rage towards him?"

"I saw him flirt with Sandra and I was annoyed but not murderous."

"I put it to you Mr Rogerson that you did indeed hate the man, that you were determined that your wife was not going to be another notch on his bedpost."

"Sandra wouldn't have gone along with him..."

"So why were you so angry then?"

"I wasn't angry, just annoyed."

"Humph," spoke volumes.

Salma took up the questioning. She smiled at Jim and said, gently, "Jim, we can understand perfectly how you felt. What man wouldn't feel angry at another man coming on to his wife?"

"Yes, I was angry. I admit that."

"When did you begin to have thoughts of getting rid of him?" Salma asked quietly.

"I didn't think of getting rid of him. I just made up my mind to talk to him, tell him I'd seen him, knew his game and warn him off."

"And that didn't work, did it?" Frank pushed his face into Jim's. "So you killed him."

"I did not kill him. I didn't."

Jim was sweating in real earnest now. He took out a handkerchief and wiped his face.

Salma continued, "No one would blame you Jim. I'm sure a jury would sympathise with you.

"I know your game," Jim spluttered. "You're being nice to me to see if you can get me to admit something I didn't do."

This was true. Salma, blaming her failure on the day's date, spoke into the tape:

"Interview with James Rogerson ending. 8.56am."

She and Frank left the room.

In the room next door, Ralph was being treated in a similar way though Fiona had been the 'nasty' one and had been on her own, with Penny standing at the back as a witness. When she had had no success, she left and Davenport came in and took over. He had opted for the good guy role as he knew Ralph personally because of his daughter's friendship with Ralph's daughter.

"I hate to have to say this Ralph but you're the one with the best reason for getting rid of your brother. As far as we know he didn't rape anyone apart from Sally."

"I know it looks bad but honestly I didn't know till a couple of days ago and if I had known before that, I'd probably have punched him, not killed him. I didn't like him much but he was my brother, for goodness sake."

"Where were you when Santa arrived?"

"I was coming downstairs from the bathroom when the doorbell rang. I saw Sally open the door - one of the twins was with her - and saw Santa come in. I just assumed that Sal had organised it and I went on into the kitchen to get some more mixers for drinks. I went into the lounge and started getting peoples' drinks topped up. I remember you asking for a soft drink this time."

"I remember that now, Ralph. Have you any idea who the murderer could be?"

"Not a scubie doo, I'm afraid. The only person who went outside must have been Jim when he went to get his camera but why on earth would he want to kill my brother? I don't suppose he raped Sandra too?"

"Well if he did, neither she nor Jim is admitting it."

"Colin?"

"You know him better than I do. Is he the type to get madly jealous?"

"This is the first time I've seen him with a woman and he certainly looked thunderous when Brian patted Aimee's bottom. I think we all saw that. That was one thing about Brian, he didn't hide his amorous feelings but you don't murder someone for flirting do you?"

"Maybe there was more to it than that."

Davenport knew that there had indeed been a sexual encounter between Aimee and Brian, at the Busby Hotel if he wasn't mistaken but in fairness to Colin he did not tell Ralph. Enough that his fiancée had left him, without everyone knowing that she had been unfaithful to him too. He would only bring that out into the open if Colin was found to be guilty.

"Could one of the twins have killed his father? One was with Sally you say when she let him in. Which one?"

"I couldn't see from a distance. The only difference between them is that Ian has a small scar on his forehead. Anyway why would either John or Ian want to kill his Dad? It's ridiculous."

"Maybe wanted something and Brian wouldn't give it to him."

"What? They got everything they wanted, too much if you ask me but that's not the point here."

Davenport signed out, switching off the tape and escorting Ralph to the station door.

"On a lighter note, would you bring Hazel up to our house tomorrow if Pippa is OK? Say in the afternoon, around two?"

"Yes that would be fine. With or without her bike?"

"Wait and see what the weather does. Can she stay overnight?"

"Can't see why not. I'll run it past Sal first in case she has anything planned for Hazel but I'm sure it'll be OK."

The two men shook hands and Davenport turned back into the station. Ahead of him he could see Salma and Frank and Jim Rogerson. He could tell from their body language that things had not gone well. Jim was walking stiffly towards Davenport and Salma looked crest-fallen, Frank belligerent, his role of bad guy still uppermost in his mind.

"Sorry you had to go through that, Sir, but you weren't the only one," Davenport told him.

At that moment the swing doors swished open and Colin came through looking nervous.

"Hello, Mr Ferguson. PC Selby and I would like a word with you. Frank please take Mr Ferguson to interview room 1. I'll be with you shortly. Don't start till I'm there."

Davenport shook hands with Jim Rogerson and Jim left, catching up with Ralph in the car park where they exchanged their experiences.

Davenport and Frank went through the routine with Colin and got no further with him. He admitted to wanting to punch Brian Ewing when he saw him pat Aimee's bottom. When asked, he said that they had met Brian in the Avenue at Mearns Cross some days before the party and as always, Colin said quite bitterly, Aimee had lit up as she always did when she met an eligible man.

"Could they have met up at some time?" asked Davenport, knowing full well that they had done so. "Maybe when she was here before?"

"It's possible I suppose. I was at work during the day. Mum took Aimee about but I think she did go off on her own a couple of times."

"Did you murder Brian Ewing, Colin?" Davenport asked quietly.

"Until Aimee went back home with, I presume, a former lover, I was kidding myself on that things were fine so, no, I didn't kill him Inspector."

Davenport thanked him for his cooperation and the young man left looking marginally better than he had done when he arrived.

The team met in the Incident Room and pooled their results. They had all drawn a blank.

"Are we definite that Arthur was killed to keep him quiet about the first murder?" Davenport asked.

"Yes," they chorused.

"Right, we'll concentrate first on Brian Ewing's murder."

Davenport wrote on the white board alongside the photograph of Brian's dead body;

PEOPLE WITH THE OPPORTUNITY TO KILL BRIAN

Underneath this he wrote:

Colin
Jim
Ian/John
Sandra
Aimee
Charles
Fiona
Jean
Diana
Hazel
Pippa

"We can discount Sally and one twin who met Santa at the door. I am now ruling out Ralph as I remember him pouring drinks after Santa arrived. Carol had no motive, as she could have given Brian a divorce and come off well out of it. She didn't need to kill him. Jean knew none of them before the night of the party and wasn't the age bracket to entice Brian so I'll take her off the list."

"Sir, we can take off you, DS Macdonald and Pippa surely?" said Penny eagerly.

"Thank you, Miss Price," Davenport grinned at her.

"And surely we can take off Diana?" asked Frank. "She's too small to stab a man to death."

"Right. I agree."

"So that leaves the following." Davenport rubbed out some names and they were left with:

Colin
Jim
Sandra
Aimee
John/Ian

"Now a second list. Those who were contacted by Arthur Mackie before he died":

Jim
Sandra
Ralph & Sally
Carol & family.

"It would appear that he didn't ring Colin and Aimee so do you agree that we take them off the first list too as the person who killed Arthur killed Brian first?"

Again a chorus of, "Yes Sir."

"So that leaves Jim, Sandra and John or Ian." Davenport concluded.

"Sir, I can't see any reason at all for either John or Ian to kill their father," said Fiona.

"Me neither," said Penny.

"Nor me," agreed Frank.

"Or me, Sir," Salma said.

"Right if we leave the twins off the list we're left with either Jim or Sandra Rogerson," Davenport concluded "and I can think of no reason for Sandra to commit the first murder, though she might have aided in the killing of Arthur Mackie if Jim asked for her help."

"Do we arrest Jim Rogerson then, Sir?" said Penny anxious for action.

"I'm tempted, especially with the chief constable breathing down my neck. Jim Rogerson is the only one whom we know for sure left the house around the crucial time."

"Sir," said Salma timidly. "Would you think I was daft if I said leave it till tomorrow. I don't think Friday 13th is a good time to make decisions."

Frank hooted.

"I knew you were superstitious when you avoided that ladder this morning, Sarge."

Salma looked embarrassed.

"Not for that reason Salma but I'm not going to make any decision till Monday. Let's have lunch and then get our interviews written up. Maybe two days away from the firing line will clear our heads."

CHAPTER 50

Fog everywhere. He was choking in it. He peered about trying to see Pippa but she had gone. Then the fog cleared and he saw her but it wasn't her any more. It was someone else wearing her clothes. He called out but his voice made no sound and the figure waved at him and cycled off.

Charles woke drenched in sweat, on Sunday morning, calling out Pippa's name. He looked at the bedside clock. It was 6.20 am. He got out of bed and walked quickly to his daughter's room. He knew that it had been a bad dream but he needed to be sure that she was OK. She was lying with one arm outside her duvet which was a new one, white with lots of little colourful flowers. She had informed him that she was now too old for childish duvet covers. Another era of her childhood gone. He gently lifted the arm and put it back under the cover. She muttered but did not wake. It took a lot to wake Pippa even when it was time for her to get up. His shout had gone unheard. There was no sound from Hazel's room.

The day before, Ralph, true to his word had folded Hazel's bicycle, put it in the boot of his car and driven up to Newton Mearns. Charles, promising to drive Hazel back the next day, waved Ralph off and shooed the two girls in for a quick lunch of their favourite fish fingers and peas with oven chips, ordered by Pippa the day before. Lunch over, he put both bicycles in his boot, thanking his lucky stars that he had a car with a large boot, picked up his video camera and drove them to Rouken Glen where he sat well wrapped up by the boating lake while they raced round it a few times before asking to go to the playground in another part of the park. They wheeled their bikes there and left them with Charles while they played on the chute and merry -go- round and used the climbing frame.

As it was a cold day, the park was quite quiet so Charles got them to cycle round the lake again and he brought out his video and took some footage of them both racing round. They were both happy as each had won one circuit of the pond. That over, they decided to go to Boaters for a snack as the exercise and cold air had made them hungry. Once inside, they took off their helmets and two rosy-cheeked faces looked at him and asked if they could have hot chocolate and a muffin each, Hazel choosing a blueberry one and Pippa one of the chocolate chip variety. Charles contented himself with a skinny latte to which he had been introduced by Fiona a few weeks ago. They had both decided that they needed to lose some weight before the summer holidays.

Snack finished, he once again folded up both bicycles and put them in the boot and they drove back home.

"Pippa, I'm going to ring Fiona and see if she'd like to come and keep me company this evening as you've got Hazel for company. OK?"

"Fine, Dad. We're going upstairs until mealtime. Will Fiona come for her meal too?"

"No I don't think pie and beans with chips - again - would tempt her, pet. I'll suggest she comes up around 7pm."

Charles went to the phone in the hall and managed to get Fiona who was back from her weekend shopping and was delighted to come up later.

"I've got Hazel Ewing for the evening and a stopover but they'll be upstairs out of our way. Maybe we could firm up our ideas for summer."

Charles hung up and, going into the lounge, picked up his Guardian newspaper and spent a good hour trying to complete the cryptic crossword which being Araucaria or Paul on a Saturday was always difficult. Today it was Araucaria. It had been him on Monday too this week, unusual as he was usually reserved for the weekend when people had more time. The Monday one had however been quite straightforward for that setter, prompting a few letters on Wednesday saying how the writers had been delighted to conquer an Araucaria crossword. Maybe in revenge he had set a particularly hard one this Saturday and Charles decided to delve into the sports' section and leave the crossword till Fiona arrived. She did The Herald crossword every day if she had time and might have some fresh insight into these difficult clues.

Upstairs, Pippa and Hazel were filling in their crime notebooks with the extra information which Pippa had overheard, neither having done anything till they could both be together. They added Wendy Hamilton to their list.

"Why would she want to kill Uncle Brian?" asked Hazel.

"Maybe she had a husband who might want to kill him," Pippa explained

"Are you sure your Dad mentioned Ian and John?" Hazel sounded grumpy about this and Pippa felt bad about having to say yes he did.

"I still think it's going to be a jealous husband," Hazel said. "I heard Mum and Dad talking the other night and they said that Uncle Brian could have made Colin or Mr Rogerson angry."

"Anything else?" Pippa asked.

"No, he saw me at the door and stopped talking about the murder."

"Hazel, what's 'rape'?" Pippa asked.

"Why?"

"Well I heard Dad say that your Dad would be annoyed about your Mum's rape."

Pippa had not meant to tell Hazel this but in the excitement of the moment and wanting to know more than her pal, she had told her after all. She need not have worried as Hazel did not know what the word meant either.

"Do you think I should ask Mum?" she inquired now.

"No," Pippa was determined, "She would want to know where you had heard it and I don't want Dad to know I was listening."

"Let's just add it to Mum's bit in our notebooks and hope we can find out. Did you try the dictionary?"

"Yes but I couldn't understand what it said there either," admitted Pippa.

They spent a few minutes writing in their jotters then Charles called up the stairs that dinner was ready and, leaving the jotters on Pippa's bed, they hurried downstairs, hungry again.

They helped Charles with the washing up and sat down in front of the TV and were still there when Fiona arrived. Charles took her jacket and went upstairs to put it on a bed, choosing Pippa's as her room was nearest. He saw the open jotters on the bed and, glancing casually at one, saw the word 'rape' written in big childish letters. He picked up the jotter and read, "Mum had a rape which might have annoyed Dad."

Feeling puzzled and a bit guilty about reading Hazel's jotter, Charles flicked through the pages. He picked up Pippa's jotter, read it and realised what the youngsters had been up to.

Angry with them both, he hurried downstairs and confronted them in the lounge. Fiona had never seen him so angry and certainly not with Pippa.

"Pippa. Have you been listening in to my conversations with Fiona? What's this?"

He thrust the jotter under Pippa's nose.

Pippa was angry too and upset about being shouted at in front of her friend and Fiona.

"Daddy, you shouldn't read my private jotter!"

"I didn't know it was private and it's Hazel's jotter but that's not the point. You should know not to be nosey about my job." Charles's voice was loud and Hazel looked frightened. He looked over at Fiona who was feeling embarrassed for the two girls and wished she hadn't been in the room.

"Fiona, these two have written down all they know about the murder and the people involved. Pippa must have listened to us talking when you were up here. Did you know she had?"

Fiona felt that she should have told him about Pippa overhearing them at work but Pippa spoke up, "Daddy, I'm sorry. I shouldn't have listened when you and Fiona were talking. We wrote the rest from what we knew from being at the party."

Pippa obviously did not want her Dad to know about her overhearing at the station, so Fiona kept quiet once again, grateful that she did not need to get the youngster further into trouble and Pippa threw her a look which said, "Thank you."

"Have you shown these jotters to anyone else?" Charles demanded.

"No," said Pippa.

Charles had calmed down.

"Well, no harm done as long as you haven't shown these jotters to anyone else. It would get me into trouble if anyone thought I'd talked in front of either of you. Do you understand that Pippa?"

"Yes Dad. We haven't shown them to anyone else. Honest."

"I'm going to burn these jotters and I want you to promise me not to do anything like this again."

"I promise Dad."

"And you Hazel."

"I promise too, Mr Davenport. We just thought we might be able to help."

"Well we'll say no more about it then. Off you both go upstairs. I'll call you both down for cocoa about 9 o'clock before bed."

Once the girls had gone and making sure that the door was shut, Charles said, "I don't think they knew what rape meant. He showed Fiona where Hazel had written that her Mum had had a rape, and Fiona agreed with him.

"What will you do if one of them asks you what it means?" she inquired with a wicked smile on her face,

"I'll just say that it's something they'll learn when they're older but I think they're both too chastened to ask that right now. At least I hope so. Maybe I'll send them to you if they do," he said, getting his own back.

They called the girls down for cocoa at 9 pm and the two went to bed without a murmur, no doubt to chat for some time before falling asleep. Charles and Fiona made no mention of the case and talked instead of the holiday. They too had learned a lesson that night. Charles wired up his video camera to the TV and they watched the short bit of footage of the two youngsters on their bicycles that day, Fiona commenting on the fact that she could not tell which girl was which as, in their helmets with their hair covered, they looked so alike.

In the cold light of dawn the next day, Charles realised that this must have been what caused his nightmare of Pippa turning into someone else.

CHAPTER 51

"Go on, Diana, tell us all about the murder. We want to hear all about it." It was just another variation of the many requests she had had since returning to school but this was probably the most demanding and most cruel one. It came from the girl Diana hated most in school, Kathleen Kingston-James who had been the one who had treated her the worst since her brothers had left. She was in the fifth form and had, Diana thought, chased after John but been knocked back. She had taken this out on Diana in various ways and she was the main reason Diana wanted to leave the school. She was a tall, well-built girl and now loomed over Diana.

"Come on," Kathleen said again. "We're not leaving till you tell us."

They had cornered her in the common room, the junior common room but being prefects they had a right to be there, overseeing the young ones. There were four of them, all big girls and there were none of Diana's friends around as they were all busy with their usual weekend hobbies which of course Diana did not have, having always gone home at weekends. She had been sitting trying to read when they had found her in the late afternoon.

There was nothing for it but to tell them what had happened. Someone had obviously got the news from home as it seemed to be common knowledge in school.

"We were all at a Christmas party a few days before Christmas and someone killed my Dad."

She stopped, feeling the tears pricking the backs of her eyes.

"Oh, we know that stupid!" said one of the girls.

"Who killed him?" asked Kathleen, sticking her nose inches from Diana's face.

"I don't know. The police haven't found out yet."

"Well tell us who was there, at the party."

"There was Mum, Dad, me, John and Ian, my Uncle Ralph and Aunt Sally - it was their party - and my cousin Hazel and her friend Pippa and Pippa's Dad and his girlfriend. There was a man who works with Uncle Ralph and his fiancée and Dr Mackie and his friend Jean and two of Uncle Ralph's neighbours, Jim and Sandra."

"How did it happen?"

"The door rang after some games and it was Santa..."

"Ooh Santa! Bet you still believe in him, Diana Ewing," laughed Kathleen.

"No I don't," stated Diana hotly. "It was meant to be fun, at least that's what we all thought but the man in Santa's clothes was the murderer."

"So will you be able to afford this school now that daddy's dead?" Kathleen's words like hot needles pierced Diana's brain. She got up and tried to push her way through the ring of girls surrounding her chair but one pushed her back into the chair.

"So no daddy to collect you every Wednesday now? Will mummy come instead then?" Kathleen's best friend had taken up the taunting.

"No, my mother won't come for me. It was Dad who wanted me at home, not Mum."

The words were out before she could stop herself.

"Oh daddy's girl are you? And now he's not here. Shame."

Diana felt the tears coming. She knew that this would only encourage them but she could not help it.

"Boo hoo, cry baby. Diddums hasn't got a daddy now."

Given strength from somewhere, Diana got up and shoved at the two girls immediately in front of her. They staggered and fell back and Diana was out of the room and running for the stairs before they could get their wits together.

"Leave her alone. She's not going anywhere. We'll continue with you later, Ewing!" Kathleen called after her.

Once in the bedroom which she shared with another girl in the same year as herself and who was out riding just now, Diana rang her brother Ian. Ian was just setting out for the town of Stirling to meet with John and some friends in a pub there. He went back into his room and sitting on the bed he tried to console his young sister, telling her that she had to stand up to these older girls or else tell one of the staff.

"I don't know why they hate me so much, Ian," she whimpered down the phone.

"Who is the worst? Do I know her?" asked Ian.

"Her name's Kathleen Kingston-James and she has three friends who copy everything she does."

"Oh her! She fancied John and kept hanging round us. He told her to get lost. I guess that's what's made her hate you."

"Ian, will you try to persuade Mum to let me leave here and go to school near home. Please!"

"OK, Sis. I'll try to convince her the next time I'm home. Now I've got to go. I've got folk waiting for me."

Ian hung up. He wished that he and John were nearer Diana and wondered if he should have promised to go there in the evening. Grabbing his jacket which he had thrown over the nearest chair, he left the room once again and made his way quickly to the pub where he told John what had happened. John was less sympathetic.

"Look, Ian, she'll have to defend herself. If you dive up there she'll expect you to do that every time she phones you for help."

Ian, while worrying about his sister, knew that his brother was right. He did not go up to the school.

Later that night Diana, woke from another nightmare, the same one she had been having since the night of the party in which her father was in a river and kept drifting past her as she tried to grab hold of him. Each time she grabbed his clothes, the clothes came off and he floated away. This time it was even worse as she grabbed his arm and it came off. She hoped she had not called out as she sometimes did but her roommate was sleeping peacefully. Diana got up and dressed herself in a pair of black trousers and a dark sweatshirt. She put on her trainers and quietly took her anorak from the wardrobe. Tiptoeing across the room, she opened the door and slipped out. There was a night light shining in the upstairs corridor and in its light she made her way to the stairs and through some corridors until she came to one of the back doors. The key was hanging up as it had to be in case of fire. She unlocked the door, opened it and edged out, shutting the door behind her.

The worst part was negotiating the long driveway as there was a milky shine from the moon and a teacher might be looking out. Keeping to the side of the path where there were hedges, she reached the gate without any alarm. The train station was not far from the school and, looking at the timetable on the wall, Diana saw that there was one more train that night. It left in fifteen minutes and was going to Edinburgh. It would have to do.

Keeping in to the wall, she waited, like a highwayman on his horse waited for an unsuspecting traveller and when the train came into the station she slid quickly towards the nearest carriage, grateful for the days of unmanned stations. The train snaked out of the station and she sat back and sighed with relief. She had escaped.

CHAPTER 52

Carol, never an early waker, was rudely woken on Monday morning by the strident ring of the telephone on her bedside table. She groaned and stretched out her hand to pick up the receiver, glancing at the time. 8.15am.Who on earth wanted her at this ungodly hour? It was Diana's housemistress with the news that Diana had gone missing.

"Missing? What do you mean, missing?"

"She's not in her bedroom, nor in the bathroom on her floor and no one has seen her since she went to bed last night."

"She must be somewhere. Have another look and call me back."

Carol lay back on her pillows and her shoulders slumped. Really, Diana was causing her nothing but trouble these days. Brian had spoiled her, babied her in fact and now she had hidden herself away somewhere, no doubt to get some attention. Well she was not going to get round her mother the way she did her father. If this was a ruse to get picked up and brought home, then she was out of luck.

Finding herself unable to sleep again, Carol got up, went down to the kitchen and made herself a coffee. She was wondering whether to get dressed or try to sleep again when the phone rang once more. This time it was Diana's head teacher.

"Mrs Ewing. We're really worried about Diana. We've instituted a search in the school and in the grounds and there is no sign of her. The girl she shares her bedroom with said that she was very upset yesterday evening and we think her anorak and trainers are missing. I think we should call the police."

"Drat the girl," thought Carol. "As if we don't have enough to do with the police already!"

To the head teacher she said, "Don't you think it might be a bit early for calling the police, Mrs Chambers? She's probably hiding somewhere. It might be a cry for help. She's been very upset since her father's ...death."

Mrs Chambers, not anxious to have the police on the premises, agreed to wait till lunchtime so Diana who had spent the night on a bench outside Waverley Street Station in Edinburgh had caught a train to Stirling, eaten breakfast in a cafe outside the station there and made her way to the university before anyone reported her missing. As her head teacher, having received Carol's permission to contact Perth police, was describing her lost pupil, Diana was endeavouring to find her brothers.

It took some time before she was given directions to the halls of residence and the call which came from their mother arrived just as she found her way to the third floor.

She knocked on the door marked 'Ewing I' and 'Ewing J'. The door was flung open and a distraught John was standing there.

"Ian," he said into the room, "she's here" and he folded his sister into a bear hug. Ian appeared beside him and taking Diana from John's arms he shook her, telling her he loved her and telling her she was a stupid girl at the same time.

Not wanting to waken anyone else on the floor, they took their sister inside and soon she was telling them of her journey from Perth to Stirling. They made her a cup of tea before phoning their mother to tell her that her daughter was with them safe and sound.

"I'll phone the school," said Carol, "and the Perthshire police. Can you bring her home today John?"

"Do you want to speak to her, Mum?" John asked, thinking for the umpteenth time what a cool customer his mother was.

"Yes, put her on."

Carol was surprisingly gentle to Diana. She had been thinking while she waited for news that maybe sending Diana to a local comprehensive might not be a bad thing. It would save money and also stop the girl whining.

"John and Ian will bring you home, Diana and we'll have a talk about school."

"Are you angry, Mum?" asked Diana in trepidation.

"No, darling. I was worried. That's all. Now I'll get off the phone and ring Mrs Chambers and the police. See you later today."

Asking friends to take notes for them at lectures, the twins took Diana home later that day. Carol gave her an affectionate welcome and after lunch for them all, they retired to the lounge where Carol, trying not to seem too keen, asked Diana what she wanted to do about school.

"I don't think Mrs Chambers would be happy to have you back after this, Diana."

"I don't want to go back, Mum. Some of the older girls were awful to me about Dad and even the nicer ones wanted to know all about what had happened. Can I go to Hazel's school, the one she'll be going to when she's old enough I mean?"

"No, darling. I'd rather you went to Mearns Castle. It gets a good reputation and it's nearer for you. Anyway, by the time Hazel gets to secondary you'd be in third year."

"I could go with Pippa and her dad. Please Mum. It would be easier to start a new school knowing someone I knew would be coming there."

"I'm sure Mr Davenport and Uncle Ralph and Aunt Sal wouldn't send their kids to a poor school, Mum," Ian piped in.

"Diana could get the bus to Clarkston and Mr Davenport could pick her up from there, on his way from Mearns to Shawlands," John added his tuppence worth.

"Let's leave things just now. I think you could do with the rest of the week at home," said Carol with, for her, rare concern for her daughter. She had for once really looked at Diana and seen her pinched, white face. She had taken Brian's death very hard, Carol realised for the first time.

Ian and John decided to go back to university the next day and took Diana off to the back lounge while Carol made them all lunch of gammon, tomatoes and hard - boiled egg. In the afternoon they walked round The Orry and Ian treated them all to afternoon tea at the Wishing Well, even Carol who for once did not refuse to eat because of her current diet. She decided to order Chinese take-away for their dinner, trying to lighten what might have been a gloomy meal as Diana was beginning to look despondent at the thought of her two brothers leaving again in the morning.

After dinner, while the young ones watched TV, Carol rang Sally and told her what had happened. Sally was horrified and called Ralph to the phone.

"Poor wee soul," were his first words. "She can't go back there Carol, you must see that."

He was astonished when his sister-in-law agreed with him. She asked him if he was happy with the secondary school that Hazel would be going to.

"Bradford High School? Yes. I've heard some mixed reports about it but I've been up to a parents' night for new pupils and I was very impressed by the head teacher and some of the principal teachers. Are you seriously thinking about sending Diana there? She wouldn't be in the same year as Hazel you know and the travel would be difficult. Williamwood High is near you and it gets a very good reputation."

Carol thanked him and rang off. She went into the back lounge and asked the boys to switch off the TV. She told Diana what her Uncle Ralph had said and was surprised when Diana accepted that it would be pointless to go to the same school as her cousin as they would never be in the same classes. Diana had been thinking and had realised that some of her 'home' friends went to Williamwood and it would be better to have friends in her own year. Hazel and Pippa might not have wanted her to muscle in on their friendship.

"OK Mum," she said now. "I'll go to Williamwood. Just please don't make me go back to Oakwood."

Carol agreed and they spent what had been their happiest evening together since the murder and all went to bed reasonably content, even Diana who had spent only unhappy nights since her Dad had died.

CHAPTER 53

There was a quiet excitement in The Rogerson house. Sandra had been waiting for what seemed ages for Jim to get home from work. He was usually home around five o'clock but naturally when she wanted to talk to him, he was late.

At a few minutes after 5.30, she heard his car in the driveway and ran to open the front door. Jim opened the back door of the car, picked up his briefcase and a bottle of wine, then, seeing Sandra waiting at the open door, he shut the car door and hurried to where she was standing.

"Hi, San. Everything OK?"

"Yes very OK, Jim, at least I think so."

"Here's some wine for dinner. I thought we needed a bit of cheering up after the last few weeks."

"Does that mean that the police don't suspect you any more, love?"

"I'm afraid not. I'm sure I'm still number one suspect because I went back for that ruddy camera.

No, it's just that I felt we deserved something nice for a change."

By this time they were in the kitchen and Jim was shrugging out of his heavy coat. It was a long walk from the hospital car park to the building which housed the gynaecological unit so he always wore a thick coat in winter. He went out into the hall and hung the coat up on the pegs by the door then went back into the kitchen. Sandra was pouring two glasses of wine. She held one out to him.

"Couldn't wait till dinner eh? Becoming a bit of a lush," he teased her.

She smiled and he thought again how wonderful it was to have his lovely, happy Sandra back. He did not know what had gone wrong over Christmas and he did not care as long as it did not happen again. There was a time a few weeks ago when he had thought that Sandra had been having an affair with Brian Ewing and one dreadful night when he had lain awake wondering if she had murdered Brian. When he had come back with the camera, she had not been in the lounge. Could she have donned the Santa suit and got rid of the philanderer, maybe to keep him quiet about their affair? He had never found the courage to ask her or to tell her his fears.

Standing holding her wine glass, Sandra looked at Jim and wondered again if her mild-mannered husband could have murdered Brian. She too was afraid to ask and pushed the thought way down in her brain as she prepared to tell him her news.

"No, not a lush, darling. In fact I think maybe I shouldn't have this wine at all. You're the very person to tell me. Could a glass of wine harm our baby?"

"Our baby... San...what baby?"

"It's maybe being a bit premature - sorry Jim bad pun - but my period is late, about a week only but you know how regular my periods are."

"Could set my watch by them, I've always said."

Jim put down his glass on the kitchen table and, eyes shining, he grabbed Sandra round the waist and, mindless of her glass of wine, spun her round and round till she was almost dizzy. The wine slopped out of the glass and spilled on the floor.

"Jim! Watch out! I know I didn't want the wine but don't waste it."

Calming down a bit, Jim held up his own glass which he had taken from the table.

"Here's a toast. To our baby."

"To our baby," echoed Sandra. "Oh, Jim I hope I'm not wrong but I'm sure I'm not. I feel different somehow."

"Well if you're wrong, we'll have plenty of fun trying to make sure you are soon," said her husband, folding her into his arms.

Later that night, lying in his arms she wondered if she would ever tell him about her short fling with Derek. She thought not as it would only be to make herself feel better at the risk of making him feel bad.

Dining room table versus their own baby. It was not a contest.

CHAPTER 54

Diana's mood swung back to one of unhappiness as soon as her brothers had left for Stirling. She needed someone to hold her and tell her she was special. Not only that, she could not see any of her friends as they were all at school and would, she knew, have homework in the evenings. They would be unavailable till the weekend and she needed company now. Her mother, after the rare burst of understanding and sympathy, had gone back into her personal world, phoning a friend to arrange lunch and simply ignoring her daughter, assuming that the girl would be able to entertain herself. Diana mooched about the house. It was not even weather for a walk being misty and wet, a typical January day. Diana was not a reader like her cousin and Pippa, preferring action to books. Her father had been taking her round the golf course and she had been showing promise. He had been delighted as his sons had forsaken him recently and he had thought that Diana would fill their shoes, given time and practice. People looking at the quiet girl would have been surprised to learn that she was sporty rather than bookish whereas her cousin, who was full of fun and never sat still except with a book, was a reader though not such an avid one as her friend Pippa.

Diana found one of her mother's magazines. She turned to the problem page and for a few minutes was engrossed in one letter which was from a woman whose husband had left her. She had asked what she should do to take her mind off him and been advised to go to Singles' Clubs and try to find herself a new partner. The agony aunt had thought that she should show her husband that she did not need him anymore. Diana was puzzled. Is this what her mother would do? Would she look for another husband? Diana hoped not. She did not want anyone to replace her father.

The other letters were about things Diana knew nothing about though she read one about someone who had pain during intercourse and Diana wondered if that meant her period as she had some pain during hers. Diana was naive for thirteen and had never had a friend close enough to discuss such things. The idea of asking her mother filled her with dismay. She looked at her watch. Nearly three o'clock. Her Mum would be back soon.

She thought back to the first letter. It had given her something to think about and she sat quietly for some time before going up to her room and putting on her anorak and outdoor shoes. She was almost at the front door when she had another thought and went back up and, removing her anorak, changed her clothes. Her mother had called out that she would be away for a few hours. It had not dawned on her to invite her daughter to have lunch with her and a friend. To her, Diana was still a child.

Diana caught a bus on Glasgow Road. This took her to Muirend where she alighted and walked through to Newlands. It was a long walk but she did not mind as she had a purpose which lent wings to her feet. For the first time since her Dad's death she felt almost happy.

Her ring on the doorbell went unanswered and she remembered that both her aunt and uncle would still be at work and Hazel would be at school. One more look at her watch told her school would probably be over and just at that moment a car pulled up and Hazel got out. Pippa's Dad had given her a lift home as he always did if he could get away from work on time to meet Pippa at the school gate. Charles saw a young girl waiting in the porch, didn't recognise Diana and assumed that it was another friend of Hazel's.

"Diana! When did you get here? Do Mum and Dad know you were coming? They never told me," Hazel greeted her cousin.

"No they didn't Hazel and Mum doesn't know either. She was out when I left but I'll phone her on my mobile later when I think she'll be in."

Hazel thought how grown up her cousin was, making her way down from Newton Mearns by herself without permission. She looked at her with a new respect as she took her house key from her purse and let them both in. She told Diana to take off her anorak and took her up to her bedroom, telling her to wait there while she went down and got them both a glass of milk and a chocolate biscuit. Diana told her all about running away from school and about how she was to go to Williamwood High School next week, once her Mum had been to the school and sorted things out. Hazel was flatteringly awed by what her cousin had done. Diana who was so timid and quiet had done something really brave and Hazel felt guilty about the times she had made fun of her.

When Sally arrived home about half an hour later, she found the cousins deep in discussion and assumed that Carol had dropped Diana off, in typical Carol fashion not checking up first that it suited Ralph and Sally. Hazel had gone out of the room when Sally said to Diana, "When did your Mum drop you off, Di?"

"Just as Hazel arrived home, Aunt Sally."

"How long are you staying?"

"Can I stay till Uncle Ralph comes home? I want to see him about something. Mum is coming for me at six." This last part was an invention. Diana wanted to see her uncle really badly and she had planned nothing for after that. It was easy to tell Hazel when she came back in that she had rung her Mum and was staying till about six o'clock as Sally was busy making dinner and paid little attention to the chat of the two youngsters.

Ralph arrived home minutes before six. He picked up his daughter and gave her a big hug then did the same to his niece. Telling Sally that he would wash and change before dinner he went off to his room. He was followed by Diana who slipped out of the kitchen after him, telling Hazel that she was going to the toilet.

When he came out of his en suite bathroom, he was surprised to see his niece sitting on his bed.

"Hello, Di. Did you want something? I'm just going to get changed."

"Uncle Ralph, do you love me?"

"Of course I do pet."

"I mean really love me, the way Daddy did?"

"Yes Di, just like your Daddy did though I know it's not the same for you. I can't replace your Dad."

"Yes you can, Uncle Ralph," said Diana and moved towards him.

Minutes later she was out of the front door and running as if all the demons of hell were after her. Ralph stood at the door. He had taken off his shoes while talking to Diana and stood in his stocking feet shouting out into the blackness, "Diana! Come back! Please! Come back!"

Sally, hearing the shouting, came hurriedly out of the kitchen with Hazel.

"What's wrong Ralph? Why are you shouting for Diana? Where's she gone?"

Ralph ran back into his bedroom and put on his shoes.

"Phone Carol. Get her down here. Hazel, come in the car with me and we'll see if we can find your cousin."

Carol, when contacted, had been going through a worrying time as once again it appeared as if her daughter had run away. When she had come home from her afternoon out, the house was empty and there was no note from Diana. At first she had assumed that Diana had gone to a friend's house but as time passed she had rung these friends and discovered that they had not seen Diana since she arrived back from boarding school. Not wanting to once again contact the police for what might be a false alarm, she had gone to the shops in Mearns Arcade where her search had proved fruitless. She had just been on the point of ringing Charles Davenport, when Sally called, telling her that

Diana had come down to them but had indeed now run away.

It took Carol twenty minutes to reach the house in Newlands, by which time Ralph had returned without Diana and was facing a barrage of questions from his wife.

"Get the police, Sally," he was saying.

"Hi, Carol. I'm just telling Sally to get the police. I don't know where Diana's gone and she was very upset when she ran off."

"Why was she upset Ralph?"

"I can't tell you right now," said her brother-in-law, throwing a glance at Hazel, "but I'll tell you all once the police arrive."

With that Sally and Carol had to be content.

CHAPTER 55

Charles frowned. Something was worrying him and had been for a while, since his nightmare about Pippa to be precise. He could not shake off the feeling that there was something he should be remembering. Was it to do with the case or was he just being foolish?

The phone call about Diana having run away came through to the desk and the PC there went along immediately to Davenport's room. There was no one there. There was no sign of DS Macdonald either so he found Salma.

"Serge, there's been a 'phone call about a missing girl and ..."

"John, you'll have to give that one to another section. We're still tied up with the Christmas murders."

"I know Serge but I recognised the name. It was Ewing and the man did say to tell the DCI but he's not here and neither is DS Macdonald."

"Did the man leave a name and number?"

"Yes. His name was Ralph Ewing and I wrote down the number. Here it is."

Salma phoned Davenport at home and explained the problem.

Davenport had the number in his diary and immediately rang Ralph who told him that Diana had run away.

"I don't want to give you the details over the phone. Could you come over to my house as soon as possible? Carol is here. I can tell you both at once. Diana ran away from my house so she should be in the Newlands' area. She's very upset."

Davenport asked for details of her clothes but all Ralph could say was that she had on no coat and was wearing a white dress.

"Is that the same dress she wore at the party and at her dad's funeral, Ralph?"

"I think so. I'm hopeless. Sorry."

Davenport rang Salma back.

"Salma, take Penny and Frank and any other available PCs and do a search round about Ralph Ewing's house in Newlands. Diana Ewing has run away from there. She's wearing only a thin white dress and is very upset about something. I'm going over to Ralph's house now to find out more. He wouldn't explain over the phone."

It took him about twenty minutes to drive over to the Ewing house. Ralph was at the open door waiting for him. He took Charles into the lounge where Carol, Hazel and Sally were sitting.

"Hazel, upstairs. Now."

It was not often that her Dad sounded so severe. Hazel did not even think of complaining but moved off fast. When she was gone, Ralph shut the door carefully. He faced the others, his face ashen and puzzled.

"Carol this is going to sound terrible to you but please hear me out completely before you say anything."

"Can I just tell the Inspector that Diana did this the other night, ran away from school? She managed to reach her brothers at Stirling University and might try to go back there again though I don't know why she felt she needed them again," said Carol.

Davenport got on his mobile and told Salma to check the train and bus stations as Diana might try to get to Stirling then he turned to Ralph.

"OK, tell us what happened."

"When I got home tonight, Diana was here. I gave her and Hazel a big hug then went off to change my clothes before dinner. I had taken my shoes off and used the ensuite toilet. I came out and she …Diana…was in the room."

He gulped and seemed to be looking for words.

"I asked if she wanted something and she asked me if I loved her. I said of course I did and she said something like, 'Do you really love me, like Dad did?' I said yes I loved her just like her Dad did but I knew that it wouldn't be the same for her. I think I said that I couldn't take the place of her Dad."

He stopped again. Davenport thought he had never seen a man look so haunted. "What did she say then?"

"She said...she said... 'Yes you can Uncle Ralph' and moved towards me. I thought she wanted another cuddle and put my arms round her and she...she..."

"She what Ralph?"

"I'm sorry, Carol, she put her hand to my trouser zip and pulled it down."

"What?" exclaimed Carol and Sally, in unison.

"I pushed her away and did it up and she said, ' Why will no one let me love them?' and ran off. I had no shoes on so I ran to the door and shouted out into the dark. Sally came out and I asked her to phone Carol."

"And you, Mrs Ewing. What did you do?" asked Davenport.

"I'm afraid I assumed when I got home and found Diana gone that she had gone to a friend's house. When that proved wrong, I went to the shopping centre. When I couldn't find her there, I was just about to phone the police, you Inspector as I know you, when Sally rang. I came straight down. Ralph why on earth would she do what she did? Diana is such an innocent, always younger than her years."

Sally nodded, "I often thought our Hazel knew more about the world than Diana."

"So we can only assume that Diana wanted to have sex with Ralph and when he knocked her back she was distraught and ran off."

"I've never given her any encouragement. You have to believe me," Ralph said horrified.

" 'Why will no one let me love them?' Are you sure that's what she said Ralph?" asked Davenport.

"Yes."

"So that means she must have tried it on some other man. I wonder who? Did Diana have any men friends, Carol, or any boyfriends?"

"Not that I know of," said Carol, "as I said, she was always so innocent, never seemed to understand a risqué joke."

"Well, we'll find out when we find her," Davenport comforted the adults. "Meanwhile I think you should ring John and Ian and see if they can throw any light on this."

Sally led Carol out into the hall and then left her there to contact her sons. Luckily John had his mobile switched on so Carol spoke to him for a few minutes. She came back into the lounge.

"John was as puzzled as we are. He said he would ask Ian when he got back to the halls of residence."

"I think, Mrs Ewing, that you should return home in case Diana makes for there. Ralph and Sally you stay here please. If my team find her, they will bring her here and contact me."

Davenport rang Salma again, telling her that he had no more news about Diana. He told her that he didn't think she would return to her uncle's house but she might go home to Mearns. She might have headed for Stirling to find her brothers. He told her to try the station and bus stops."

"I'm going home. I had to leave Pippa with a neighbour."

Frank had gone to the local station. There was a train due and the last one into the Central had gone about twenty minutes ago. Diana could have caught that. Salma told him to get off to the Central and try to find out if a young girl wearing only a thin, white dress had purchased a ticket for Stirling. Penny was dispatched to Buchanan Street Bus Station with the same instructions. Two other PCs were instructed to keep searching round the Newlands' area. Salma herself went back to the Ewing house to ask if they had a recent picture of Diana. Sally found one taken in the summer of Brian standing with his arm round his daughter and Salma went back to the station to get copies run off. She rang the PCs doing the searching and arranged to meet them outside the local train station where she gave them each a copy of the photograph and started them off on a house-to-house enquiry.

It was Penny who found Diana. The woman at the ticket booth in Buchanan Street had noticed a young girl wearing only a white dress but had been too busy to follow it up. She remembered giving her a ticket for Stirling and directed Penny to the bus stance, telling her that the Stirling bus would be leaving in six minutes. So it was that Penny, boarding the bus, found Diana sitting huddled up at the back of the bus. She was shivering and tearful and it took all of Penny's persuasive powers to get her off the bus. It was only by promising to take her home to Mearns that Penny got the girl into the police car. As soon as they set off, she phoned Davenport who agreed to meet them both at Diana's home. He in turn rang Ralph, then Salma who contacted Frank and the other two PC searchers.

Charles had picked up Pippa from the neighbour, an elderly woman who had done this for him only once before. He thanked her and took his daughter home. On the kitchen table lay Pippa's school photographs. They had been looking at them when the phone call had come about Diana.

"Do you want to buy any Daddy?" Pippa asked now.

"Yes, I'll buy one for Mum. I imagine we get these to keep, don't we?"

"Yes. Do you think I look OK in them?"

"Yes pet, you look lovely."

Reassured, Pippa skipped into the lounge and switched on the TV and Charles started their rather late evening meal. Penny's phone call came as they were eating it. Not wanting to ask the neighbour again, Charles rang Fiona at home. She had had her dinner and professed herself willing to babysit Pippa after he had told her the happenings of the evening. Pippa was happy to see Fiona and they spent some time talking about their favourite chalet school books and looking at the school photographs

"Your Dad has still not shown me his train set, Pippa," laughed Fiona as they stood in the kitchen waiting for the milk to boil for Pippa's before-bed cocoa.

"I'll remind him, Fiona," promised Pippa. She took her cocoa and went up to bed to drink it there. Fiona followed her up.

"Does your Dad let you read in bed?" she asked her young charge.

"Yes but only for fifteen minutes," said the honest youngster.

As Fiona was turning away to go back downstairs, Pippa asked her, " Fiona, Dad said I looked lovely in the photographs but Hazel's Uncle Brian said I was beautiful. What do you think?"

Not wanting to over flatter her but knowing that she was indeed a pretty child, Fiona settled for that word.

"I think beautiful isn't a word to use for a person your age, Pippa. I would say you are very pretty."

With that Pippa had to be satisfied. Fiona stored up this titbit of information for Charles when he came home.

CHAPTER 56

Davenport arrived at the Ewing house in Mearns before Penny and Diana did, having not had nearly so far to come. He found Carol, not in her usual cool state but upset and very confused.

"Mr Davenport. Why would Diana do what she did to Ralph? Has he been abusing her?"

"I don't think so Mrs Ewing, otherwise he wouldn't have reacted the way he did and she wouldn't have run away."

"But what would make her do it?"

"I have no idea. Hopefully, she'll talk to us when she gets home."

"I rang the boys so they know she's safe."

Carol began pacing up and down like a caged lioness. She was feeling so guilty about going out socialising without checking that her daughter was OK. To stop her prowling, Davenport asked if she would make them both a cup of tea and they were sitting drinking this in silence when Diana arrived home with Penny.

Carol opened the front door. She tried to take Diana in her arms but the girl would not let her, merely pushing past her mother and making for the stairs. Charles went up after her but as soon as he arrived in the bedroom doorway, she started to shake uncontrollably.

"Diana. We have to talk. What..."

"Don't come near me. I don't want you near me."

She was almost hysterical. Carol appeared behind Davenport but if anything this made Diana worse.

"I want Ian. I want Ian."

Going back downstairs and convincing Carol to go with him, Davenport asked Penny to go up. Being nearer in age to Diana she might get the girl's confidence. If that failed he would have to get a doctor in to give her something to calm her down, then try again.

Penny did not go right into the room. She stayed at the door and spoke from there:

"You've been having an awful time pet. Can I come in and try to help?"

Diana muttered, "Come in but you can't help. No one can."

Penny went in and sat on the bed beside her.

"Uncle Ralph's very upset. He doesn't know what he's done to upset you so much."

"I just wanted him to love me like Dad did."

A light went on in Penny's brain. She would have to be very careful here.

"Diana, did your Dad love you in a very special way?"

"Yes."

"And you wanted your Uncle Ralph to do the same, tonight?"

"Yes."

"Have you tried to get anyone else to love you like that?"

"Yes, John and he wouldn't either. I hate him. I prefer Ian now."

"Did Ian love you like your Dad?"

"No, I was scared to ask him."

Now came the difficult part. Penny braced herself.

"Can you tell me what your Dad did that was so special?"

"Promise you won't tell Mum. Dad made me promise not to tell Mum or John or Ian. He said they would be jealous of him loving me more than them."

The sad story unfolded.

The first time Brian had gone to his daughter's bedroom, she had been asleep and woken to feel him stroking her arm. He had told her to be quiet then got into bed beside her. He had taken off her pyjama jacket and stroked her breasts, telling her that they were beautiful, that he had never seen anything so beautiful. He had told her how much he loved her but that this was to be their secret. When asked when this had happened, Diana could not be definite but said that it was around the summer after her thirteenth birthday.

"Dad said I was beautiful. It was wonderful. No one had ever told me that before. He bought this lovely dress for me at Christmas. At first I didn't like it, it seemed old fashioned but Dad said it made me look like a princess. I wore it to his funeral and I wore it tonight to make Uncle Ralph love me but it didn't work. Why didn't it work?"

The look she gave Penny was one of confusion and hurt and Penny balked at trying to explain to the young girl that what her Dad had done was wrong and that her Uncle had done the right thing in rejecting her advances. She said instead, "What did John say when you asked him to...love you, Diana?"

"He said it was wrong but how can love be wrong?"

"How often did your Dad come into your room, into your bed, Diana?"

"Every Wednesday and every Saturday. He came up to school to take me home on Wednesdays because he missed me so much."

Penny was silent for a moment. She remembered that her boss had told them that Carol was certain that Brian had found a replacement for Wendy and here she was pouring out her heart - it was his daughter, Diana!

Diana was continuing, a dreamy expression on her face.

"Daddy bought me two beautiful nighties. He said I was too beautiful to wear ugly pyjamas. Hazel still wears pyjamas you know. She's so young. I bet Uncle Ralph doesn't love her the way my Dad loved me or... maybe he does and that was why he couldn't love me as well. Do you think that was why?"

"Er..." Penny didn't know what to say. She felt that she could harm this young girl even further by saying the wrong thing right now.

"Diana what did your Dad do on those nights?"

"He touched me in what he called my special place and then not long before he was ...killed, he did what he called making special love to me. It hurt a bit the first time but the second time it didn't. I didn't really like it but he said I would get to really enjoy it."

"Did you tell anyone about this?"

"Yes, I told John and he would probably tell Ian."

"What did John say?"

"He didn't say much at all, really. I asked him if he was jealous and he gave a funny laugh and said no, he wasn't jealous."

"Can you remember when you told John?"

"I told him on the Thursday morning after Dad brought me home for the holidays. The school term didn't finish till the Friday but Dad said I could have some extra days off."

Penny realised that she could not be expected to deal with all this on her own.

"Diana, I have to go downstairs for a minute. Why don't you get out of your lovely dress and put on something warmer. I'll come back if you want me to."

A sullen look had replaced the dreamy one.

"Come back if you want. I don't care. I want Ian." She began to cry softly and Penny turned to go downstairs with a heavy heart.

"Remember don't tell Mum what I've told you. Promise," the weeping girl choked out.

"I promise, Diana."

Davenport looked up as Penny came into the lounge.

"Well PC Price. Have you found out anything that might help us understand what happened tonight?"

"Yes, Sir." Penny turned sympathetic eyes on Carol Ewing. "I'm very sorry Mrs Ewing but I had to promise not to tell you."

As Carol started up from her seat, looking angry, Davenport spoke.

"Mrs Ewing. Penny can't break her word to Diana, you must see that, but if you leave the room now, I promise that I will tell you myself later."

Realising that she would have to be content with that, Carol left the room to sit in the kitchen.

"Well Penny?"

"Sir, Diana's Dad was abusing her but she liked it. She thought it made her special. She's quite a plain girl isn't she, Sir and Brian told her she was beautiful."

"When did this start?"

"She said about summer time. Sir, she told her brother John the night before the party."

"You realise what this means, don't you Penny?"

"Yes Sir, it gives John or Ian or both a motive for killing their father."

Davenport pulled furiously on his ear lobe. He wished he had Fiona here with him right now.

"Go back up and stay with her, Penny. I know it's a lot to ask of you but try to comfort her. I have to tell her mother, you know that but I'll do it once you've gone upstairs so that you can honestly say to her that you have not told her Mum."

Once Penny had gone, reluctantly, upstairs, Davenport went into the kitchen and told Carol bluntly that her husband had been abusing their daughter. There was no easy way to break such news.

"I think she went over to her uncle's tonight to try to get him to love her in the way that Brian had been doing. When he rebuffed her advances she ran off. I'm afraid it will be better if Diana doesn't know that you know about this. Can you keep up that pretence, Mrs Ewing?"

Carol nodded. She had caused this, she thought, by refusing to sleep with Brian. He had turned to other women and then finally to his own daughter. She shivered with revulsion.

"Why didn't she tell me?"

"I imagine Brian would tell her that you wouldn't believe her or if, as we suppose from her actions tonight, she had come to enjoy the abuse, maybe he said you would be jealous. I don't know. Now if you'll excuse me, we'll have to leave you both. I really don't know how you're going to deal with this. I suppose that you *will* have to tell her that I told you but I would be grateful if you would make sure that she knows that PC Price did not tell you. That's only fair."

Davenport went to the foot of the stairs and called for Penny who looked very relieved when she reached the hall.

"She's calmed down a bit, Sir. I suggested that she got ready for bed and she's doing that now."

"Maybe leave it till the morning to speak to her, Mrs Ewing. It might be easier in the cold light of day."

Carol nodded.

Davenport and Penny went out to his car and he drove them both to his house, asking Penny if she minded not going home right away.

Fiona was sitting in the lounge, reading the paper. She looked startled when she saw their faces.

"You two look as if you've both shared the same nightmare," she said.

"We have indeed done just that," Charles told her and went on to tell her what had happened.

He expected Fiona to make some reference to the murders; she was usually quick on the uptake but she surprised him by saying, "God, that could have been Pippa!"

"Pippa! What do you mean?" Charles was horrified. Was Fiona suggesting that he could abuse Pippa?"

"Sorry, Charles. I meant that Brian Ewing could have been planning on abusing your daughter too. He had certainly started to groom her."

"Explain yourself," Charles barked, startling Penny who had never seen her boss so angry.

Fiona told him about Pippa showing her the school photographs and asking Fiona if she thought she was beautiful. She said that Hazel's uncle had told her at the party that she was beautiful.

"I laughed and said that she was pretty rather than beautiful," Fiona explained. "She went up to bed and when I went up to get her empty cocoa mug, she said that he had told her she must come over and play with Diana some time."

"The bastard!" Davenport was quietly cold now. "He deserved everything he got."

With a meaningful glance at Penny, Fiona reminded him that he was not the judge and jury. It was their job to find the culprit, not to say whether or not it was a justifiable killing.

"Sorry, folks. You're right of course Fiona. What we haven't told you is that Diana confided in John the day before the party."

"So you think that John...?"

"Or Ian, as he would certainly tell his twin brother, or both together most likely. Yes I think they killed their father."

CHAPTER 57

Davenport informed Grant Knox, the chief constable, the next day, that he felt sure closure of the case was imminent. The chief constable's meek secretary had been replaced since his last visit and he vaguely remembered being asked to contribute to her leaving present. The new one could have been Knox's twin sister in attitude. She did not smile and her voice was frosty and disapproving when Davenport told her that he did not have an appointment.

He did this at 9am then, gathering his team in the Incident Room, he told Salma and Frank what they suspected. Penny, uncharacteristically, had not been eager to tell them and she sat very quietly as her boss enlightened the other two.

"Salma and Frank, write up any details of what you did last night and Penny, I'm afraid you're going to have to write up your conversation with young Diana Ewing. I've alerted the Stirling police and they are going to bring John and Ian Ewing to Glasgow."

Davenport and Fiona had discussed this earlier and she had agreed that Penny should be the one to be present at one of the interviews as her boss thought that it would be better if she was occupied today. Fiona and Salma would interview the other twin.

"I'm sorry Selby. Hope you don't feel that you're being left out. You will of course be informed of the outcomes of both interviews."

Good-naturedly, Frank grinned.

"Give all the work to the women, Sir. I'm all in favour of that."

"Thanks Frank, and Frank..."

"Yes Sir?"

"If you have time today, get a haircut. I can hardly see you for that floppy lock of hair over your face."

Davenport smiled as he said it. Frank smiled back. He tugged at his left earlobe and even managed to raise a smile from Penny who recognised this take-off of the DCI.

It was nearly midday before John and Ian Ewing were brought into the station. John was taken into interview room one and Ian into room two.

After the usual formalities, Davenport spoke to John. John was looking scared. He twisted his hands together in his lap and cleared his throat nervously before asking why they had been brought here.

"Last night Mr Ewing... sorry you don't like to be called that do you," said Davenport remembering an earlier conversation. "Why is that?"

"I'm not old enough for the Mr bit," said John.

"I put it to you that you didn't like your father who was Mr Ewing and that is why you don't want to be named that," Davenport retorted.

"Why would I not like my father?"

"Because he abused your sister, Diana, John. That's why."

John was startled and showed it. He ran his hand through his hair and stammered, "A...bused? Diana? When?"

"It's no use, John. Diana told us she told you. She told you the day before the party and I think you thought of killing him at that moment."

John, realising that he had given himself away by pretending not to know about the abuse, fell silent.

"Who killed your father? You or Ian?"

"Me, Sir," said John quietly. He put his head into his hands. Penny saw his shoulders shake. Davenport let him cry for a while before questioning him about his father's murder and that of Arthur Mackie.

In interview room two, Fiona had not been so lucky. Ian had admitted to knowing about the abuse and had claimed that he and John had confronted their father and told him to stop what he had been doing or they would inform the police. She and Salma could not shake him on that. Fiona whispered something to Salma and she slipped out. She went into the other room and spoke to her boss before returning to room two. She spoke quietly to DS Macdonald who spoke to Ian:

"Ian. John has confessed."

"No he hasn't. We didn't do it so he wouldn't confess."

At that moment Davenport entered the room. Fiona spoke into the tape machine to say that DCI Davenport had come in then she sat back and Davenport continued.

"Ian. John has admitted killing your father. He says that he also killed Dr Mackie..."

"He didn't kill Dr Mackie. I did that."

Ian realised how easily he had been trapped and groaned.

"Would you like to tell me how both murders happened, Ian? Stick to the truth please. I have John's version remember."

John and Ian were put into separate cells under the first floor of the station and Davenport called a meeting of his team in the Incident room. John had confessed to both murders. It had been his idea. Ian had helped him by pretending to be him to make it appear that both of them were present in the lounge at the time when Santa was there. Asked how he knew where to get the Santa suit, John had told him that his father had helped out a few years ago (before Child Protection had tightened things up, Charles hoped) by being Santa at the Sunday school party. Ralph had asked him, having been asked by Jim Rogerson and not wanting to do it himself as Hazel was to be present. John and Ian had gone with their father when he went to pick up the suit.

It had been Ian who had gone to the door with Aunt Sally to let Santa in. It had been easy for John to put the suit into the bin outside then slip into the queue for food ahead of the others as Ian had hurried the other young ones in ahead of them too. Ian told him later that he had pretended to be John changing the CD over.

Asked why they had killed Arthur Mackie, John explained that the doctor had phoned to ask to speak to John and Ian and the next day they had gone to his house.

"Luckily for them, the nice old guy had also asked to speak to Carol to ask how she was so we didn't suspect that he had called specifically to speak to the boys," said Davenport.

"Arthur had told them that he knew it was Ian who had claimed to be John changing the CD because Ian had run his hand through his hair, showing the small scar which he had got through a snowball having a stone in it when he was younger and they lived in Shawlands and Dr Mackie was their GP. Brian had brought Ian to the doctor who had sent them off to the hospital to have it stitched."

Davenport continued, "Dr Mackie came straight out and asked John and Ian if they had murdered their father."

"We admitted it and told him why and he said he understood but would have to inform the police," said John, "so I killed him."

"But it wasn't John who hit Dr Mackie over the head with the candlestick," Davenport informed them now.

Frank managed to resist the temptation to say, "In the lounge with the candlestick, by Professor Plum." He did not think anyone would appreciate his humour at that point.

"It was Ian." continued Davenport. "Ian confessed to that once he knew that John had admitted to killing their father. John had been willing to let Arthur Mackie tell us as he was finding it very hard to live with what they had done but Ian decided to share the guilt and keep them safe. He let Arthur Mackie leave the room to telephone and hit him over the head with one of the candlesticks.

Davenport sighed. "It's a horrible case this. Those two young boys hated what their father was doing to their sister. They did what they thought was best. John regrets it now but Ian doesn't, yet he committed the worst crime. Poor Arthur Mackie didn't deserve to die. Had they killed only Brian, a jury would surely have been lenient towards them but Arthur's death is a different matter."

"Sir," said Penny. "Diana said she had asked John to love her. Did he say anything about that?"

"Yes, Penny. Apparently Diana went to his room one night and simply climbed into bed beside him. He was horrified and told her to go away and never come into his room again. He said she avoided him after that and Ian became her favourite."

"Did she not try it on with him then?" asked Frank.

"It seems that she didn't, maybe because she'd hit on the idea of going to Ralph."

"I suppose charades and people divided into groups made it easier for them to give the idea that they were both present?" said Fiona.

"Yes. John said he planted the idea of charades into Hazel's head during the evening and she asked for it."

"Did you have any inkling that it was them, Sir?" asked Fiona.

"Something bothered me that night we watched the video clip of Pippa and Hazel on their bikes. You said that they couldn't be told apart with their helmets on because their clothes were so similar. When John was talking about how easy it was for he and Ian to pretend to be each other I remembered that someone, I think it was their cousin Hazel, had told me that they always wore different clothes except when they wanted to play tricks on their teachers when they were at school. Yet they wore the same clothes to the party. That should have alerted me."

"No use thinking that now."

In her attempt to cheer Charles up, Fiona forgot the ' Sir' but only Frank noticed.

"What now?" asked Salma.

"Now I'm afraid we have to inform the commissioner and have the boys bound over for trial."

"Poor Carol. How on earth will she cope with this?"

Fiona felt pity for the woman.

"That and having to see that Diana gets help. She'll be distraught with her father dead and her brothers in prison as they surely will be." Penny hated the end of a case like this one.

"Well I'm off to tell Carol now. I'll make an appointment to see Mr Knox after that. Fiona, would you come with me. I doubt that Carol Ewing will need female comfort but you never know. Right, team, case over."

He and Fiona left the room and for once Frank's cheery whistling of "Over the Sea to Sky" did not irritate him. It was a sign that things were going to get back to normal.

THE AUTHOR

Frances Macarthur lives on Glasgow's South side with her husband, no children and no pets. She is a retired English teacher who taught in two of inner Glasgow's Comprehensive Schools.

After retiring in 1998, she took up writing crime novels set around her former stomping grounds of Pollokshaws, Shawlands and Newlands and her present abode in Waterfoot.

She holidays with her husband every year in Penang, Malaysia where a later book is set.

She puts her love of crime fiction down to the fact that her mother read them avidly and passed on her love of them, along with a love of cross-words and other word puzzles.